"I'd like to kiss you."

The blunt words were out before Ross could consider their tone. But he wouldn't call them back even if he could have.

"Oh…" Jenna managed.

"I mean, it seems logical." *Right, and physical attraction has nothing to do with it,* a more candid part of him mocked. "That way, we'll have a better basis to, ah, make our decision."

"So you haven't reconsidered? You're still thinking about marriage?"

"I am," he assured her. "But right now I'd just like to kiss you."

He lowered his mouth to hers, taking in her subtle floral scent and reminding himself that this was only a kiss. But that didn't mean he couldn't savor the moment. At last he forced himself to lift his head, drop the hand still cupped around her silky-smooth chin and take a step back. "I'm prepared to suggest that we take this…all the way."

Jenna stared up at him, her own breathing far from even. "All the way?"

"To the altar."

HER NECESSARY HUSBAND

Sharon Swan

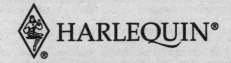

HARLEQUIN®

TORONTO • NEW YORK • LONDON
AMSTERDAM • PARIS • SYDNEY • HAMBURG
STOCKHOLM • ATHENS • TOKYO • MILAN • MADRID
PRAGUE • WARSAW • BUDAPEST • AUCKLAND

For my agent, Pam Hopkins,
with many thanks for all her support.

ISBN 0-373-16983-3

HER NECESSARY HUSBAND

Visit us at www.eHarlequin.com

Printed in U.S.A.

ABOUT THE AUTHOR

Born and raised in Chicago, Sharon Swan once dreamed of dancing for a living. Instead, she surrendered to life's more practical aspects, settled for an office job, concentrated on typing and being a Chicago Bears fan. Sharon never seriously considered writing as a career until she moved to the Phoenix area and met Pierce Brosnan at a local shopping mall. It was a chance meeting that changed her life, because she found herself thinking, what if? What if two fictional characters had met the same way? That formed the basis for her next novel, and she's now cheerfully addicted to writing contemporary romance and playing what if?

Sharon loves to hear from readers. You can write to her at P.O. Box 21324, Mesa, AZ 85277.

Books by Sharon Swan

HARLEQUIN AMERICAN ROMANCE

*Welcome to Harmony

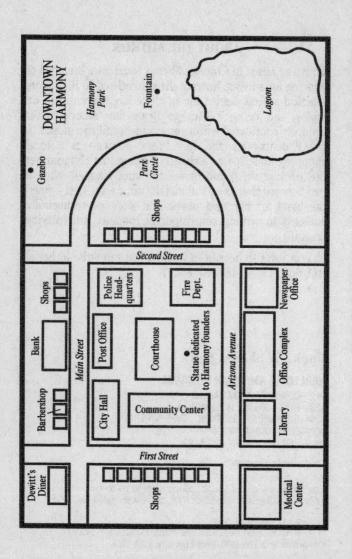

DOWNTOWN HARMONY

Harmony Park

• Gazebo

• Fountain

Lagoon

Park Circle

Shops

Second Street

Shops

Bank

Barbershop

Main Street

Police Head-quarters

Post Office

Courthouse

Fire Dept.

City Hall

Community Center

• Statue dedicated to Harmony founders

Arizona Avenue

Newspaper Office

Office Complex

Library

First Street

Dewitt's Diner

Shops

Medical Center

Chapter One

Something told Jenna Lorenzo that Ross Hayward would not be hiring her as his live-in housekeeper the minute he opened the front door.

Only moments earlier she'd been admiring that door, painted the palest of yellows, and the wreath of sage green leaves topped with delicate dried flowers that hung under a high arch gracefully etched into the smooth wood. Like the rest of the modern two-story home built of narrow bricks shaded a pristine dove gray, the door was a tribute to conservative elegance. Even the well-trimmed front lawn with its neatly shaped borders of low plants sporting a quiet mix of early September blooms was designed to bid visitors a gracious welcome.

Serene, Jenna thought. That was the word that came to mind. She had never worked—and certainly never lived—anywhere quite like this place.

And she wouldn't be working, or living, here. The polite smile that didn't quite reach the deep-set navy eyes of the tall man standing in front of her had her all but positive of that.

"Come in, Jenna," he said in a low voice she'd by no means forgotten from the initial interview he'd conducted several days earlier at Dewitt's Diner. Despite the business nature of the lunch, she'd felt at ease in the familiar setting, having indulged in one of the downtown diner's juicy hamburgers along with a mound of crisp fries many times with her friends when she was growing up in Harmony, Arizona.

She didn't, however, feel anywhere near that same level of ease right now. The truth was that when it came to casually comfortable surroundings, the Hayward home was an entirely different matter.

Just how different Jenna realized full well the moment she stepped into the entryway and found herself confronted by a landscape of sheer white. Carpet, walls, ceiling. Even what living room furniture she could see through an arched opening at one side of the hall featured a white-on-white design. Only a group of pastel prints simply framed in silver and hung at well-spaced intervals provided any hint of true color.

Everything sparkled in the sun slanting through lacy white curtains. Nothing was out of place. It was a scene straight out of a trendy home magazine.

But this was real life, and there were children living here. "How in the world does it stay clean?" Jenna wondered out loud.

"We've learned to be careful," the man at her side said.

The attractive man at her side, she couldn't help thinking as they made their way to the living room. At one time, as had many girls in town, she'd had a major crush on the Golden Boy—which was how her adolescent eyes had come to view him—with his sun-streaked brown hair and flashing grin. Somehow it had only seemed natural when he'd started dating Cynthia Morgan during his high school days.

A slim blonde with the lightest of blue eyes, Cynthia

had swiftly become the other half of the Golden Couple—a couple some had envied for their popularity. They'd married shortly after both graduated from college, Jenna had learned from friends on her recent return to Harmony. It had been, by all accounts, an excellent marriage, one that had quickly produced a beautiful baby daughter, and eventually another.

And then, almost three years ago, Ross Hayward had tragically lost not only his wife but also his mother when the car Cynthia had been driving skidded off a snowy road and crashed.

"Have a seat," he said. "I'm glad you were able to spare me some time this morning."

Jenna settled herself on a long sofa while her host chose an overstuffed chair across from her. A chrome-and-glass coffee table with smoothly curved lines as quietly refined as the rest of the room occupied the space between them.

"Actually, I was waiting for your call," she admitted. "When you said you'd get back to me, I wasn't sure if you'd want to meet again." And when he had called her at the home of a friend where she was currently staying and invited her to come over, she'd imagined she was well on her way to being offered the housekeeper's job. Until she'd seen his expression.

Now even his polite smile had faded. "I meant to get in touch sooner," he said, "but I had some things to consider."

What things? Jenna couldn't help wondering as she folded her arms across the front of her deep tangerine pantsuit. No ready answer came to mind, but there was no denying that her prospective employer—most likely *ex*-prospective employer—looked far from overjoyed at the moment. He also didn't look quite as much like a businessman today.

Then again, it was Saturday. Even the top guy at Hayward Investments was allowed to dress down on the weekends, she supposed. Not that his cream-colored knit shirt and well-ironed khaki pants were anywhere near as casual as faded denim, but the outfit still displayed some impressive sights. Strong shoulders snugly outlined by smooth cotton and forearms left bare to reveal lean muscles dotted with swirls of crisp hair readily indicated that this man didn't spend all his time behind a desk.

Jenna dropped a brief glance down, half expecting to find gleaming leather loafers to complete the picture. Instead she saw no shoes at all, merely dark socks.

"We generally take off our shoes when we come in," he told her, obviously noticing the direction her gaze had taken.

"Ah, yes, the white carpet," she summed up with a nod. She dropped another look down, this time at her black pumps.

"You're a guest, so you get to keep yours on."

The wry statement had her chuckling. "Thanks," she said.

Her host cleared his throat and leaned back in his chair. "I know your qualifications are top-notch."

But... He didn't say it; she heard it, anyway. And what more could *she* say? He'd checked her references before their lunch. Three couples in the Denver metropolitan area combining dual careers with a bustling family life had confirmed that she'd run their busy households and done a bang-up job of it at a time when they'd needed someone like her most.

Jenna could only agree.

During the seven years since she'd left Nevada—

where her father had relocated her family when she was sixteen—for the high plains of Colorado, she had put talents learned at her mother's side to good use. Combining them with her own love of tackling new challenges, she had built a solid career for herself despite the lack of a college degree—a career she'd still be pursuing in the Denver area if the urge hadn't hit to revisit her birthplace in Arizona during an unexpected break between jobs.

And then there'd been no question of a permanent return. As she'd come around the last curve on a winding highway lined with tall pines and gazed down on the small, sun-splashed city rimmed by a chain of low mountains northeast of Phoenix, something inside her had recognized it as...home. After more than a dozen years she was home, and she meant to stay.

"Look," she said, deciding it was time to stop skirting the issue, "I'll admit I'm more than getting the feeling that for some reason you don't think I'm right for this position."

And maybe it wasn't right for her, she mused, all at once aware of precisely how attractive this specific member of the male species was—not to the female half of the population in general, which was probably a given, but to her in particular.

Good heavens, she couldn't still have a crush on Ross Hayward, former Golden Boy. That would be ridiculous.

"Why don't we just declare this visit over?" she suggested, then slanted a sidelong look out a curtained window and waited for the expected agreement.

Rather than simply concurring, however, the man seated across from her held back a grimace at her abruptly brisk tone. He hadn't meant, Ross thought, to be quite so obvious about having reservations where this woman was concerned—reservations resulting from a recent conversation he had no trouble recalling.

"People are bound to talk if a widowed man still in his early thirties hires a single woman in her twenties as a live-in housekeeper," Tom Kennedy, Harmony's veteran police chief, had pointed out when Ross had stopped by police headquarters for a brief chat after his initial interview with Jenna. And hard on the heels of that statement, Ross remembered, the longtime friend of the Hayward family had gone on to share some news.

"Normally, I'd say it's your choice on whether to just ignore the gossip," Tom had told him. "But voters gossip, too, and you know our mayor is pushing seventy, and I've heard he may not decide to run again. That means we could wind up with another Hayward in the mayor's office next year, provided you're interested."

And he was interested. Ross couldn't deny that. His grandfather had been the last Mayor Hayward, and it was a sure bet that the old man, rest his stubbornly upright soul, would have counted on his direct descendant and the sole grandson to bear the Hayward name to try to follow in his footsteps. Especially since the old man's only son had already left a black mark on the pages of the family history.

Ross knew it could be argued that he had been an upstanding citizen of Harmony right from the day he'd been born into one of the founding families first to settle the city. For generations most Haywards had been dedicated to getting things done and had won respect for their achievements. As time passed, some residents had even come to expect Haywards to set an example of what good stock and hard work could accomplish.

What no one had expected a Hayward man to do was to walk out on his wife of many years and head off to

Southern California to live the life of an aging playboy. Which was exactly what his father had done, Ross thought grimly. And if he hoped to be mayor in spite of Martin Hayward's hardly admirable behavior, it could only be smart to look after his own good standing in the community.

So, taking all of that into account, he'd been having a devil of a time making up his mind about whether to offer Jenna Lorenzo the job.

There was no question that he needed to fill the position—and fairly soon, what with Myra Hastings having to leave at the end of the month to care for her elderly mother full-time. But replacing his middle-aged housekeeper with a younger person who, while perhaps no true beauty, was still a striking-looking woman, might not be the wisest course he'd come to recognize.

And now that woman had just handed him an easy out.

The thing was, for some reason he found himself reluctant to take it. Not yet, anyway.

"Let's not be too quick to throw in the towel," he told her.

A fast frown formed on his visitor's brow as she pulled her gaze away from the window. "I don't understand. Either you want to hire me or—"

"Daddy!" a young voice wailed, breaking into the conversation. A rosy-cheeked blonde dressed in a pink cotton top with matching pants soon appeared in the doorway to the living room. She was a six-year-old bundle of usually cheerful energy. Yet despite her angelic looks, Ross knew full well she could sometimes be as mischievous as a pint-size imp.

"My daughter Katie," he explained to his guest before fixing his attention on his youngest child. "What's wrong, sunshine?"

Katie brushed back a small tear as she ran to him. "Pandora lost her hair again!" She held out a doll wearing a well-worn yellow satin gown and sporting a jumble of deep auburn curls.

Ross studied the object in question. It was a collector's item more than a child's toy, but his mother had presented it to Katie on her third birthday, anyway, with the warning to be careful when she played with it. Reality had, of course, stepped in; the doll had clearly seen better days. Nevertheless, Katie continued to favor it over most of her other toys.

"We'll try to glue it on one more time," he said, lifting his gaze from the delicate porcelain forehead sadly lacking a wide fringe of bangs. "Where's the part that fell off?"

"I don't know. Myra said it could be in the vacuum cleaner, 'cause she cleaned this morning." Katie's lower lip trembled. "Can you get it out, Daddy?"

Ross held back a sigh. "Even if I could find it," he explained as gently as possible, "it would probably be in too bad a shape to save it."

"But you could," Jenna pointed out as she entered the discussion, "cut off some of what's left and make a new hairdo."

Him? Provide a doll with an entirely different hairdo? Ross couldn't even imagine it. "I'm not sure I could do that if my life depended on it," he admitted dryly.

"Could *you?*" Katie asked, spinning around.

Ross sat forward. "Katie, this is Ms. Lorenzo," he said, completing the introduction.

Jenna smiled softly. "Pleased to meet you, Katie. May I see your doll for a minute?"

"Sure." Katie took a seat beside Jenna and handed Pandora over. "Do you know how to do hair stuff?" She studied the woman next to her with a doubtful tilt of her head.

"Mmm-hmm." Jenna's smile took a knowing slant. "I wear my hair straight back like this," she explained, smoothing a hand over the thick coil at the nape of her neck, "because it's long, and this is the best way to keep it neat."

"How long?"

"Almost to my waist."

"Wow." Katie's eyes went wide. "How do you wash it?"

"It takes time," Jenna allowed. She inspected the doll. "One of my sisters has hair this color. And another one has naturally curly hair she keeps short, like yours."

Katie folded her small hands in her lap. "How many sisters and brothers have you got?"

"No brothers. Three younger sisters. And I helped all three fix their hair while they were growing up."

Katie mulled that over. "Maybe Pandora could wear her hair like the twins on the TV show I watch sometimes after school."

"You might be on to something there," Jenna agreed after a moment, clearly recognizing the show in question when Ross had no clue. Myra wouldn't, either, he knew, despite the fact that she was here every day when his daughters got home from school.

His current housekeeper was a fine person in her own right who cooked good, healthy meals, kept his house sparkling clean and could be trusted without question to watch over his children whenever he was away. Yet, for all of Myra's virtues, taking time from her busy day to watch a kid's television show with Katie on occasion would simply not have occurred to her.

But it obviously would to Jenna.

While a spirited discussion of how the new hairdo might be best achieved continued, Ross found himself wondering how his visitor would look with her own midnight-dark hair spilling past her shoulders and down her back.

Exotic, he decided. Yet classically female, as well. In fact, her oval-shaped face with its straight nose, high cheekbones and fine, creamy skin—not to mention those chestnut-brown eyes that slanted up slightly at the corners—would probably look right at home in a painting by one of the old masters.

As to the rest of her, he couldn't make out enough to judge. Both of the tailored outfits he'd seen her in so far were by no means formfitting. Still, although she was several inches shorter than his own six-feet-plus, *petite* wasn't the word that came to mind. Not when he suspected that a full figure with plenty of curves might be lurking out of sight.

Whatever the case, she'd been in his thoughts ever since their initial meeting. Something about her had captured his attention, that was plain. Something that might turn out to have little to do with her qualifications as housekeeper, if he wanted to investigate the matter further.

One thing for certain, when it came to her qualifications, she *was* the right choice to run his household, as he'd concluded soon after she'd offered her credentials. If he'd had the least lingering doubts about that, the way she was currently chatting so easily with Katie would have routed them once and for all.

Too bad Tom Kennedy had hit the nail on the head,

Ross thought, recognizing that more than ever as his hooded gaze silently told him in no uncertain terms just how striking Jenna Lorenzo was—how vivid, how…alive she looked against a backdrop of almost total white. People were bound to talk if she moved in and took Myra's place. Despite Harmony's genuinely friendly atmosphere, gossip was a fact of life.

And the truth was that even if he chose to ignore the gossip, he was a long way from certain he'd be doing the fair thing by subjecting this woman to it.

Logic said to just tell her face to face that it wouldn't work out and to thank her for her trouble, which he'd undeniably been of more than half a mind to do when she'd arrived on his doorstep. On the other hand, something that went beyond pure logic was still urging him not to let her go so easily.

Ross frowned at the knowledge that he had to make up his mind before his prospective housekeeper decided he'd left her hanging long enough and walked out on him.

JENNA SOMEHOW FOUND herself seated at a round, glass-topped kitchen table, a pair of shiny scissors and a small tube of clear glue set in front of her on a gray-and-white-checked place mat. Moments earlier she'd learned that the deep blue eyes belonging to the youngest member of the Hayward household could be very persuasive when attempting a woeful look. Even before Katie had followed it up with a whispered, "Please," Jenna had suspected that her immediate future would include treating Pandora to a new hairdo.

Probably only an objection from the man now seated beside her would have changed her fate, she reflected as she placed a silver-gray linen dishtowel trimmed in lace around the doll's neck. Instead, Ross had merely suggested that they adjourn to the rear of the house, where he'd again played host, offering refreshment and providing what materials she needed to get the job done. Then he'd settled into a chrome-backed chair in his not surprisingly gleaming kitchen and seemed to sink into his thoughts, as he had during most of their time in the living room.

What was he thinking so hard about? Jenna had to wonder. And was she going to be offered the position or not?

"Myra's gonna be surprised to see how Pandora looks when she gets back." Katie tucked small feet snuggled into pink socks under her and leaned in from her seat at Jenna's other side. "Do you start cutting now?"

"Mmm-hmm." Jenna sat the doll on the table, picked up the scissors and carefully began her task, her eyes narrowing for a better look. Her thoughts drifted to the brief meeting that had taken place in the hallway outside the kitchen just before Myra Hastings, a tall, thin woman with short salt-and-pepper hair, had left to visit her elderly mother who remained hospitalized after a stroke.

The housekeeper's greeting could hardly be classified as warm, not when she'd explained, oh, so primly, that it took a great deal of effort to keep a home like this in tiptop shape. Plainly she knew, although Ross hadn't said as much during his introduction, that Jenna had applied to replace her. And the older woman wasn't exactly impressed. The question was: how much would Myra's opinion count with her employer?

Certainly he didn't seem any happier now than he had earlier. No, *less*, Jenna concluded, slanting a glance his way. But even with the corners of his mouth turned down and a deep frown marring his brow, he still looked good to her.

Probably too good.

"There, I think that's enough off," she told Katie, mustering a cheerful tone for the little girl's sake. "Now we'll glue on some new bangs and cut them on an angle, just like the television twins wear theirs."

When the job was finally done, Katie clapped her hands and wasted no time in offering her judgment. "Pandora looks neat!"

"She looks very nice," another young voice politely chimed in from behind Jenna. Startled, she turned around to find herself being calmly studied by light, clear blue eyes, a sight that instantly reminded her of the woman Ross Hayward had married. This slender-as-a-reed girl with straight, shoulder-length blond hair could only be Cynthia Morgan's child.

The man of the house proceeded to introduce his eldest daughter, Caroline, who shook hands with the quiet courtesy of someone far older than her own ten years. Again he made no reference as to why their visitor was there. This time it had Jenna more than suspecting that the children weren't aware of her status as a potential employee, as Myra plainly had been. They probably thought she was an acquaintance of their father's.

Or a girlfriend.

No, not hardly, she informed herself in the next breath, belatedly reminded of what seemed to be common knowledge in Harmony—there had been no woman in Ross Hayward's life since his wife's death. As far as his children were concerned, their current visitor was no doubt a friend, and the most casual kind, at that. Which was fine with her, Jenna thought. And she would be fine, as well, regardless of whether she got this job or not.

"I recently moved back to Harmony after being away for several years," she told Caroline, summoning a smile, "and I'm very glad I did."

The girl's own soft smile broke through. "It's a good place to live, isn't it?"

"Yes."

"It's cool," Katie added.

Caroline straightened a fold of the powder-blue shirt-waist dress she wore with ballerina-style blue slippers and looked at her sister. "Cool means the weather," she said in a small lecture. "It has nothing to do with a city."

"Does, too," Katie quickly countered, lifting her little chin.

Well acquainted with how easily sibling arguments could erupt, although she couldn't imagine her own lively family ever butting heads over something as formal as a question of grammar, Jenna stepped into the breech. "Whatever the case," she said, "Harmony happens to be where I was born a *loo-ong* time ago."

Ross leaned back in his chair and found his mood lightening as the stretched-out word, issued with an exaggerated flutter of his visitor's dark lashes, had both girls abruptly giggling. The sound was music to his ears.

Yes, he reflected with assurance, this was exactly what the daughters he loved more than anything in the world needed, and what had been behind his thought to hire a younger housekeeper in the first place. They needed someone who could joke with them on occasion as well as care for them. Someone who could offer a female perspective on things and fill a gap he couldn't hope to fill. His daughters could only benefit from having a young, vibrant woman in their lives, no question about it.

And so would he, he knew. But in his case, it would have to go beyond having someone around to take care of his household. He wouldn't satisfy any of the private needs that had begun to build inside him by hiring a housekeeper, any housekeeper. He needed something else. Something more.

Hell, what he really needed was a wife.

Which, in his more candid moments, he'd been telling himself for a while now. Not only would it give his daughters a motherly influence and provide some physical comforts for himself, it could also lead to more children, maybe even the son he would desperately like to have while he was young enough to do a good job of being a father to an active boy. Marrying again, and sooner rather than later, might well be the best solution all around, he'd conceded more than once. Trouble was, no single woman of his acquaintance even stirred his interest…except the one who had recently returned to Harmony. The more time he spent with Jenna Lorenzo, the more he was beginning to recognize that fact.

"Daddy, are you *that* old?"

Ross brought his attention back to the discussion, realizing he'd missed a turn in the conversation. "What?" was all he could ask in response to Katie's question.

"Ms. Lorenzo said you were older than she is," Caroline explained in her usual calm manner.

"Way older is what she said," Katie tacked on.

He shot Jenna a look and found her eyes lit with amusement, as though she hadn't been able to resist that little zinger. "If four years is *way* older," he said dryly, "then I suppose I am."

With that issue cleared up, Katie jumped to her feet. "I'm gonna put Pandora to bed for a nap."

Jenna removed the towel from the doll's neck. "Better let her sit up awhile longer to make sure the glue's set."

"Okay. I'll sit her in her rocking chair."

Caroline reached for the scissors and glue. "I'll put these away, Dad."

Ross nodded to his eldest child. "Thanks, princess."

"You have two wonderful daughters," Jenna told him when the children had left.

"I'm in total agreement on that score." He sat forward and rested his forearms on the table. "And what can I say but thank you?"

She switched around to fully face him and frankly met his gaze. "You could say whether I'm going to be offered the job."

Well, this was it, he thought. Despite her qualifications, he knew the chances of that particular relationship working out were slim to none. Added to his earlier reservations about offering her the position, seeing her in his home had led to his viewing her in a different, and far more personal, light. The sheer truth was that he'd become too aware of her as a woman, and a desirable one at that, to regard her as merely an employee.

He released a gusty breath. "No, I'm afraid not."

"All right," Jenna said after a silent second. She gave him the briefest of smiles as she scooted back her chair. "You must have things to do. I won't take up any more of your time."

Ross knew he could have summoned a courteous smile in return and seen her to the door. With his contacts, he could even have offered to help her find another job. And he would, in fact, have done both without hesitation—if he could have actually stood back and watched Jenna Lorenzo walk out of his daughters' lives. Out of his life.

But he couldn't.

Every instinct he had—instincts that had served him well in the business world—had begun to tell him in no uncertain terms that he could only benefit from doing his damnedest to further another sort of relationship with this striking-looking woman. A private relationship.

"If you'll give me a few more minutes," he said before she could step away from the table, "I'd like to discuss, not the housekeeper's position, but something else entirely."

Her brow furrowed as she looked down at him. "What else is there to discuss?"

He met her question with a blunt one of his own, deciding to just plunge in. "Would you consider going out with me?"

Even as he watched, a blank expression wiped every trace of emotion from her face. Moments passed before she issued yet another question.

"I came here to talk about a job, and you're asking me out on a date?"

"Yes." Jeez, how did he put what he was thinking into words when he was still groping his way through it in his own mind? "But it could lead to…something more. And I don't mean an affair," he added before she could misunderstand him.

While his body wouldn't have protested much—not with this particular female—he knew that an affair was the last thing he wanted to start. It wouldn't provide what his children deserved to have in their lives. Or what he needed beyond the rewards of a purely physical relationship, for that matter. Because, if he chose to look to what the future might bring and view things from a strictly practical standpoint, taking a lover also wouldn't help in conducting a mayoral campaign.

No, it all boiled down to the fact that what he had to have to meet both his current and potential needs was a—

"Then what do you mean by, ah, something more?" Jenna asked, her tone wary as she broke into his thoughts.

"What I mean is…" He met her gaze, noting that her frown had not only reappeared but deepened. She hardly looked ready to go out with him at the moment, that was for sure.

If he didn't get on with this, he told himself, she'd be headed for the door. He hadn't missed the barest hint of temper glinting in her eyes; he had a temper himself, although he seldom displayed it. It also hadn't escaped his notice that in addition to her growing irritation with his drawn-out explanation, she was fast coming to the conclusion that he was acting strange.

And after he said what he was about to say… Hell, she just might think he was flat-out crazy.

But he was saying it, anyway.

"If we started seeing each other and it goes well," he told her, measuring out the words, "how would you feel about possibly marrying me?"

Chapter Two

Jenna's jaw dropped. In the next instant she sank back into her chair and hit the seat with enough force to snap her mouth closed and rattle her teeth. Then she stilled completely and groped to take in what she had just heard.

How would she feel about marrying him? *Him?* Ross Hayward, once half of the Golden Couple, talking about walking down the aisle again with her. *Her?* No, he couldn't have meant it!

"I must," she said, finding her voice at last, "have misunderstood you. You weren't—you couldn't have been—talking about the two of us and…marriage."

He studied her for moment. "I was."

Now she had to suck in a breath, a big one. As her lungs filled, a short study of her own told her that he really did mean it. His watchful expression was far too serious to reach any other conclusion. Good Lord. Even in her wildest adolescent dreams, she'd never imagined that this man would ever consider asking her to marry him.

Then again, he wasn't asking now, she reminded herself as the brain she normally put to good use began to recover from the undeniable jolt to its circuits. He'd mentioned *possibly* getting married, which was a far cry from an actual proposal.

"Maybe I'd better go into a few more details as to what I had in mind," he said.

She cleared her throat. "Details," she couldn't help but say, "would be good."

He sat forward and propped his elbows on the table. "First off, I'd like to get something straight. I'm not currently involved with anyone, and I take it, since you just recently returned to Harmony, that the same is true in your case."

"It is," Jenna agreed. Not only wasn't she currently involved with a man, she had, in fact, been extremely careful for some time when it came to personal relationships with the opposite sex. The truth was, she'd been burned once, badly, and she had no wish to repeat the experience. She dated on and off when it suited her, but live-in housekeepers didn't have much chance for a private life, and she'd accepted the restrictions.

"Then since we're free in that regard," Ross continued, "marrying each other could have some definite benefits for both of us."

She was slowly getting his drift. "You mean that, rather than just a housekeeper, you'd have a wife to take care of things around here."

"You're right, of course," he conceded, "but more than that, I would have a mother for Caroline and Katie."

"And that's important to you," she summed up, all at once sure of her words as she looked him straight in the eye and saw the clear reality of the matter reflected in his gaze.

"It is," he confirmed. And with that quiet acknowledgment, he went on to explain how he felt his daughters needed a younger woman's influence in their lives. "I think it's going to be even more important as they get closer to being teenagers," he added, "and Caroline's already on the brink."

Jenna could hardly disagree, remembering how her own mother had dealt so well with her four girls. "I can't deny that the mother-daughter relationship is important. Having a large family meant that both my parents had to work to make ends meet while I was growing up, and I remember how I sometimes couldn't wait for my mother to get home—for more reasons than one, I'll admit, as I got older. As the eldest child, I was often in charge of the younger girls once I was big enough to take on some responsibility, and it wasn't always easy."

He nodded. "That's why I would prefer a stay-at-home mom for my kids, and in this case, living on my salary alone wouldn't pose a problem."

"No, I expect not," Jenna replied. Which, she realized, was an understatement. Haywards had been among the more successful of Harmony's residents for many years. None had ever been truly wealthy, but comfortably well-off would certainly apply, especially when compared with such families as the Lorenzos. The city didn't have a bad side of town, so Jenna couldn't honestly say she'd been born on the "wrong side of the tracks" from Ross Hayward. Nevertheless, a social gap remained between them. At least it would in some people's eyes.

And now he was suggesting they date with the possible goal of marriage? Her eyes narrowed of their own accord. "Are you *sure* you don't want to hire me as housekeeper?"

For the first time in many minutes, his lips curved in a smile. "I'm sure." His gaze never wavered from hers.

"And the position we're currently discussing would be far more permanent, when you think about it. You would have a secure future, financially and otherwise."

And what about love?

Jenna didn't voice the silent question. She didn't have to. She knew this man loved his daughters; that was more than apparent. But his emotions weren't involved in the bargain he'd just put forward. How could they be when he'd only really known her for a matter of days?

She was certain he didn't remember her or her family from their earlier years in Harmony. He had no clue as to how she had once mooned over him, right along with most of the girls her age. To him, she was a known quantity in the fact that she had a history here, but he didn't actually know *her*.

Of course, despite that, he obviously believed she had certain qualities that went hand in hand with being a good parent. And when it came to a wife…

"So what you're suggesting is a potential marriage of convenience?" she asked very carefully.

"Not exactly." He exhaled a short breath. "It might be based somewhat on convenience, I'll admit, but I'd want it to be a real marriage in every sense of the word."

There was no mistaking the candid look in his eyes. "You mean, a…physical relationship."

"Yes."

The single word had her pulse fluttering. "I see."

"But I wouldn't push you on that," he added. "Even if we became husband and wife, I'd give you however much time you needed to feel more comfortable with the situation."

"I see," she repeated after another brief pause.

"I'll also be up-front about the fact that I'd like to

have more children. Would you like some of your own?''

"Yes," she replied, this time without hesitation. She couldn't deny that she had hoped to have children some-day.

"Good," he told her. "If we do decide to make that a, uh, joint project, it would be up to you to set the timetable, although I'd personally prefer not to wait too long to have another child." He paused for a beat. "For now, all I'm asking is that you give this whole matter some thought."

"Maybe you'd better give it some more thought first," she found herself saying with blunt directness.

His sudden grin was wry. "I promise you I haven't gone off the deep end. I'm one of the most sound and sensible of the Haywards. You can ask just about anyone in this town."

She didn't have to. Successful businessmen hardly made a habit of acting on a whim, and Jenna had to concede that the reasons he'd given for getting married again were logical enough.

"Have you considered how your daughters would feel about your remarrying?" she asked.

His expression sobered. "I'm not saying that the change wouldn't have its rocky moments. There are bound to be some. But everything I've done since the day they were born has been with their happiness in mind, believe me."

She believed him. In fact, his solemn tone made her wonder if he had already given up some of his own happiness in exchange for theirs. No, that was ridiculous, she told herself in the next breath. This man had been part of the ideal family. Whatever happiness he'd lost had been stripped from him by fate when he'd lost the perfect woman to share his life.

Jenna sighed to herself. How would that woman's successor, no matter who she was, ever be able to compete with perfection?

"So YOU DIDN'T get the housekeeper's spot, but he wants to possibly offer you the job of *wife*." Peggy O'Brien's aquamarine eyes were wide, the flush of excitement on her cheeks nearly as red as the shiny curls brushing her shoulders. "What in the world did you tell him?"

"I finally agreed to think about it." Jenna lounged back in a well-worn recliner set in one corner of a cozy family room, thinking that the O'Brien home, a ranch-style house located on a cheerfully rowdy street in a middle-class neighborhood filled with children, was usually a place that promoted relaxation. Unfortunately it wasn't having that effect on her tonight.

She'd waited until Peggy's five-year-old son, Tyler, had been put to bed and her loving husband, Jack, was puttering in his workshop off the garage before sharing that day's startling events with her longtime friend from grammar school. When Peggy and Jack had invited her to stay with them during her job search, she had readily accepted.

"You have to think about the chance to marry Ross Hayward?" From her seat on a plump chintz sofa, Peggy crossed her arms over the front of the white T-shirt she wore with jeans and shook her head in wonder. "He's got everything going for him, Jen. Looks, smarts, an excellent reputation in the community and a good income coming in from his business. He is definite husband material and—" Peggy wiggled a reddish brown eyebrow ''—the man is probably one heck of a lover, as well.''

''He's also a man who isn't madly in love with me,'' Jenna reminded her. ''As I've explained, this wouldn't be a traditional marriage. More one of convenience, in fact, than anything.''

''Hmm.'' Peggy's gaze narrowed thoughtfully. ''Does that mean separate beds?''

Jenna cleared her throat. ''Maybe in the beginning,'' she replied, ''but he frankly expects that to end at some point.''

''So the relationship wouldn't be minus the normal physical aspects,'' Peggy summed up. ''Probably not for too long, at any rate. Which means you'd have the opportunity to find out exactly how good a lover he is.''

At the moment Jenna couldn't imagine sharing a bed with the man who'd rendered her speechless that day. ''I won't be finding out anything if he never actually proposes. Or if he does, for that matter, and I decide to decline.''

''So, let me get this straight,'' Peggy said. ''You actually think you can turn this guy down?''

Because she was a long way from sure of the answer, Jenna countered with a question of her own. ''Why not? Most people, even the least romantic of them, would probably think twice about entering into this kind of marriage, you know. Plus there's the fact that I'm me. And he's…him.''

''If you're implying that you weren't born high enough on the social ladder for him, Jen, my temper is going to get the better of me.''

Peggy's staunch defense of her—their—less-than-upscale roots had Jenna smiling a truly genuine smile for the first time in hours. ''No, I'm not implying that,'' she said. "But you can't argue the fact that Ross Hayward and I were born into very different kinds of families."

Peggy raised one delicately boned shoulder in a shrug. "So what? Diversity isn't necessarily a bad thing. Could be the Haywards would even profit from some new blood being added to the mix."

"They seem to be doing just fine with the mix they have." Jenna had to say it. "As far back as I can recall, they've been a good-looking bunch, and the two young girls I met today are certainly no exception."

"Yes, 'angelically fair' would describe both whenever I've seen them around town, I agree. But then, how could they miss with the combination of genes from their father and…" Peggy's voice trailed off as she steepled her fingers and tapped them together. "I think we're getting to the heart of the matter here," she continued after a second. "Unless I'm badly mistaken, your reluctance to consider the many merits of strolling down the aisle with the biggest catch in town has a lot to do with who he married first."

Busted, Jenna reflected with a rueful twist of her mouth. "Okay, so maybe it does. But, my Lord, Peg, he had Cynthia Morgan to come home to every evening." *And to go to bed with every night.* "You have to remember how she always looked—and acted."

"Uh-huh. The stunning blonde with the polished poise most of our particular group would have given our eyeteeth to have at the time we were going through our awkward stage," Peggy said. "Then again, she was older than we were."

"Don't kid yourself," Jenna advised. "Cynthia never had an awkward stage. She probably entered the world holding her tiny head high and greeting the doctor who delivered her with a gracious smile.''

''And you're thinking that she'd be a hard act to follow,'' Peggy surmised with a shrewd glance.

Jenna could hardly deny it. ''Sure, I am. What woman who knew her could resist thinking along those lines?''

''Maybe none—but *you're* the woman he's at least considering making wife number two,'' Peggy reminded her. ''And not because he'd have any trouble finding someone else to wear his ring if he wanted to put the least bit effort into it, as we both know. Instead, though, he's apparently setting his sights on you. Whatever his reasons, that has to count for something.''

''Yes, it does,'' Jenna acknowledged. Truth be told, she couldn't help feeling flattered. Not that it would be wise to get too caught up in that feeling, her more practical side told her. Still, no matter what it said, her pulse picked up a beat every time her mind drifted back to that afternoon.

To *him*.

''You can handle whatever you have to if you take that walk down the aisle,'' Peggy declared, regaining Jenna's attention. ''Ross Hayward isn't the only one who has a lot going for him.''

''Oh, if the whole thing ever came to pass, I can deal with the cooking and housekeeping part,'' Jenna said with confidence, although honesty forced her to admit, privately anyway, that Myra Hastings might not be an easy act to follow, either. Not when it came to maintaining a spotless house decorated mainly in white—or as much of it as Jenna had seen, anyway.

''You can handle the mothering part, too,'' Peggy assured her. ''You not only helped raise your sisters, but from what you tell me, you've had recent experience riding herd on kids, as well. Heaven knows, you already have Tyler wrapped around your finger. You didn't scream when he pulled out the fake spider that looks real enough, goodness knows. It's made you tops on his list.''

"He's a great kid," Jenna pronounced without hesitation, and fully meant it.

Peggy grinned a plainly proud grin at that compliment to her offspring. "Thanks. Watching you with him, it's easy to see that you like children, and I'll bet they generally like you, which goes a long way toward what's needed to make a good mother, at least as far as I'm concerned."

Jenna mulled that over for a second. "I guess you have a point there. To me, caring about kids—not just caring for their needs—has to be a prime ingredient in what makes a good mother. And stepmother, too," she added firmly.

"I don't see you as a wicked one, that's for sure," Peggy murmured with a twinkle in her eye.

But would the two girls she'd met hours earlier come to view her in that light? Jenna knew that was the real question. There might well be rocky times ahead in that area, as their father had frankly conceded. Nevertheless, as he'd also contended, they would ultimately benefit from having a younger woman in their lives. It by no means had to be her, Jenna readily admitted, but having someone around to fill that role would be a plus.

Peggy sat forward. "And now we come to the wife part."

"Yes, well." Jenna ran her tongue around her teeth. "That particular subject is far from clear at the moment."

"You don't have to be Cynthia," Peggy assured her, reading her like a book. "You just have to be you."

"I *can* only be me," Jenna replied, realizing the truth of that. When all was said and done, she was who she was, and she'd been comfortable with that for some time. Nonetheless, she also recognized that who she was might suffer in comparison to what many would consider a sterling example of perfect womanhood.

Jenna Lorenzo was by no stretch of the imagination perfect.

"So are you at least going to give this whole thing some real thought?" Peggy asked.

"I suppose I'll have to," Jenna said with a wry curve of her lips, "because the man in question has already talked me into going out with him for dinner on Friday night."

Peggy's grin came back full force, lighting up her elfin face. "Well, if nothing else, you'll be going out on a date with Ross Hayward. At one point in my life, I would have stood on my head and sung every rowdy rock tune I knew—backward—to be able to do the same."

Jenna had to laugh. "Me, too, as well you know."

But that was long ago, and the upcoming event wasn't precisely the normal kind of first date. It wouldn't be a casual get-to-know-you occasion. Or only on the surface, perhaps. Underneath, far more serious matters were in the balance, ones that would demand answers before too long.

With Myra Hastings leaving in a matter of weeks, Ross Hayward had no choice but to make some arrangements. He would either be hiring another housekeeper—which wouldn't be her, Jenna knew. Or he'd be taking a wife—which might be her.

In fact, he seemed more than willing to consider her for the latter position. The woman she'd become realized it was so, even if the girl who would always remain a part of her still couldn't quite believe it.

HE WAS RUSTY at this dating business.

Ross couldn't help but acknowledge that truth as he pulled out a chair for Jenna at one of the quieter eating spots in Harmony. He'd been out of college for only months the last time he'd ventured on a date as a single man. Not long afterward, he'd become a husband, and then years later, a widower with little desire to ask any female out.

Nevertheless, despite his lengthy break from the dating scene, the Mountain Meadows Café had seemed like a good bet for tonight. Not as starchy as the dining room at the Founders Club, where he continued to maintain a membership yet seldom visited these days. And not as casual as the diner where he'd chosen to conduct a job interview with the woman seated across from him, her deep burgundy evening suit providing a colorful contrast to both his own charcoal-brown suit and the pale table-cloth.

"This is nice," she said, glancing around. Her small ruby earrings sparkled in the flickering glow of the single candle resting in the center of the table.

Again she wore her hair caught back in a thick coil at the nape of her neck. And again he wondered how it would look flowing like a dark waterfall down her back.

He also had to wonder if he would ever find out. If he would ever get the chance the run his hands through those gleaming strands. If…

Ross took in a breath and reined in his wandering

thoughts. "The view is one of the best around," he told his companion.

"It has to be." Jenna studied a picture-postcard scene through the wall of clear windows beside her. Even in the growing darkness, enough light remained to make out the tall pines dotting the side of a low mountain.

"Would you like a cocktail or some wine to start things off?" he asked.

She opted for white wine, and he ordered a bottle of Chardonnay when the young waiter approached. He'd decided to join her despite the fact that a premium brand of Scotch on the rocks was his usual drink, one a long line of Hayward men had favored. Even his father, he thought, hadn't broken with tradition there.

Silence fell between them on the waiter's departure, as if neither knew exactly what to say next, until Ross picked up his menu and offered some comments on meals he'd enjoyed at the Mountain Meadows in the past.

"I don't think you can go wrong with any of the fish selections," he said. "The last time I was here, I had the grilled salmon and certainly didn't regret it."

"As it happens, I like fish." Jenna studied her menu. "Even tuna fish is a hit with me. I used to have to fight a cat I once had for it. I swear Bingo had a sixth sense that brought him running every time I opened a can, no matter how quietly."

"Was that when you lived in Nevada?"

Jenna looked up and hesitated for a brief moment. "Yes. What made you think that might be the case?"

He lifted one shoulder in an offhand shrug. "Bingo, cards, gambling. They seem to fit."

"I suppose so." She closed her menu. "I'm going to take your recommendation and try the salmon."

He decided on the pan-fried trout and again searched for a subject of conversation once the wine appeared and their orders were taken. He could have asked Jenna more about her days in Nevada—would have, if he hadn't noted how she'd put a subtle yet swift end to the earlier conversational turn.

A sign that she'd rather not discuss that particular time in her life? Could be, he concluded, mindful of the fact that there were times in his own life he had no wish to discuss, either.

He finally settled on food as a safe bet. "What do you like to cook?"

"Pasta is one of my favorites." Jenna sipped her wine. "Goodness knows, I ate enough of it when I was a kid. My mother makes the best red sauce ever. I learned from watching her, so I'm pretty good at it myself." She paused. "Can you cook?"

"Not really. Then again, my mother never had a great deal of interest in that area, either."

She met his gaze. "I assume you had a housekeeper to take care of kitchen duties when you were growing up."

"Uh-huh. We had several over the years, as a matter of fact." *But none of them ever looked like you,* Ross added to himself.

"And after you got married?"

He ran a long finger down the smooth stem of his glass. "Cynthia preferred to run her own household," he said. And then it was his turn to change the subject, because his former marriage was one of the things he'd just as soon not discuss. "How do you like the wine?"

Whether conscious of it or not, Jenna returned his earlier favor by readily going along with the switch in topics. "It's excellent." She glanced down at her clear goblet and the golden liquid it held. "Very smooth."

As the evening continued, Ross couldn't help but wish he were half as smooth when it came to wining and dining a woman. But all in all, it wasn't going too badly, he decided when they'd done justice to two good meals and lingered over after-dinner coffee. Thankfully they'd found one subject that seemed to suit them both when it came to maintaining a steady flow of conversation, and that was Harmony itself.

It almost—but not quite—kept his thoughts from drifting to something he'd been asking himself in the back of his mind since halfway through dinner.

When they arrived back at the house where Jenna was staying, should he kiss her good-night?

Ross cleared his throat. "I'll never forget when we had the record snowfall," he said in another bid to silence the nagging question for which he had no firm answer. "I must have been around twelve, and I remember standing chest-high in one of the drifts."

Jenna sipped her coffee. "That was the year it was nearly over my head in spots."

"And did you build the biggest snowman you could, as I did?"

"Mmm-hmm. My sisters and I made fast work of it, too, since snow seldom lasted for long here. We tied a bright red scarf around his neck, as I recall, and thought he looked very dashing—until he started to lean to one side and promptly fell over. Then we consoled ourselves with a snowball fight."

"I recall a few of those myself," he told her. "Being an only child, I relied on my friends and a cousin around my age to provide a satisfying battle. We usually wound up half burying each other in the stuff."

Jenna laughed, and found that it felt good. Somehow the thought of very young Ross Hayward covered from tip to toe with snow put her more at ease. It wasn't like her to let her nerves rule, which they mostly had since he'd arrived on the O'Brien doorstep to pick her up. She usually had a much better hold on them.

Certainly her escort had done nothing to foil her efforts in that respect, either. This might not be quite the normal version of a first date, but so far he'd made no reference to the startling suggestion he'd come up with days earlier. She could only be thankful that he hadn't brought it up again, because at this point she was still a long way from sure how she would respond if he actually wound up proposing.

At the moment it was far easier to put herself to the task of being a genial companion. With that in mind she kept up her end of a casual conversation, which remained centered on the past as they talked about the grammar school they'd attended and the first-grade teacher who'd taught several generations of the city's residents.

"I haven't seen Miss Hester since I got back," Jenna said. "I wonder if she'd remember me."

"My guess is she would," Ross replied. "Although she's over eighty now, she's still as sharp as a tack. I think she really runs half the town, although no one will admit it."

"That doesn't surprise me. I could never get away with anything with her," Jenna confessed.

He leaned back in his chair. "Neither could I, despite the fact that we're related, at least through marriage."

Now Jenna was surprised. "You are?"

"Yes. My grandfather married Hester Goodbody's sister."

Harmony was indeed, she thought, a small community. "I do know that your grandfather was mayor at one time."

"That's right. And," he added, "there's a possibility that I'll be running for that office, too, provided our current mayor decides not to run for reelection."

"Would you really want to do that?" she had to ask, again surprised. He'd seemed content with his business career.

"My grandfather would have wanted it," he told her.

But that wasn't the question she'd asked, Jenna noted.

She also noticed the lack of any mention of his father. And maybe that wasn't quite so surprising. She'd heard about the events that had taken place during the time she'd been away. As far as her friend Peggy knew, the distinguished-looking man Jenna had little trouble recalling hadn't set foot in Harmony since he'd abruptly walked out on his wife in favor of, as rumor had it, a far different lifestyle in California. As to the woman he'd left behind, she had immediately filed for divorce and had refused to discuss the subject in public right up to her death.

It wasn't long before Ross paid the check and took a last sip of his coffee. "Ready to go?"

Jenna nodded and gave herself a mental pat on the back. She'd relaxed and had even managed to enjoy herself.

As he had before, Ross steered them both through the cheerful maze of small, candle-lit tables with a light grasp on her elbow. And as before, Jenna felt the barest grip of his long fingers right down to her toes. So much for relaxation, she reflected as sheer awareness had her shoulders tensing once more.

Sudden thoughts of how the evening might end surfaced as they left the restaurant and walked across the parking lot to her escort's late-model blue sedan. If this were an ordinary first date, Jenna knew that something she hadn't considered until now could well be taken as a fitting way to wind things up.

A kiss—a brief kiss—was almost customary.

Then again, even if this were an ordinary date, could the prospect of locking lips, even briefly, with Ross Hayward ever be judged an everyday average event? *Not hardly,* she acknowledged to herself. *Not by you.*

But then, he might not even be considering a kiss.

HE WAS GOING FOR IT. Or he was if he got the chance. If she didn't slip away from him and head inside the minute they arrived at their destination, Ross thought as they started down a short walkway where a child's tricycle was parked on one side of the path.

"Nice night," he said, keeping his voice low as he glanced up at a black sky sprinkled with stars.

"Yes," was her soft reply.

"Cool but pleasant."

"Yes," she said one more time as they reached a plain oak door lit by a small overhead lamp. She looked up at him and held out her right hand. "Well, thank you again for din—"

"I'd like to kiss you." The blunt words were out before he even considered the tone of them. But he wouldn't call them back if he could have. If he hadn't said something, he'd probably be looking at that door closing behind her in a matter of moments.

When she just stared at him, brown eyes gleaming in the darkness, he cleared his throat. "Given the situation, I think we should find out what it would be like."

"Oh."

"I mean, it seems logical." *Right, and physical attraction has nothing to do with it,* a more candid part of him mocked. He ignored it. "That way, we'll have a better basis to, ah, make our decision."

She studied him for a silent second. "So you haven't reconsidered? You're still thinking about marriage?"

"I am," he assured her. "And I'm still of the opinion that, if we decide to go through with it, it would have benefits for both of us. But right now, I'd just like to kiss you. May I?"

She released a short breath. "Okay."

The word was scarcely out when he lifted one hand to cup her chin. Then he lowered his mouth to hers, taking in her subtle floral scent and reminding himself that this was only a kiss. It wouldn't—couldn't—lead to greater intimacy. Whether there would even be an opportunity for any real body-to-body, skin-to-skin intimacy between them remained to be seen.

But that didn't mean he couldn't savor the moment. And he did exactly that as he deepened the kiss just slightly, just enough to discover that he'd like to take it deeper still, much deeper. Instead he made himself settle for a gentle exploration of a mouth far softer than his own. As he lingered, his blood heated despite the cool breeze, and in a matter of seconds he had to work at keeping an invisible fist tight on his control, denying feet ready to take a last step to get even closer and hands that wanted to wander. All of him, in fact, wanted many things, none of which he could have.

Which he would never have, not with Jenna, unless he became her lover. No, unless he became her husband.

He needed, he reminded himself, a wife.

At last he forced himself to lift his head and to drop the hand still cupped around a silky-smooth chin. Inhaling a rough surge of air, he took a brief step back to let his senses clear. It was hard to believe that a kiss, even an undeniably potent one, had been enough to have him making up his mind about something that would change the course of his life. But it had.

"I know you're probably not ready to hear this," he said with a huskiness he couldn't hide, "but I'm prepared to suggest that we take this…all the way."

Again Jenna stared up at him, her own breathing far from even. "All the way?" she repeated carefully.

"To the altar."

There, it was out. And he found he had no regrets. He'd made his choice, although the woman still pinned under his gaze needed some time to make hers. That was plain enough by the way her eyes had gone wide with what might have been shock.

"You don't have to say anything now," he told her. "I'll call you in a day or two so we can make plans for another date and talk about it more."

Jenna merely nodded once in reply. As she let herself into the house, her escort turned and left with a final wave. Moments later she was inside, leaning against the door she'd closed behind her.

She could still feel the imprint of his mouth on hers. Still taste the pure, tangy maleness of his questing tongue. Still smell the light, woodsy scent of his cologne. Still… Heavens, she was still tingling all over.

Peggy poked her head out of the doorway to the family room. "Good grief, what happened to you?"

"What?" Jenna blinked.

"That was my question, friend." Peggy walked down the narrow hall. "What in the world happened? You look like you've been knocked for a loop."

Jenna took a steadying breath. "I'm…fine."

"Sure, and I'm a rock star." Peggy crossed her arms over the front of her T-shirt. "Is Ross Hayward responsible for that stunned expression on your face?"

"I suppose so," Jenna had to concede.

"What did the man do?"

"He, uh, kissed me." *Right before he floored me by proposing on our first date.*

But she was keeping that last fact to herself for now, Jenna decided. He really had asked her to marry him, hadn't he? Yes, although he hadn't actually done it in the most traditional of manners, his meaning had been clear.

"And that's the effect his chiseled lips have on the female half of the population?" Peggy's brows climbed. "I'm impressed." She paused to take another survey of her friend. "If he's looking anywhere near as staggered as you are, wedding bells could be in your immediate future."

Jenna pushed away from the door and was grateful to find that her knees were no longer in danger of folding. "Only if I agree to go along with it," she managed to counter.

Peggy shook her head over that statement. "I think you're a goner, Jen. If he can have you looking like that with no more than a kiss, how can you turn him down?"

Choosing to duck a question she knew she'd have to face far sooner than she expected, Jenna only shrugged in reply. "I'm heading off to bed," she said as the need to be alone grew.

"All right, see you in the morning." Peggy stepped aside. "After that stunning experience, you'll probably have some terrific dreams," she added with a sly smile.

But that prediction proved to be wrong, and later that night Jenna was wishing she actually could dream—

about anything—as she stared up at the ceiling in the small guest bedroom. At least it would mean she had finally fallen asleep. It seemed that as hard as she tried to shut it down, her mind remained on full alert and filled with questions.

What she had to do to win any prospect of peace was to try to come to some conclusions, she decided at last.

So, did she really want a husband? she asked herself. She had to admit that she'd always expected when she was growing up to have one at some point. Her parents' happy marriage had been a wonderful example.

But did she want that husband to be Ross Hayward, former Golden Boy and possible future mayor?

Well, as the man himself had pointed out days earlier, their marriage would provide her with financial security. Which wasn't a matter she could take lightly, Jenna knew, after growing up in a household where money was usually scarce.

And, as he also hadn't hesitated to mention, it would give her children. Another thing she couldn't take lightly, because she'd spoken no more than the truth when she'd told him that she wanted children.

The problem was that she had learned something tonight. Something that had been made plain to her even before Ross, who was obviously a man of action, had rendered her speechless once again by staring down at her with frank directness and suggesting that they take it all the way…to the altar.

Up until hours ago she had privately skirted the issue of an intimate relationship with Ross and how it might affect her. Now she knew that what he could make her feel as a woman was far more powerful than any teenage crush. Even if they became husband and wife, it wouldn't be easy for her to allow it to become a real marriage in every sense, not when it could lead to her coming to care too much for him. Because if that happened and he wasn't able to return her feelings as time passed, her heart would be on the line—as it already had been in another relationship, with far from happy results.

So what did she do now?

You take a chance, an inner voice told her, *because you can't turn him down, not when there's at least hope that it could someday become a genuinely caring marriage on both sides.*

Jenna sighed the softest of sighs, somehow, deep at the core of her, recognizing that silent statement as the simple truth. She could toss and turn for still more hours on end, even continue to rack her brain for days, but it all came down to one undeniable fact.

Both the starry-eyed girl she'd once been who had viewed an all-too-attractive Hayward male from a distance, and the levelheaded woman she'd become who had just experienced the impact of his closeness, simply couldn't say no. Not to him.

So the next move was hers, she knew, and there was no point in waiting for the man in her thoughts to call. Instead she would place a call herself. And then she would say words that would change her life forever.

As impossible as it would have seemed only a short time ago, Jenna Lorenzo was going to marry Ross Hayward.

Chapter Three

"So you're really going through with this?" Adam Lassiter asked as he faced Ross across the gleaming surface of a large, dark walnut desk.

"I am, trust me." Ross reclined in his tan leather swivel chair. As the rest of his corner-office furnishings, it was practical, comfortable and modern in design—all of which his current guest ignored in favor of frankly studying him.

The engagement announcement had been printed in the local paper that morning, and his phone had predictably rung off the hook until he'd given in to an urge for a little peace and quiet and asked his assistant to hold his calls for a while. Then his tall, dark and nattily dressed cousin had arrived on the scene.

Days earlier Ross had called to notify some closer family members before the news became public, which had led to Adam's unexpected appearance. In fact, the man who made an excellent living as a hot-shot business consultant in the Phoenix area had driven a considerable distance to come to Harmony.

Adam braced elbows covered by the well-tailored jacket of his steel-gray suit on the arms of a beige tweed visitor's chair. "I told the Lassiters when you asked me to be your best man that if you said you were going to do it, it was a good bet you would. But they refused to believe it until I rescheduled several appointments so I could come here and look you in the eye.''

''Uh-huh.'' Ross hid a smile. ''And how is my aunt Doris?''

Adam's grimace was swift and wry. ''Okay, so maybe my mother was the chief skeptic. The truth is that if she wasn't up to her elegant neck in getting things ready for a major charity auction back in Scottsdale, she'd probably be here instead of me.''

''I assume,'' Ross said, ''that I'll see her at the wedding.''

His grimace turning to a grin, Adam replied, ''I don't think wild horses could keep her away, especially when the bride is somewhat of a mystery woman.'' He paused for a beat. ''When do the invitations go out?''

''Soon. As I told everyone, the wedding is the last Saturday of this month.''

Adam frowned. ''It's none of my business, I'll admit, but I have to wonder why the rush.''

''Why not? You know I don't hesitate over most things once I've made up my mind,'' Ross said in the mildest of tones.

And that was all he'd say on the subject. The bargain he'd made with his future wife was, as far as he was concerned, private. Only a few people knew that his intended bride had first applied for a housekeeper's position, and he saw little reason to spread the word. No, he was keeping mum on that score, even though he and this particular cousin were near the same age and had been especially close until Doris Hayward Lassiter had gone along with her husband's plan to achieve bigger and better things in the corporate world—and its various society connections—by moving their family to a larger city.

"Hmm." Adam lifted a hand and ran it through his expertly cut hair. "I suppose even the best man doesn't get to meet the mystery lady until the big day."

"It won't be long," Ross assured him, keeping his tone mild.

Silence reigned for a moment. "How are Caroline and Katie taking the news?" Adam ventured at last with a probing look.

Ross suspected the question held more genuine concern than his normally unruffled relative usually displayed. Maybe because Adam had a young child of his own, a son he saw mainly during the summers since the boy lived back east with Adam's ex-wife.

"It was a surprise," Ross acknowledged, "but they seem to be dealing with it as well as can be expected."

Maybe he would have liked at least a bit more enthusiasm on their part, he reflected, but he could readily understand why they'd both been unusually quiet since he'd sat them down and told them as gently yet straightforwardly as possible about his plans after Jenna had called. He'd been more than a little surprised himself, he couldn't deny, when she'd agreed to marry him without much debate. But surprises aside, things would settle down and his daughters would be grateful to have her in their lives. It was just a matter of time.

As for himself, he was damned grateful to have her in *his* life, and for more reasons than one after the potent first kiss they'd shared. So far, it was the only real kiss circumstances had allowed, but he had expectations of getting more, much more. Not that he hadn't meant it when he'd said he wouldn't press her. Still, he hoped he wouldn't have to wait too long to get everything he wanted…because he wanted it all.

"You look just a tad on the eager side, cuz." Adam's soft laugh came from low in his throat. "This woman you're keeping under wraps must be something."

Ross lifted a brow. "I suppose you could say that."

"Aha. No further explanation required. I read you."

"You always were quick on the uptake, cuz," Ross countered, repeating the nickname they'd once used on a regular basis to refer to each other.

Adam rose to his feet. "Well, I'll report back to the family and tell them that things are still on track. Is it going to be a big wedding?"

Ross got up and came around his desk. "It's already bigger than we initially planned on," he said as he walked his cousin to the door, "but it won't be too big."

IT WAS GETTING BIGGER every day, Jenna reflected with a rueful twist of her lips as she addressed a stack of envelopes that would hold thick, ecru-colored cards edged with a scalloped border. With desktop publishing, it was hardly astounding that professional-looking invitations could be produced so quickly, but who would have thought that one of the most popular—if by no means the grandest—spots in town to get married would be available for a Saturday event on such short notice? Yet that had indeed been the case, as her friend Peggy had wasted no time in finding out, and after that discovery the guest list had rapidly multiplied.

Like rabbits, Jenna thought.

Her family was coming, of course. They'd plainly been startled—or maybe downright amazed—at the news when she'd placed a call to Nevada, but they would be here. At least her parents and youngest sister would make it. Both of her other sisters simply couldn't. One was attending chef's school in Europe after winning a scholarship, and the other was due to have her first child only days after the wedding.

The bride's family was merely the start, however. Even the groom's was just the tip of the iceberg.

Besides his daughters, Ross had no immediate family still living—except for his father, whom he had firmly declined to invite. But Harmony was home to several more distantly related Haywards, plus many others who considered themselves longtime friends of the family. And, as it turned out, a whole bunch of them wanted to come.

They all wanted to attend a wedding that wasn't quite the average version of the traditional celebration. Except none of the people primed to celebrate knew that.

"Why couldn't we have just been married at the courthouse as we'd first thought and be done with it?" Jenna mumbled to herself as the phone on the kitchen counter rang. With Peggy and Jack working and their son in school, it was up to their houseguest to answer, so she rose from the square oak table set in one corner of the room and lifted the receiver. "O'Brien residence."

"How's it going?" a deep voice asked.

As usual, her pulse picked up a beat in response. Jenna wondered how much time would pass before it remained comfortably steady in reaction to what was an increasingly familiar, if undeniably pure male, sound. After all, she and Ross had not only talked on the phone several times in recent days, they'd also seen each other most evenings, mainly in the company of his daughters.

"I'm getting writer's cramp," she complained half-heartedly as she leaned against the counter. "Are you sure we can't conveniently forget these invitations and sneak off to the courthouse instead?''

His chuckle was low and amused. ''I'll admit things seem to have snowballed, but we can handle it.''

Well, he could handle it, Jenna knew, at least when it came to the extra expense. Ross had already assured her that he could afford it. He had originally been determined to pay for everything, and he'd mostly had his way. She'd only insisted on buying her own wedding outfit, and he'd given in on that point. Their first compromise, she thought.

Wondering how many more they'd be called upon to make in the future, she said, ''Okay, so we can't sneak off. I'll just keep writing.''

''Don't forget that we're taking Caroline and Katie out for pizza tonight.''

''I'm looking forward to it,'' Jenna replied, and meant it. Maybe this time, she thought, she'd even be successful at getting Ross's daughters to do more than manage a short response to a direct question while aiming wary glances her way. Before much longer she would be caring for them on a day-to-day basis. She had to hope they would have become better acquainted by then. Katie, with a chattiness that had seemed to come naturally on the day they'd first met, probably wouldn't hold back for long before allowing a friendlier relationship to develop. Not too long, at any rate. But Caroline...

A fleeting frown crossed Jenna's brow. She wished she felt more confident that problems didn't lie ahead there. Not that Caroline had ever said anything in the least troubling. No, Ross's eldest child had impeccable manners. Nonetheless, her calm gaze had displayed an unmistakable coolness on the few occasions when her eyes had actually met those of the woman about to become her stepmother. But that didn't mean Jenna planned to stop watching for a hint of something warmer to form.

"I'll concentrate on pumping up my appetite so I can tackle my share of the pizza," she added, determined to remain optimistic when it came to the children.

"Okay, we'll pick you up at six." Ross paused for a moment. "Any progress on the wedding outfit?"

"I'm going shopping tomorrow." *Again*, she might have added. At the moment she was torn between a knee-length, cream-colored dress she could wear on other occasions and a floor-length model made of rosy silk that wouldn't be as practical in the long run. She'd already tried on both at one of Harmony's downtown boutiques. Neither was expensive enough to give her much pause, but she hadn't been able to make a final choice.

"Don't worry," she told him, "I'll show up wearing something appropriate. If I didn't, my father, who can be a stickler for the proprieties when he wants to, would refuse to walk me down the aisle."

"Then I take it you'll be decked out in more than a paper bag."

That had Jenna laughing out loud. Thankfully, while he could still rattle her with a casual touch, and far too easily as far as her nerves were concerned, he also had a sense of humor she had no trouble enjoying. "My father will insist on it," she assured him with mock gravity.

It won her another low chuckle. "He sounds like a sensible man. I'm looking forward to meeting your family."

She could have responded in kind—but didn't. The truth was, she could have done without meeting a whole group of Ross's relatives at the same time, especially when many of them had to be wondering about the hasty marriage.

"I'm sure the Lorenzos can't wait to meet you," she said instead.

If he noticed the lack of any mention of his own family, Ross made no comment, and the conversation ended seconds later.

Before Jenna could resume her seat at the table, however, the front doorbell rang. She smoothed a hand down the front of the oversize teal sweatshirt she wore with matching cotton pants and went to answer, walking with characteristic purpose. She didn't amble often, certainly not when there was work to be done, and she still had those invitations to finish.

Opening the door, she found someone standing there who looked much the same at eighty as she had back when Jenna had been a member of her first-grade class. Hester Goodbody's silver hair might be even more wispy now, but nothing had dimmed the good-natured intelligence gleaming in a pair of memorable blue eyes framed by gold-rimmed glasses.

"Hello, Jenna," the older woman said with a soft smile.

Jenna had to smile herself as she took a step back. "It's great to see you, Miss Hester. Please come in."

As she shut the door behind them, Jenna noticed for the first time that her visitor had a long cloth garment bag draped over one slender arm clad in a skillfully crocheted sweater.

"I won't be staying long," Miss Hester said. "I know you must have many things still to do for the wedding."

Jenna led the way into a small living room that didn't

seem to get much use in the O'Brien household. "Please sit down."

Accepting the invitation, Hester Goodbody sat on the beige brocade sofa and placed the garment bag beside her. "You've grown into a fine-looking young woman," she said as Jenna sank into a nearby chair.

Fine-looking—not beautiful. Jenna didn't miss the distinction. Trust Miss Hester to come down on the side of simple truth.

"I hope I look half as wonderful as you do years from now," she replied with total honesty.

The veteran teacher studied her for a second. "You will. You have excellent bone structure, and nothing withstands the test of time as well as good bones." She paused. "I assume that good behavior has also won out with you."

Jenna rolled her eyes, well up to speed on the reason for that comment. "Yes, ma'am. I've learned to be a lady, although I imagine you doubted you'd ever see the day."

"You certainly could be a scamp, but a likeable one with so much zest for life." The small features of the older woman's face settled into more serious lines as she continued. "Which is why I'm delighted that you're marrying Ross. I'll think you'll be good for him."

Good for him? Although far from certain on that point, Jenna was positive of one thing. "I intend to be the best wife I can," she said with determination.

"I'm glad to hear it." A thoughtful frown creased Miss Hester's finely lined brow. "Ross seldom misbehaved in school, you know. It might be that he felt he had the Hayward name to uphold, and if that was the case, I suspect it was more of a burden than most people realized."

"I suppose you could be right," Jenna conceded after a moment's consideration. Not many would easily note a downside to being a member of a well-respected family, but the sharp-eyed teacher who probably saw more than most just might have a point.

"Anyway," Miss Hester said, "I, for one, am pleased with the coming marriage, although from what I understand you're having a little trouble deciding what to wear for the occasion."

Jenna didn't ask how that understanding had come about. News traveled fast in small cities. She remembered that well from her earlier days in Harmony. Given Hester Goodbody's long-standing residency, this woman probably had more friends—and thereby sources of information—than anyone in town.

"I've narrowed it down to two choices," Jenna told her. "I plan to take another look tomorrow and make up my mind."

Miss Hester sat forward. "I have a third alternative." She patted the garment bag with one thin hand. "I'm hoping you'll give it some consideration."

And that was how Jenna found herself viewing a wedding gown made of delicate ivory lace moments later. Long-sleeved and high-necked, it was snugly fitted through the bodice, with a narrow skirt that fell straight from the waist. A floor-length satin slip in the same ivory shade peaked through the lacy fabric and provided a subtle hint of sheen.

"It was my sister's," Miss Hester explained. "She was taller than I am—about your height, in fact. And it's close to the same size as those dresses you tried on."

Jenna arched a brow, unable to resist the urge to tease. "Which you just happened to hear about?"

"No, which I made it my business to hear about,"

Miss Hester cheerfully confessed. "My sister wore this dress when she married Ross's grandfather, but both her daughter and her son's bride, Ross's mother, chose not to wear it for their own weddings. So she added it to some other belongings she left me when she passed away."

And what about another bride?

Jenna's silent question was answered in the next breath. "Ross's late wife also preferred to go with a newer style," Miss Hester said, "which may have been a prudent decision on her part. This gown would have had to be altered extensively, given that Cynthia was taller than average and very slim. And I must say that she was a vision in pure white during the summer ceremony held on the outdoor terrace of the Founders Club. With your creamier skin tones, however, I believe ivory would better suit you," she told Jenna, and demonstrated the truth of that by holding a lacy sleeve up to her former pupil's hand.

"Yes, the color probably would be better for me." Jenna couldn't deny what seemed so evident as the delicate fabric brushed across her fingers. But how could she explain that the chance to wear what could be considered a Hayward family heirloom was something she'd never expected to be offered? And maybe never would have been offered, she thought, if Miss Hester knew the circumstances behind the upcoming marriage.

"I wasn't," Jenna said as diplomatically as possible, "planning on wearing a traditional wedding gown."

"Nevertheless, it is lovely, isn't it?" the other woman wasted no time in asking.

"Yes." Jenna could hardly contend otherwise. The gown was indeed lovely, and somehow the fact that it was from another era only added to its gracious beauty.

Miss Hester straightened to her full height, which wasn't very high. "I would consider it both a favor and an honor if you would wear it."

Looking into sea-shaded eyes that plainly reflected the truth of that solemn statement, Jenna felt herself wavering. She did love the gown. And so would her mother, who hadn't been able to afford more than a simple dress when she'd been married. Plus there was the fact that it probably wouldn't have to be altered. She could make sure no damage was done and give it back as she'd received it.

"All right," she said at last. "I'll borrow it—just for that day."

"No, you'll pass it along as I did," her companion countered in a no-nonsense tone, suddenly sounding exactly like the teacher Jenna had once known. "And I'll get my reward from the sight of a young man's face as he watches you walk down the aisle. All I ask," she added, "is that you keep it a secret until then."

Jenna knew when she was licked. "All right, Miss Hester, whatever you say."

A sudden sparkle lit in Hester Goodbody's gaze, making her look far younger than her years. "Spoken," she declared with quiet satisfaction, "like a star member of my first-grade class."

THE WEDDING COTTAGE had been the site of countless Harmony nuptials over the years. Nestled in the center of a large corner lot on a peaceful street, the two-story frame house painted a mossy green was snugly surrounded by a well-tended garden. There, a wealth of fall flowers dominated the picture, and tall, leafy trees poised on the brink of their annual autumn transformation chimed in to produce a bright scene despite the layer of thin clouds hiding the late-afternoon sun.

Accompanied by his best man, Ross took in the sights around him as he made his way from an adjacent parking lot down a winding sidewalk leading to a side door reserved for the lesser members of the wedding party, which at the moment included the groom. He knew full well that until the ceremony started, the bride was the one who counted—and with that thought in mind, he had to wonder how Jenna was making out. He hadn't spoken to her since the evening before when he and his daughters had met her family over a quiet dinner hosted by the Lorenzos. Adam, who'd arrived in town a day earlier than the rest of the Lassiters, had joined them.

"Nervous, cuz?" Adam asked as they settled themselves in a small side room. Both men wore dark suits, white shirts, subtly striped ties, and had a tiny red rosebud stuck in the buttonhole of their jackets.

"I was more on edge last night," Ross admitted, "but I think I passed the test."

"With flying colors, in my opinion," Adam remarked. "Your about-to-be in-laws are a nice bunch, and they were obviously thrilled with the girls."

But were his girls thrilled with them? Ross couldn't honestly say one way or the other. At least Katie had been more talkative than in recent weeks, and he supposed he'd take that as a good sign.

"The maid of honor is quite a looker, too," Adam continued. "Too bad she's too young for me."

"Glad you recognize that," Ross said. "Joe Lorenzo might not look kindly on any serious flirting with his youngest child, and as big as he is, a smart man probably wouldn't test it."

"Hmm. At least I got to meet the mystery woman.

And I have to say you've got good taste. There's definitely something about her that stirs the juices. I mean," Adam added hastily at Ross's lifted brow, "my juices might get stirred if she wasn't well on her way to being your wife."

Deciding to be satisfied with that concession, Ross looked in a mirror placed on a narrow wall sporting printed wallpaper in masculine shades of brown. He straightened a tie that didn't need straightening and wondered how many grooms had stood where he was standing. The last time he himself had been a groom cooling his heels in another room, his father had been his best man. Now, it was hard to even imagine that.

Just then, Judge Reynolds, a longtime friend of the Hayward clan, poked his graying head into the room. "Time to take your places, gentlemen," he said in his usual courteous fashion. "The bride and her party have arrived."

Adam grinned, displaying a handsome set of teeth. "Showtime, cuz."

It wasn't long before both men stood beside the judge at one end of a large room decorated in a garden theme as though it were an extension of its outdoor surroundings. Directly in front of them, a straight walkway displaying a length of floral-print carpeting led to an arched doorway, with long rows of wicker chairs painted a leafy green lining both sides of the aisle.

The room itself was filled with familiar faces, and the most familiar of all to Ross belonged to his daughters, who sat next to Adam's parents in the first row. He smiled at them, and Katie, dressed in cheery yellow, managed a tiny one in return. Caroline, who was partial to quieter shades of blue and wore it today, nodded her head, but didn't smile. In contrast, Hester Goodbody, looking well pleased with the day's events, met his fleeting glance with a wide curve of her thin lips from her seat behind the children.

Music began to swell from a small organ near the rear of the room, and then a shapely brunette barely over twenty appeared in the doorway wearing a floor-length dress of dusky-rose silk. A matching hair ribbon held back Sophie Lorenzo's cap of short curls. An appealing grin broke through as she approached the men who awaited her, prompting Adam to lean over to his cousin and mutter, "Are you sure she's too young for me?"

Before Ross could reply, the wedding march started, right along with a sea of whispers as the guests got to their feet. Even though he couldn't make out the words, Ross drew his own conclusions. Those who hadn't yet met Jenna were most likely speculating about what she looked like, and those who had were probably wondering how she'd be dressed for the occasion.

He had to admit to being curious himself on that last point. She'd only told him that she'd settled on something and hadn't gone into details.

At least, he thought with a wry slant of his mouth, he could be certain she wasn't wearing a paper bag.

Then he stopped thinking at all as the bride came into view. For a stark second he could only stare. Finally he sucked in a breath and widened his stance, but his gaze remained locked on the woman taking slow steps toward him, one hand tucked under her father's sturdy arm.

The gown she wore was vaguely familiar, as though he'd seen it in an old photograph, but the generous curves softly outlined beneath it won more of his attention. Now he knew what he'd only suspected might be concealed by a preference for clothing that was far from formfitting. This was a female body in all its glory, and he had to ask himself why it had been kept so modestly covered. Whatever the reason, Ross couldn't deny a wholly male interest in the latest developments even as he raised his gaze to a face framed by midnight-dark hair worn in a simple crown of circled braids threaded with small, deep red roses echoing the color of the single large rose the bride held at her waist.

His bride.

"Watch it," Adam cautioned in a low murmur, "your tongue's in danger of hanging out."

Heeding that warning, Ross cleared his throat and took in another long breath. But he still couldn't look away.

Jenna couldn't look away, either. There he was, she thought, waiting for her. *Her.* Although her eyes testified to the truth of that, a portion of her—the part most tied to memories of the distant past—continued to be amazed.

She took a final few steps, released her father's arm and finally dragged her gaze away from the man who had captured it long enough to glance up at another tall, broad-shouldered male with eyes so much like her own.

"I don't have to tell you that I'm not great with words, but I love you, baby," Joe Lorenzo said, looking a long way from comfortable in a dark suit that was a far cry from his usual working man's clothes. Nonetheless, with his thick salt-and-pepper hair and proudly erect stance he made a handsome picture.

"I love you, too, Pop." Jenna craned her neck to press her lips to the side of an olive-skinned jaw.

"I think this guy is okay, but if it turns out that he doesn't treat you right, you just let me know." And with that, Joe turned and shook hands with his about-to-be son-in-law, then took a front-row seat next to a full-figured woman who was brushing back tears.

Breaking with tradition, Jenna walked over and leaned down to kiss Eva Lorenzo on a wet cheek. Its healthy flush was several shades lighter than the wine-colored dress that brought out the auburn highlights in Eva's chin-length brown hair. ''Mama, you look as young as a bride yourself in that new outfit,'' Jenna whispered. Then she quickly moved back to stand beside the undeniably attractive groom.

Her groom.

Judge Reynolds began the short ceremony at that point, his deep voice solemn in the silence all around them. In a matter of minutes plain gold rings together with quiet vows had been exchanged. With some effort Jenna maintained an outward calm throughout the proceedings, even returning a smaller version of the dapperly dressed judge's sudden smile when he pronounced them husband and wife.

''Time to kiss the bride,'' the judge told the groom.

Which, as it turned out, was all it took to have a firm mouth exploring hers—and more thoroughly than might have been expected in front of an audience. Nevertheless she knew she wouldn't—couldn't—pull away, any more than she'd been able to look away earlier as the wedding march played in the background while she'd watched unmistakable hints of swiftly banked desire form in the navy eyes viewing her intently. It seemed that Ross did indeed want a real marriage between them, and she had to wonder how long he'd be content to wait for her to find the prospect of achieving that state less unsettling than she found it now. Still, honesty forced her to admit that she was enjoying being soundly kissed before he lifted his head at last.

"Well, we did it," he said softly, gazing down at her.

Jenna had to blink herself back to a full awareness of her surroundings to issue an even softer reply.

"Yes, we certainly did."

THE RECEPTION was in full swing by the time Ross was able to settle himself on a long stone bench in the garden. He'd spent the first part of the past hour shaking hands with his male guests and accepting kisses of congratulations from the females in attendance. He'd spent the second part listening to his best man's smoothly spoken champagne toast and doing justice to a light buffet supper served on the cottage's glassed-in porch.

Now he held a second glass of champagne and was glad to relax for a while. The day seemed to be ending well, he thought, even if it hadn't started out that way, thanks to Myra Hastings and a confrontation he had no trouble recalling.

After fixing breakfast for the last time, Myra had packed up the final round of her belongings in the first-floor bedroom off the kitchen and moved out, but not before giving her employer a private piece of her mind about his imminent marriage.

"I've held my tongue until now, but my conscience won't let me rest if I don't say that I can't believe you're marrying a woman you hardly know, and someone who first applied for a housekeeper's position, to boot. Your mother," Myra had declared with a sharp lift of her pointed chin, "would be appalled."

He'd tried to rein in his temper, given that the Hayward family had benefited from Myra's skills for many years. Maybe if she hadn't added that last haughty sniff he could have managed it. But she had, and he'd essentially told her that his personal business was none of hers, after which she'd left in a huff.

Not surprisingly, although she'd been invited to the wedding, his ex-employee was nowhere to be seen in the small crowd currently milling around outdoors. In fact, considering the crisp breeze fluttering scores of leaves, few people would probably have found the outside setting comfortable without a jacket or sweater if not for the tall, strategically placed gas lanterns that provided both heat and light.

Even with all the guests taking in the evening air, however, Jenna was nowhere in sight. She must be inside somewhere, Ross concluded with a sweeping glance around the lushly landscaped yard. She hadn't, he'd noticed, eaten much earlier, and had barely sipped her champagne.

A case of bridal jitters in action?

He had to grin at the thought, despite knowing full well that the commonly held reason for the condition didn't apply in this particular instance. No jitters were necessary, because there wasn't going to be a true wedding night.

Not tonight.

"Mind if I join you?" a low voice drawled.

Ross glanced up to find Harmony's veteran police chief studying him. "Have a seat," he said, gesturing an invitation.

Tom Kennedy sank down onto the bench and reached up to thumb back the wide brim of the cream-colored hat he wore with a dark brown suit cut along Western lines. Even dressed in his Sunday best, the sixtyish man looked more like a rancher than a longtime member of the law-enforcement community.

"Nice ceremony," Tom said.

And that was all he said, although his companion waited for more. They hadn't spoken privately since the day the chief had advised Ross to think twice before hiring a younger woman as housekeeper—the same woman he had just made his wife.

Ross twirled the stem of his glass between long fingers. "Glad you could make it."

Tom chuckled, a deep sound that rumbled out of him. "Not many folks wanted to miss it. Even our mayor showed up."

And had left after kissing the bride with old-fashioned gallantry, Ross reflected as Tom continued. "Did you hear about the announcement he made this morning?"

"No," Ross had to acknowledge.

Tom's eyes met his. "It seems what I got wind of was wrong, because the wily fox decided to run again. Guess he figured that flirting with seventy didn't make him old enough to hang it up."

Ross calmly absorbed that information. "Well, we all knew it was a possibility."

But would the grandson of another mayor have done what he'd just done if he had known that for sure? Ross could almost hear the silent question echoing in Tom's steady gaze.

Yes, something inside him firmly contended, and Ross recognized it as the pure truth. Although the prospect of an open mayoral slot might have been a factor in his decision, the knowledge that there would be no political campaign in his immediate future made not a whit of difference as to how he felt about today's events.

"I'm content with the way it all turned out," he said, meaning every word.

He had what he wanted. As a concerned father, he had someone who would be a mother—a good mother—

to his children. As a man looking to father more children, he had a woman who might well make that a happy reality. And as a healthy male still in the prime of his life, he had a female who held the power to fill his private needs—and do a damn good job of it, too, every instinct he had told him.

It might take a while for things to settle down after all the recent hubbub, he acknowledged, but no matter how long it took, he found he had no doubts about the bargain he'd just concluded.

He had done the right thing in marrying Jenna Lorenzo.

SHE MAY HAVE MADE a big mistake in marrying Ross Hayward.

Jenna came to that conclusion halfway through the wedding festivities as she viewed her image in a wide rest room mirror edged with tulip-shaped light fixtures. Not that everything hadn't gone off like clockwork, she thought. It had.

No chaos. No emergencies. No hitches. Nothing to mar the merry celebration still in progress, except that the bride was having second thoughts—big ones.

And she had only herself to blame. Despite knowing full well that this wasn't the romantic wedding many women dreamed about, she'd found herself caught up in the excitement of last-minute preparations during the past few days—a heady feeling rich with high hopes that had marched along beside her all the way to the altar, only to rapidly depart and desert her at the crowded reception.

That was when reality had set in.

Although she'd done her best to put up a cheerful front, it had been made plain to her in no uncertain terms that a trip to the courthouse would have suited the situation far better, because then the bride's and groom's respective families wouldn't have come together to make something as clear as their crystal glasses filled with sparkling champagne.

In a very basic and elemental way, the Lorenzos and Haywards were different. And so were many of their friends.

Oh, it wasn't a matter of day and night. No stark line had been drawn down the center of the large room where the ceremony had taken place and that now held the reception. But guests of the bride and groom had naturally drifted to opposite sides and definite contrasts were more than apparent.

As if to prove that point, the rest room door swung open. Ross's aunt walked in wearing silver from head to toe. Silver streaks in her stylishly cut short hair, silver satin designer suit, silver high-heeled pumps and matching evening bag. Catching Jenna's eye in the mirror, she smiled politely and crossed to the floral-patterned tiled counter with seemingly effortless grace, a talent that might well have been supplied long ago by a finishing school for young ladies.

"Hello, Doris," Jenna said, using the slender woman's first name as she'd been graciously invited to do earlier. She dredged up a smile and suspected it fell short of the mark when Doris's gaze took on a knowing glint.

"You look a bit tired," she said after a moment. "But then, I'm sure it's been a long day for you."

"I guess you could say so," Jenna replied in a neutral tone. Now that Doris's own smile had faded, Jenna noticed that the faint lines around her coral-shaded mouth were a little grim. "Is anything wrong?" she found herself asking.

Doris didn't pretend to misunderstand. She merely issued a thin sigh. "I'm afraid my nephew and I aren't too happy with each other at the moment."

Jenna frowned at the realization that it had to be a reference to Ross. "He looked fine when I saw him a while ago," she said. In fact, she thought, he had seemed well satisfied with the way things were proceeding.

"That was probably before we had a candid conversation regarding his father," Doris told her.

"Oh," was all Jenna could come up with in response.

Doris lifted a neatly shaped brow. "Since it was hardly a secret at the time, I suppose you've heard the circumstances under which my brother, Martin, left Harmony?"

"Yes, I know a little about that," Jenna answered carefully.

"Well, what most people don't know is that he remarried last summer, and his wife isn't one of the series of much younger women he had the poor judgment to squire around during his first few years in Southern California. This woman is close to his age, and during a phone call I recently received from him, he expressed a desire to bring her to Harmony for a visit." Doris paused for a beat. "Martin wants to mend fences with his son, but Ross is determined to have no part of it."

"I asked him if he wanted to invite his father to the wedding," Jenna acknowledged, "but he gave me a firm no."

Doris released another sigh. "I wouldn't even be mentioning this if you hadn't just become a member of the family. Other than my brother, the Haywards have managed for several generations to keep their personal lives private.''

Which Jenna knew to be true. Martin Hayward was much the exception rather than the rule. "I won't, of course, say anything to anyone."

Doris studied her for a second. "Actually, I'm hoping you'll say something to my nephew to try to change his mind. The problem is that Ross was taught to respect the strict standards of conduct passed on to him by his grandfather, and being Thornton Hayward's daughter, I can tell you he could be rigid in that regard. Some people would see it as a virtue, but it also means forgiveness doesn't come easily."

"Yes, I can see how that would follow," Jenna murmured.

"The result," Doris said, "is that Ross feels the entire family, and most especially his mother, Arlene, was betrayed by his father's actions. And there's no denying, of course, that Martin's behavior created a minor scandal with its share of the kind of notoriety no one relishes."

The kind of notoriety no one relishes. Jenna's frown deepened at the thought that those words would be a fitting description of something she'd been forced to deal with in what now seemed like another lifetime. "The Incident," as she'd come to think of it, had certainly generated enough negative publicity to cause her a great deal of unhappiness. Not that she had done anything terrible; she hadn't. It had distressed her family, true, but only because of their concern for her.

But how would someone who'd learned to value those strict Hayward standards view the matter?

Up until this minute she hadn't thought it important to tell Ross about a time in her past she only wanted to forget. It had, after all, happened several years ago, before she'd even embarked on a career as a professional housekeeper.

At the moment, however, she had to admit to feeling slightly uneasy about the omission, although she didn't see how she could bring it up now, when Ross had already put a ring on her finger. The timing would definitely leave a lot to be desired.

"Are you willing to talk to him?" Doris asked quietly, breaking a short silence.

She groped for a response. "If the right opportunity to mention his father comes up, I'll give it a try," she said at last.

The older woman dipped her head in an almost regal nod that Jenna knew none of the Lorenzos or their friends could have managed to achieve. "I would appreciate it," Doris said with a faint smile.

Jenna mustered a smile in return. Nevertheless, the uneasiness their conversation had prompted only reinforced her earlier doubts about her brand-new marriage as she left Doris and made her way down a short hallway. She was near the arched doorway leading to the main reception area when Caroline appeared and started past her toward the rest room without a word. As far as Jenna could recall, the ten-year-old hadn't spoken at all that day. Not directly to her.

She reached out a hand and gently placed it on a delicate shoulder. "Are you feeling all right, Caroline?"

The child's light blue eyes met Jenna's then, and there was no mistaking the fact that her usual coolly polite gaze now displayed more than a hint of hard frost.

"I know I'm not always supposed to tell people how I really feel," she said.

They weren't, Jenna realized, talking about a physical condition. She felt the tension in the girl's shoulder before letting go. "You can tell me," she replied softly. "I don't object to anyone being frank if something's bothering them."

Apparently deciding to accept the invitation, Caroline clenched her small hands at her sides and issued a stark statement. "I heard Dad and Myra talking this morning before Myra left. She said you came to be our housekeeper, but he asked you to marry him instead, and that my grandmother Arlene would be *appalled*. I know what that means. It means that if she hadn't died, if she was still here, she would be upset. She wouldn't want you to be my stepmother—and I don't, either."

With that, Caroline turned and continued down the hall, leaving Jenna to take in a long breath, hurting for the girl even as her uneasiness rose to new heights. Not only, she thought, did she and her new husband come from what she'd now begun to view as not just different backgrounds but in some ways different worlds. And not only did she have to wonder how he would judge a particular time in her past she had no power to change, his eldest and much-loved child actively disliked her.

Faced with all of the above, Jenna couldn't help but wonder how her marriage would fare. This morning, she'd greeted the day with a heady rush of high hopes racing through her. Now, the rosy glow had disappeared and something was telling her in no uncertain terms that being a wife to Ross Hayward would pose some definite challenges—starting with tonight, when she would be sleeping under his roof for the first time.

After watching him watch her walk down that aisle, she knew she wouldn't have to sleep alone. All she had to do was say the word—a word she couldn't even imagine saying. Not yet.

And since they wouldn't be sleeping together, where would they both be sleeping?

In all the excitement of the impending wedding, she'd forgotten until this very minute that she still didn't know the answer to that question.

Chapter Four

Ross stood in the shower and craned his neck back to meet the pulsing flow of warm water that streamed over his face and down his body. His all-too-eager body, he had to admit. He'd already tried—and failed—to forget the sight of Jenna deep in dreams in his bed when he'd come back from his early morning run minutes earlier.

No, make that *her* bed.

As of last night, he was sleeping on the daybed in the sitting room off the master bedroom, he reminded himself. He still had to hope it wouldn't be the case for all that long, but something was beginning to tell him that that might be sheer wishful thinking. His bride had certainly looked far from ready to welcome him with open arms when they'd arrived home from their wedding with two sleepy girls and Jenna's suitcases in tow. In fact, if Jenna had had a choice, he was dead certain that she would have opted to sleep in Myra Hastings's former bedroom off the kitchen.

"You didn't offer her a choice, though, did you?" he muttered to himself under his breath.

Then again, he hadn't had much choice himself but to show her into the master suite while the girls headed off to their rooms and to explain the need for sharing the place. Katie might think nothing of her father and new stepmother bedding down for the night in separate areas of the house, but at the age of ten, Caroline could hardly be expected to overlook it.

And, to her credit, Jenna had calmly accepted the situation. He'd only had to put his foot down about his sleeping in the sitting room while she took the bedroom. Again without much fuss, she'd headed for the master bath to change out of her wedding gown—his grandmother's gown, Hester Goodbody had cheerfully jogged his memory by so informing him at the reception. And with his wife occupied with that task, he'd hung his clothes in the walk-in closet, pulled some pajama bottoms from a chest of drawers and left her to her privacy, after which he'd spent far too much time wondering if she was managing to get any sleep.

Apparently she had.

At least he'd found her dead to the world with the white comforter pulled up to her chin when he'd cracked open the connecting door and poked his head into the bedroom shortly after dawn. Rather than so much as a toss or a turn, she hadn't moved a muscle while he'd retrieved some socks from a drawer, then grabbed his gray sweats and running shoes from the closet.

With the sun slowly rising in the sky, he'd had to be grateful when a long run through quiet streets in the bracing morning air had helped settle him down after his own night of tossing and turning. What he hadn't counted on, however, was finding Jenna stretched out on her stomach when he'd returned, with the bed coverings now at her waist and her dark hair spilling down a creamy-skinned back covered only by a silky, plum-colored nightgown.

''Jeez, how's a man supposed to react when he discovers a woman sleeping so innocently and looking way too tempting at the same time?'' Ross rumbled to himself.

Just the way you reacted, logic told him. *And now it's time to cool off and douse some of your frustration.*

Gritting his teeth, Ross accepted the wisdom of those words and switched the shower knob to cold with a swift snap of his wrist. By the time he hopped out and grabbed a thick white towel off a polished chrome rack, he was shivering—and cooled off at least enough to have the more unruly parts of him under control.

He rubbed himself dry, knotted the towel around his waist and opened a mirrored cabinet to remove his shaving supplies. Determined to keep his thoughts from straying, he faced his reflection in the mirror, slathered foam over his jaw, and set his mind to the task of planning the day to come.

"At least," he told his image, "no one will be looking for the newlyweds to leave on a honeymoon anytime soon."

He and Jenna had already silenced any expectations along those lines by explaining that with the children currently in school, the just-married couple had decided to put off an out-of-town trip. If anyone had deemed that plan to be less than romantic, no comment had been made on the subject.

Ross picked up his razor. "So, all you have to do today is say goodbye to Jenna's family before they return to Nevada and send your own relatives on their way back to Phoenix." He had to wonder how chummy the whole group would become before they left, since they'd all spent the night at Aunt Abigail's, one of Harmony's most popular bed-and-breakfasts.

Probably chummier than he and his aunt Doris would

manage to get anytime soon after yesterday's go-round about his father—which was just too bad, because he wasn't backing down.

So what if Martin Hayward had gotten married again and wanted to mend a few fences? As far as his only son was concerned, too much water had gone over that particular dam to try to stem the tide now. Let him stay in California, Ross thought grimly, or go anywhere else on the face of the planet, for that matter, as long as he keeps away from—

Just then the bathroom door opened. He turned his head to find Jenna standing in the doorway, wearing a bright violet terry-cloth robe that covered her from neck to toe. For a startled second they just stared at each other. Then she spoke in a rush.

"I'm sorry, I didn't realize you were in here."

"I'll be out in a minute," he told her, "as soon as I finish shaving."

Jenna dragged in a long breath, noticing for the first time that he held a razor poised for action in his hand. Her eyes had been too busy giving their full attention to his long, leanly muscled body clad only in a towel hitched at his hips.

"No problem," she said, and closed the door in a hurry. A few quick steps took her across the room, where she hopped back into bed, robe and all, and pulled the plump comforter over her. Not that she needed it to ward off any chill in the morning air. No, all at once she seemed to be generating more than enough heat on her own—the direct result, she more than suspected, of finding the man she'd married less than twenty-four hours earlier one towel away from wearing absolutely nothing.

Good heavens, she'd seen nearly all there was to see of him, and there was no denying that every inch her avid gaze had taken in was a sight to remember. In fact, the vivid image still fresh in her mind almost wiped out the memory of how uneasy she'd felt on awakening to find herself stretched out in a modern, queen-size bed that stood at one end of a large, white-on-white room.

Almost, but not quite.

This was the bed Ross had shared with Cynthia. Everything about the room—and the bed—indicated the truth of that. A woman had decorated this place and chosen its furnishings—the same woman Jenna still couldn't begin to imagine replacing. For that very reason, she would have much preferred using the daybed in the adjacent sitting room. Unfortunately, she hadn't been given that option.

"I'll take the daybed," Ross had told her in a soft tone underscored with the barest hint of steel. "I've slept there before, and it's comfortable enough to suit me."

I've slept there before. Yes, that was what he'd said.

As she had last night, Jenna found herself mulling that statement over. And, as it had last night, the voice of reason didn't hesitate to point out that there were times in every marriage when a spouse might sleep elsewhere with a convenient alternative close by. Even a simple cold could produce enough coughing and wheezing during the night to make sleeping apart a more practical solution.

Yes, although she couldn't envision either one of the Golden Couple laid low by anything as common as a cold, it had to be something like that.

Then the bathroom door opened and once again the man in her thoughts won her full attention. Truth be told, it was all she could do to remember to keep from staring as she got another look at a wide chest sprinkled with small swirls of hair. Although Ross had traded in his towel for a pair of blue pajama bottoms in crisp cotton, he'd lost none of his ability to make an impact.

"I'm done," he told her in an even tone, as if there were nothing at all awkward about being caught with his pants off by a woman who, if she'd been alert enough to recall that they were sharing the master bath as well as the suite, would have knocked first to find out if the coast was clear.

Jenna cleared her throat. "From now on, I'll make sure the bathroom is empty before I barge in."

He smiled a faint smile. "It wouldn't have happened if I had thought to lock the door, so don't worry about it." He crossed the room in his bare feet, holding a gray sweatshirt, matching pants and canvas shoes.

"I was out for an early run," he explained as he walked into the closet. "It's my way of staying in shape," he added, his deep voice drifting back through the doorway.

And it's certainly working, Jenna tacked on to herself as she threw back the bed coverings and got up. A few quick strides took her to the bathroom doorway. "I'll make breakfast shortly," she called.

"I forgot to mention last night that you don't have to bother with that today," he called back. "We can eat at Aunt Abigail's and say goodbye to our families at the same time."

She glanced back over her shoulder. "Don't you have to stay at the bed-and-breakfast to eat there?"

"Normally, yes, but I got a special invitation from Aunt Abigail's cook via Adam. The newlyweds are apparently welcome to join the crowd for a meal. That is, if we're not too exhausted from, ah, nocturnal activities." Ross paused. "I have a hunch my best man came up with that last comment on his own."

"Well," Jenna said, ignoring the best man's offering, "I'll at least make coffee after my shower. I hope you saved me some hot water," she added, deliberately summoning a breezy tone.

His chuckle was a low rumble that reached her even across the considerable distance between them. "Trust me, there's plenty of hot water left."

She shut the door behind her, locked it without hesitation, removed her robe and hung it on a silver hook placed on a nearby wall. Then she glanced around her, noting that the bathroom was as neat as a pin. No shaving supplies in evidence. No stray whiskers in the sparkling porcelain sink. No water dabbled on the counter. Only a damp towel now folded with careful precision and looped over a long rack near the gleaming glass shower door indicated that the place had been occupied just minutes ago.

Either Ross came by it naturally or living in this elegant house had taught him well. Whatever the case, it seemed as though she wouldn't have to pick up after him.

Which didn't mean she wouldn't be doing things for the man she'd married. Taking his clothes to the cleaner's, washing his laundry, ironing his shirts. Exactly what she'd done for other men in a professional capacity, Jenna reflected as she tugged her nightgown over her head and tossed it aside. So why was the thought of folding her own husband's underwear threatening to raise her private temperature to new heights?

Hmm. What she probably needed was a cold shower.

THE SPRAWLING, two-story home known as Aunt Abigail's sat on a winding, tree-lined street. Painted a bright cinnamon and trimmed in rusty red, the place brought thoughts to mind of gingerbread houses with frosty white roofs that remained a staple of holiday baking in Harmony. At Aunt Abigail's, however, known throughout the area for its homemade sugar-and-spice cookies, baking from scratch wasn't only a holiday but an everyday event. And Ethel Freeman, a silver-haired woman on the far side of seventy, cheerfully ruled the kitchen.

"I'm so glad you decided to accept my invitation," the cook who could have doubled for a storybook version of a doting grandmother told the newlyweds as they sat at a lace-covered table in the bed-and-breakfast's spacious dining room.

"Thanks for the offer," Ross said.

"Yes, and by the way, the food is wonderful," Jenna added from beside him, summoning a smile.

Ross dropped a glance at the large china plate he'd heaped with breakfast fare. "I may have gotten carried away, but everything on the buffet looked terrific."

Ethel beamed as she smoothed a plump hand down the front of her ruffled apron. "Enjoy every last bite. No one leaves Aunt Abigail's without plenty of good food in their stomach."

"I can well believe that," Eva Lorenzo offered from her seat next to Jenna. "It's a shame we've only been able to stay a short time after being gone from Harmony for so long, but my husband has to get back to work. There's still a healthy market for quality cabinetmaking."

Joe Lorenzo dipped his head in agreement and kept on eating with the zeal of a big man for a well-cooked meal.

"Just come up for air every now and then, Pop," Sophie, yesterday's young maid of honor, advised her father with an impish grin.

That produced a laugh all around before Ethel headed back to the kitchen with a promise to keep the silver serving dishes resting on the long oak sideboard filled and ready to challenge even the heartiest of appetites.

Ross forked up a helping of French toast laced with pure maple syrup and downed it in one swallow. He had to admit to being grateful to find himself seated with Jenna's family rather than his own relatives, who occupied another table nearby with Caroline and Katie. They'd been eager to spend more time with the girls, and he could have easily done without spending any more time right now with his aunt Doris, so it had worked out to everyone's advantage.

Now if he could only ignore the probing glances Adam kept aiming at him from several feet away, things would be fine. Trouble was, he had little doubt as to why his tall, dark and ever-well-groomed cousin seemed so curious. Adam was seeking signs of a vigorous wedding night. As to his findings, Ross could only guess. The best he could manage at the moment was a yawn— one that wasn't entirely for show, either. He had to hope sheer exhaustion would set in and he'd sleep better tonight.

"When are you two going to open your wedding presents?" Eva asked.

"You mean the ones we specifically asked everybody *not* to buy?" Jenna countered with a rueful lift of a brow.

Eva smiled a wide smile. "Yes, those, dear."

"You really didn't have to get us anything," Ross said, and meant it. He knew why Jenna seemed a long way from pleased. Theirs wasn't a typical marriage, after all, even though that was far from common knowledge. He just had to hope that no one had gone overboard on any of the brightly wrapped gifts currently stacked on the table in the Hayward dining room.

"We'll probably open them later today or tomorrow," he added, and left it at that.

"I remember we got three toasters for our wedding," Joe said, taking a break from his food long enough to reach for a crystal glass filled with fresh orange juice. "Plus several coffeemakers and who knows how many electric can openers."

Eva's smile broke through again. "We managed to use everything over the years, too."

Joe set the small juice glass that looked even more delicate in his big hand down. "With four kids, we must've toasted enough bread to feed an army."

"We ate my folks out of house and home," Sophie told Ross with another grin. "At least that's what Pop always said, even with one less mouth to feed after Jenna went off to college."

College? This was the first Ross had heard about that. "What did you major in?" he asked, slanting a glance at his wife.

"Business administration," she replied after the barest pause, "but I never got a degree."

He was about to ask why when she continued. "I decided to work full-time rather than stay in school, and a few years later I moved to Denver and got my first housekeeper's job."

Ross didn't miss the abruptly sober look Jenna's parents exchanged after that last statement. He'd be willing to bet that something troubling to them had happened between their daughter's leaving college and her move to Colorado. Something to do with a man, his instincts were telling him.

Had Jenna been involved with someone they didn't

approve of? Or was there more to it than that? Then again, why was he even speculating? He'd be wiser to remember his conviction that everyone had the right to keep past relationships private if they so chose... including him.

By the time breakfast was over, Ross was genuinely sorry to say goodbye to his new in-laws as the group pushed back their chairs and rose. "Are you dropping your rental car back at the Phoenix airport?" he asked Jenna's father as they shook hands.

Joe nodded. "Next time we visit, though, we're taking Harmony Air and cutting out the drive."

"That's right," Jenna's mother agreed as she gave Ross a farewell hug. "The cook here hasn't only been sharing a few of her recipes with me," Eva informed him, "she's also been touting the new weekend service between Phoenix and Harmony."

"We actually got to meet the head of the airline," Sophie chimed in with a sigh. "He's a hunk."

"Oh, really?" Jenna said with a wry curve of her lips.

Ross had heard that the pilot responsible for starting up a local operation at Harmony's small airport was married to Aunt Abigail's resident manager, an attractive and very pregnant redhead who had greeted the newlyweds on their arrival. "Whether the guy's a, uh, hunk or not," he told Sophie dryly, "I hope he makes a success of the business."

"Me, too," Jenna's sister replied with a playful wink. "He can fly me anywhere!"

"Does this mean I have a rival?" Adam asked as he stepped over to join the group.

Sophie dimpled up at him. "Would that news break your heart?"

Adam flashed a grin in return. "I guess I'd survive…barely.'' When that produced a round of chuckles, he turned to Ross. "Well, I suppose it's time to say so long for now, cuz.''

Ross nodded his agreement. "Thanks for being my best man.''

Adam dropped his voice to a private level as he closed in on the new groom while the bride's family lavished her with hugs and kisses. "I'll just say one more thing before I get out of your hair.'' His face settled into serious lines. "If you want to talk about it, call me.''

It took Ross less than a second to summon a blank expression. "Talk about what?'' he asked mildly, despite more than suspecting where this conversation was going. He and his cousin had usually been on the same wavelength.

"Talk about why you don't look that all satisfied to my eagle eyes,'' Adam didn't hesitate to inform him. "Not physically, at any rate. Not in the way of a man who has torn up some sheets.'' He paused. "Now you can tell me to mind my own business.''

Ross smiled a faint smile. "Mind your own business.''

Adam's mouth slanted up at the tips. "Okay,'' he replied, assuming a casual tone. "Maybe it's just my imagination, anyway.''

But, Ross thought as he headed off to offer brief goodbyes to the rest of his relatives, they both knew it wasn't.

JENNA WAS SURE that being a stepmother had its rewards. She just hadn't discovered any lately. Instead, during the past week she'd learned to her cost that being a housekeeper who watched over other people's children was not the same as being married to the man of the house and watching over his children.

It wasn't even close—as she had no trouble recalling from recent events.

First, probably owing to an increased tension in the house due to a major change in all their lives, Katie and Caroline had taken to locking horns with each other on a regular basis. Then, every time Jenna had tried to step in and smooth things over, they'd swiftly joined forces to present a united front, as though nothing were wrong…until the next squabble.

And now, with both girls holed up in their respective rooms after getting back from school, she was once again facing the fact that she was the outsider. Something had obviously happened between the time they'd left the house that morning and their all-too-quiet return to put them at odds again, but they weren't letting their stepmother in on it.

One part of her told Jenna to let the whole thing go. Maybe once their much-loved father got home and produced a few smiles, it would all blow over without her getting involved. But another part—a more stubborn part, she had to admit—urged her to step into the breach one more time. The plain truth that neither of the girls seemed close to happy these days made Jenna long to at least make things better between the two sisters.

With that in mind, Jenna knocked softly on Katie's door and opened it to find the little girl sitting tailor-fashion on her bed, still wearing the colorful top and cotton pants she'd chosen to head off to school in that morning. Her outfit was a bright splash in a room that featured nearly as much white as the rest of the home's elegant furnishings. At least, Jenna reflected, the haphazard mix of stuffed animals on the twin bed and other toys stacked on a small dresser made it look more comfortably cozy than it would have without them.

"I'd like to talk to you for a minute," she said.

Katie slowly raised her deep blue gaze to meet Jenna's. "Okay."

Jenna folded her arms over the front of the kelly-green tunic she wore with stirrup pants, crossed the room in her stocking-clad feet and perched on an edge of the bed. She was careful to keep a short distance between them and not to invade the child's space. This wasn't the time, she knew, to offer a hug of consolation, not even when Katie looked so glum.

"I know something's wrong between you and Caroline," she said as gently as she could. She was counting on the fact that this time, without her older sister around to squelch any confidences, Katie might admit to the reason for their latest rift.

One second stretched to five before Katie finally spoke in a small voice. "She's the teacher's pet 'cause she gets good grades all the time. And I don't. Not always. But she just says I have to try harder, and I *am* trying." A tiny sigh broke through. "Sometimes we don't like each other very much."

Where have I heard this before? Jenna asked herself, recalling other children—even some from her own family—saying exactly the same thing about their siblings. "Well," she said matter-of-factly, "sometimes I didn't like my sisters, either."

Katie looked at her. "You didn't?"

Jenna offered a brisk nod. "Sometimes I thought they were a real pain."

The child's deep blue eyes widened. "You did?"

"Uh-huh." Jenna's gaze didn't waver. "But that didn't mean I didn't love them—because I did, always."

"Oh."

"And that's what you have to remember when you

and your sister don't agree on things. It may not be easy to like everyone all the time, but you can still love them.''

Katie mulled that over for a minute. "I guess."

Jenna rose, deciding she'd done what she could to make her point. "Want to come downstairs and watch television?"

"I'll think I'll stay here and play," Katie said after a moment's consideration. While she didn't look quite as glum as before, she also didn't offer any smiles as she reached behind her and grabbed up a stuffed dog—half as big as she was—sporting a shaggy coat of black hair.

Fluffy. By now, Jenna knew that was the dog's name. Only weeks ago, she thought, she and this little girl had first met, yet so much had happened since. Back then she'd been a visitor and both of Ross's daughters had offered ready smiles.

"See you at dinner," she said, doing her best to hang on to an upbeat tone as she left and closed the door behind her.

A few steps took her to Caroline's room. Again she knocked before entering. It didn't surprise her to find the ten-year-old seated on a small wicker chair resting next to the bed with her nose buried in a book. It would be something educational, Jenna concluded without a doubt. She had to wonder if this child had ever read a comic book in her life.

"I'd like to talk to you for a minute," she said for a second time.

Neither woman nor child had so much as mentioned their meeting in the hallway at the wedding reception, and Caroline had since gone back to being painfully polite to her stepmother. "All right," she agreed. She straightened a fold of her blue jumper and set her book in her lap.

Where she'd treaded softly with the youngest Hayward, Jenna stood where she was and decided to be a bit more blunt this time. "I just had a conversation with Katie. She said you and she don't like each other all the time."

Caroline met Jenna's gaze but said nothing.

"And I told her that even though sisters might not always get along, it's loving each other even when you don't agree that counts." Jenna aimed a glance around the room. Here, little broke the unrelieved whiteness of the furnishings and carpet. Whatever toys Caroline had were kept neatly stored in her closet.

Something drew Jenna's gaze to a photograph framed in gleaming silver on the dresser. A stunning blonde smiled confidently into the camera, as though she had no doubt of how it would record her beauty. It was the woman who had given birth to Caroline, of course.

"I'm sure your mother would have agreed with that," Jenna said, once again looking at the girl. "She wouldn't want her daughters to be at odds too much, I bet, and even when they were, she would want them to remember that family is the most important thing." Jenna paused. "Katie looks up to you, Caroline. She may not always get the same good grades you did when you were her age, but she's smart enough to take pride in doing the best she can. If you'll try to remember at least some of what I just said, I think the two of you may get along better in what I know is a difficult time."

Again Caroline remained silent, but Jenna saw by the way the girl's expression grew thoughtful that something was being mulled over, and fairly intently, too. *That's right,* Jenna mused, smiling to herself as she left the room, *let those little wheels in that excellent brain turn. A whole lot of good could come from it.*

She descended the stairs at a fast clip, somehow feeling more lighthearted. Maybe, just maybe, she wouldn't be the outsider for too much longer. At least she couldn't help feeling more optimistic. Things were looking up.

A prime piece of beef flanked by fresh vegetables was roasting in the oven. The plump strawberries she'd bought today would serve as a light dessert. And her husband would come home to a house as sparkling clean—or nearly as clean, anyway—as when his former prim-and-proper housekeeper had ruled on the domestic front.

Yes, all in all, things were looking better.

Jenna's smile didn't falter as the front doorbell rang. It only disappeared after she pulled open the door and saw the older couple standing on her doorstep, both wearing raincoats although the wet weather promised for that night hadn't yet blown in.

She didn't recognize the woman with a pleasant face framed by short, stylishly cut brown hair. However, Jenna had no trouble recalling the woman's tall, lean and distinguished-looking escort, even though she hadn't seen him in many years.

"You must be Jenna," Martin Hayward said.

"Yes," she replied carefully, all but positive where he had come by that information. A conversation with Ross's aunt Doris was the obvious solution. "I'm—"

"I know who you are, Mr. Hayward."

The sudden bend of his thin lips was wry. Gradually it widened to reveal well-formed teeth that held much the same gleam as the bright silver streaks at his temples.

"Then let me introduce my wife, Rosemary," he said with unruffled courtesy.

Jenna acknowledged the introduction with a small nod as Martin spoke again.

"May we come in?"

Sucking in a quiet breath, Jenna groped for a response. "Ross isn't home from work yet," was the most neutral reply she could manage.

Martin accepted that news with no change of expression. "I expect he'll be home soon, though."

"Yes," she acknowledged after a beat.

"I'd like to wait for him, if I may."

And what did she say to that? A flat-out *no?*

Jenna resisted the urge to sigh long and hard, realizing she simply couldn't turn this man away and shut the door without a qualm. Whatever their disagreements, he was her husband's father.

"All right," she said at last. "Please come in."

And please, she added to herself, let Ross understand that I had no other choice.

Chapter Five

Ross parked his sedan next to Jenna's maroon compact in the three-car garage attached to the Hayward house, thinking that it was good to be home. With a few economical movements he slid out from behind the driver's seat, reached back inside to retrieve his navy suit jacket and leather briefcase, snapped the car door closed, and then walked swiftly toward the door opening into a rear laundry room.

From long habit, he automatically removed his black wingtips and left them in a narrow space beside the washer, then loosened his striped silk tie and shouldered his way through a swinging door leading to a back hallway. The hearty smell of something cooking drifted past the entrance to the kitchen, making his stomach growl in appreciation.

Yes, it was damn good to be home, he told himself as he walked past an empty family room toward the front of the house—especially after a long day spent with his chief accountant studying third-quarter financial results.

Not that he'd get to head upstairs and change out of his business clothes quite yet. The Haywards had company. He already knew as much from the sight of a late-model sedan parked in the side driveway when he'd pulled up. He had to wonder who it belonged to, since he hadn't recognized the car. But he'd find out soon enough, he reflected with assurance, catching the sound of low voices coming from the living room.

"Harmony is still the lovely little city I remember," a deep male voice was saying as Ross got close enough to make out the conversation. A voice, he had to admit, that sounded all too familiar.

No, it couldn't be, was his first thought.

But it was, he discovered an instant later as the group seated there came into view. Occupying one of the over-stuffed chairs, Jenna faced a man and woman sitting across from her on the long white sofa. The woman was a stranger to Ross, but the man was another story. Everything inside him clenched as he halted dead in his tracks and issued a grim statement that rushed out of him without so much as a second's hesitation.

"What the hell are you doing here?"

Martin Hayward looked up with a quick jerk of his head. Then he rose slowly to his feet. "Hello, son," he said, his tone calm, his expression solemn. "It's good to see you. I know Doris told you I had remarried. I wanted to introduce my wife."

Ross kept his gaze fastened on his father. "Does she know that you walked out on your last wife?"

Martin dipped his chin in a brief nod. "I've explained to her what happened, yes."

Ross entered the room, dropped his briefcase on the carpet with a thud and tossed his jacket over the back of Jenna's chair. "And she still decided to take a chance on you?" He shook his head. "She must be one brave lady."

The woman seated on the sofa stood at that point, sending the hem of her tan raincoat dropping to midcalf.

Ross conducted a short study, taking in the fact that she might well have been born close to the same time as his late mother. There, however, any resemblance ended. This woman, for all that she held herself with quiet dignity, would have faded into the shadows standing next to the tall and stately Arlene Hayward.

"I believe I'll wait for you in the car, dear," Martin's second wife told him. "I don't think this is going well."

As though she agreed with that judgment, their hostess got up and showed the woman out. "I'm sorry," Ross heard Jenna murmur before the door closed with a quiet snap that broke the stark silence building in the room.

It wasn't until Jenna returned, moving past him with what might well have been wary steps to resume her seat, that Ross fisted his hands at his sides and again addressed his father. "You don't have to stick around, either," he said, making no bones about it, "because I'm not changing my mind when it comes to having anything to do with you."

"I was afraid of that," Martin replied after another beat of silence, "but I had to try."

"So you tried," Ross snapped. "Let's leave it at that."

"I suppose I'll have to," Martin murmured. Defeat seemed to settle on his broad shoulders with those last words. "I wasn't planning on returning to Harmony for good, you know. My home and the brokerage firm I've formed will remain in California. I just wanted to heal the breach between us if I could and be able to visit you and my granddaughters from time to time."

"It's not going to happen," Ross informed him in no uncertain terms.

"No, I can see that…now."

Martin turned to take a few slow steps toward the

front entryway, then halted and looked back. "Perhaps the way I did it was a terrible mistake, but I simply couldn't stay with your mother any longer, Ross." He paused and met his son's eyes. "I think, if you'll give it some consideration, you'll understand what I mean," he said. "I think they were a lot alike."

And with that, Martin Hayward walked out, leaving Jenna to frown in puzzlement as she wondered about his final words. *I think they were a lot alike.* She was still mulling the matter over when Ross fixed his gaze on her.

"Why did you invite him in?" he asked, clipping out the words.

Now that his anger was clearly directed at her, Jenna felt the beginnings of her own temper rising. She already knew by his reaction to his father's appearance that the chances of his understanding her earlier dilemma were slim to none, but she tried for a reasonable tone anyway.

"He showed up out of the blue," she said, "and I couldn't just close the door in his face when he asked if he could come in and wait for you."

Ross crossed his arms over his chest. "Did you think about how I'd feel, finding him here?"

Deciding to meet the situation head-on since he was plainly far from in favor of beating around the bush, she got up and squared her shoulders.

"Yes, I thought about it." *Even worried about it more than a little while I was waiting for you to get home.* Rather than voicing that last thought, she merely added, "Nevertheless, I couldn't do anything but what I did."

Rather than concurring or disagreeing with that staunch contention, he issued another terse question. "Did Caroline and Katie see him?"

"No. They've been in their rooms since they got back

from school. Katie's playing with some of her toys and Caroline's reading.''

He lifted a hand and raked it through his hair. ''Well, thank God for that much, anyway.'' Again he met her gaze. ''If he comes back here and I'm not home, I expect you to keep him away from the girls.''

''I will, since that's what you want,'' Jenna agreed, although she doubted Martin Hayward would return. If that breach was ever going to be healed, his son would now have to make the first move. She was all but positive of that.

''You know,'' she said, again groping for a reasonable tone, ''when all is said and done, he's your father and he always will be. And,'' she continued, ''he'll always be your daughters' grandfather, too.'' Something they could have used, as far as she was concerned, given that their maternal grandparents were a lot farther away than California. As she'd learned since her return to Harmony, Cynthia's well-to-do parents, who'd had their only child late in life, had retired and moved to an oceanside community in Florida some time ago.

''To my way of thinking,'' she added, forging on with determination, ''Caroline and Katie don't have that many close relatives still around to give up even one who wants to get to know them.''

For a moment Ross just stared at her with a steely gaze, as if he couldn't quite believe that she was butting heads with him over this issue. But she was his wife, Jenna reminded herself, not his employee, and he'd have to accept the fact that she was entitled to her opinion.

''Well, to *my* way to thinking,'' he countered at last, his tone even curter than before, ''they don't need the kind of relative who once turned his back on everything the Haywards have always stood for in this town.''

That said, he grabbed his jacket from the back of the chair, picked up his briefcase in one fluid motion and swiftly became the second Hayward male to walk out of the room. Even in his stocking feet, the sound of his footsteps made an impact as he pounded his way up the stairs to the second floor.

Jenna wouldn't have been surprised to hear the door to the master suite being slammed. Instead, an uneasy quiet descended on the house. She knew that maintaining a casual conversation over the dinner table tonight would be a challenge, one she and Ross would both undoubtedly meet because Caroline and Katie would be there.

As to what would happen tonight when they were finally alone, she could only hazard a guess. What she did know was that she couldn't apologize for what had happened. If Ross chose to lose his temper again, well, so be it. She just had to hope she could keep a hold on her own.

One thing was certain, Jenna thought, the new bride and groom wouldn't be making up in the time-honored way. Slipping between the sheets together had ended plenty of confrontations, but it wouldn't be ending this one. In fact, the prospects of the Hayward marriage being consummated anytime in the foreseeable future seemed dimmer than ever.

Jenna headed back to the kitchen, forcing a spring into her step. She had a roast to get out of the oven, and she planned on eating her share of the meal she'd prepared, even though her appetite had deserted her. If she was going to do battle later that evening, wisdom said she'd be better off doing it with something substantial in her stomach.

She just hoped it didn't lead to an all-out war.

IN THE END, there wasn't even a battle.

But maybe there should have been, Jenna decided as she entered the old yet well-maintained brick building that had been home to Harmony's main post office for many years. A small skirmish, at least, might have cleared the air.

As it was, she and Ross had started being almost as painfully polite to each other as Caroline continued to be to her stepmother. And all that politeness was getting on her nerves.

The only truly good thing that had happened during the past few days was that from all appearances the two children in the household were getting along better. Whether her own efforts had prompted it or not, Jenna had to be grateful for that much.

"Well, if isn't the new Mrs. Hayward," a soft voice said as Jenna approached the rear of the high-ceilinged room to buy stamps. She found the familiar aquamarine gaze belonging to the woman behind the thick marble counter trained on her.

"Have you gotten used to being called that yet?" her friend Peggy O'Brien asked.

"No," Jenna replied with complete honesty.

Peggy, who'd been with the postal service long enough to be considered a seasoned employee, glanced down at the large stack of small, cream-colored envelopes Jenna held. "That's quite a load you've got there."

"They're thank-you cards, for the wedding presents."

Peggy's sudden grin was on a sly side. "I've been waiting to hear what you thought of mine."

Jenna had no trouble recalling the O'Brien family's gift, which had consisted of a skimpy black silk teddy edged with see-through lace for the bride and matching black silk boxers, minus the lace but with a red heart embroidered in a very strategic area, for the groom. As his-and-her sleepwear went, it was a memorable addition to both the bride's and the groom's wardrobe.

"I was glad there wasn't a crowd around when I opened it," she said with feeling.

That Caroline and Katie had been within viewing distance on that occasion had been more than enough—not to mention their father. Fortunately only the newlyweds had gotten a good glimpse of the gift in question before she'd hastily stuffed Peggy's offerings back into the box bearing the name of one of the trendy boutiques in town.

"Thought I'd go with something personal," Peggy told her oh, so innocently.

"It was personal, all right," Jenna agreed dryly.

"Well, I wasn't going to get you something for the house. Not *that* house. I'm sure the Hayward residence has everything it needs, and then some."

Jenna could hardly deny the truth of that. In fact, the house now had far more than it needed, thanks to the generosity of the wedding guests, a generosity that had only made her uncomfortable, considering the circumstances.

"You didn't have to get us anything," she reminded her friend.

"I know I didn't have to. I wanted to." Peggy paused for a beat. "How did everything fit, by that way—comfy enough to sleep in or, er, whatever?"

Jenna met that deliberately offhand question with a quelling frown.

"Just wanted to make sure I got the right size," Peggy continued in the mildest of tones, looking far from fazed. "I'm fairly certain I did in your case, but Ross—" her gaze took on a playful glint "—well, I simply had to guess."

And had enjoyed guessing, Jenna had little doubt. "Everything is still in the box, if you must know, where it may well stay for a good long while."

Peggy lifted one delicate shoulder in a shrug. "Or maybe not."

Don't get your hopes up in that regard, Jenna could have advised. Although she said nothing, a soft sigh broke from her throat before she could swallow it.

"Aha," Peggy said, her expression turning thoughtful, "do I detect trouble brewing? And," she added in the next breath, "could it have anything to do with the latest news going around that Ross's father was seen in town a few days ago?"

Jenna had to sigh one more time. "Has anyone ever told you that you can be too darn perceptive?"

Peggy lifted a hand and absently brushed a stray red curl from her forehead. "Only my darling husband. And only when I catch something he'd rather I didn't notice—like another tool he can't seem to resist showing up on our credit card bill. What a plumber needs with so much woodworking stuff I'll never know."

Since Jenna didn't know, either, she merely offered a shrug.

"Tell you what," Peggy went on, "it's almost time for my lunch break. If you're not in a hurry to get home, why don't we stop at the taco stand by the police station and get something to go? We can find ourselves an empty bench by the courthouse and talk some more."

"All right," Jenna agreed after a moment's consideration, deciding that talking frankly to a good friend would be a welcome change from treading her way carefully around the man she'd married. "My treat."

Peggy's grin was back. "Of course, it's your treat. After all, you're the one who landed one of the very successful Haywards."

Yes, she had, Jenna thought. And she still had to wonder if that had been a mistake.

IT HADN'T BEEN A MISTAKE, Ross told himself as he left his third-floor office and started down the polished mahogany stairs he usually opted to take instead of the elevator. Although the small downtown office complex had been modernized in recent years, the staircase dated back to his grandfather's days. Thornton Hayward had seldom chosen the elevator, either, even when the arthritis brought on by his steadily advancing age had crept up on him.

The old man had known his own mind.

So did his grandson.

And marrying Jenna had been the right thing to do.

Despite the uneasy and always well-mannered truce between them that sometimes had his teeth clenching, Ross had to believe that. He just needed to walk off some of the frustration with the situation that had been building for days, which was why he hadn't gone directly back to work as usual after the club sandwich he'd finished at his desk.

His assistant, who was never shy about expressing her opinion, had approved.

"Some fresh air in the middle of the day never hurt anybody," Thelma Carter had remarked on his way out.

Although the sharp-eyed woman who'd worked at Hayward Investments for many years might well contend that she was past the age of kicking up her heels, something that sparked to life in her shrewd gaze every now and then told Ross that there had been a time when she'd put her youth to good use—probably more than he had in the past, at any rate. Which, he had to admit, wouldn't be all that hard to do. He'd seldom raised any major hell, even when he was away at the eastern college a long line of Hayward men had attended.

The same college he wanted his son to attend. Provided he ever had a son, he reflected as he crossed a small lobby and stepped out into the crisp, unpolluted air that was one of the reasons for Harmony's longstanding popularity with visitors.

As usual, Ross's gaze was drawn for a moment to the tall bronze statue dedicated to the city's founders that stood in front of the stately stone courthouse facing the office complex.

"That's why you can take pride in being a Hayward," his grandfather had told him, pointing to that same statue on more than one occasion. "We put our brains and our backs to good use in order to build this place and make it what it is today."

Ross had to smile at the memory as he started across the street with the intention of taking a short walk around the grassy, tree-dotted spot known as Courthouse Square. Then his smile faded when he caught sight of two women seated on one of the several wrought-iron benches that lined a narrow sidewalk winding through the area. They were so engrossed in their conversation that they didn't even hear him approach.

"Hello," he said in a deliberately mild tone when he was three feet away. He watched them both jump in response.

His wife's friend Peggy was the first to recover and offer a welcoming grin. He'd seen her at the post office from time to time but had only recently become acquainted with her on a personal level. If his memory was on target—and it usually was—she and her husband were the wedding guests who had presented the newly-weds with a gift he well remembered. He'd barely had time to picture the bride wearing that little black silk number before it had been whisked out of sight by a wide-eyed Jenna.

"Hi, yourself," Peggy said. "Taking a walk?"

"Seemed like a good day for it," Ross allowed.

"Mmm-hmm." Peggy glanced up at a blue sky sprinkled with small white clouds. "Mother Nature came through again."

"Yes." He doubted the conversation he'd interrupted had been about anything as general as the weather, but whatever the subject, his arrival had probably put an end to it.

As if to confirm as much, Peggy rose to her feet. "My lunch break's almost over. I'd better be getting back."

Ross shoved his hands into the pockets of his trousers. "Nothing like a determined woman to keep the mail running."

Peggy issued a soft chuckle. "You got it." With that, she turned and walked off with a final wave. "See you later, Jen."

"'Bye," Jenna said, offering a brief wave of her own.

Then it was time for husband and wife to trade guarded looks. "Mind if I sit down?" he asked.

"Please do," she replied in the same all-too-courteous tone they'd both been using for days.

He nearly winced before he caught himself. Maintaining a hard-won nonchalance, he sat and stretched his long legs out in front of him. And now what? he asked himself. A comment on how the plant life in the area seemed to be flourishing after the recent rain? A rehashing of this morning's forecast, which had predicted more sunshine for the rest of the week?

Hell, you can't go on like this, Hayward.

Ross blew out a gusty breath. This might not be the ideal place, but it would have to do. He shifted to face the woman at his side. His temper had gotten the better of him, and now it was time to pay the piper.

"I'm sorry," he said.

That won Jenna's attention in a hurry. She met his gaze head-on. "For what?"

"For coming down on you like a ton of bricks when I got home and found my father there."

"Oh." She studied him for a long moment while birds chirped in the surrounding trees. Finally she spoke. "I know you were upset."

"More like furious," he admitted with a wry twist of his lips.

For some reason that confession had her mouth curving up at the corners. "Yes, well, I think that would describe it, too," she said dryly.

What she didn't say was that she was sorry, as well, for welcoming his father into the house. He couldn't help but note that omission when silence again built between them. She clearly still felt she'd done the only thing possible.

It wouldn't have surprised him if she also remained firm in her opinion that he should heal the breach with his only living parent. But on that subject, he remained every bit as firm. Not that he was bringing the whole thing up again. And he had a hunch Jenna wouldn't, either—at least not anytime soon—which suited him just fine. As far as he was concerned, the less said on the matter the better.

"Have you had lunch?" he asked.

She nodded.

He ran his tongue around his teeth. "How about heading over to Dewitt's? We can have a milkshake for dessert."

The fifties-style diner was known for its malts and shakes, and it was the best peace offering he could come up with at the moment. The last time he and Jenna had been there, he'd been conducting an initial interview for the housekeeper's position. Now, if she accepted his invitation, they'd be walking into the place as a married couple.

"Okay," she said after a beat, just as he'd hoped she would. Rising, she tugged down the hem of a long fisherman's knit sweater that was even less formfitting than the tailored outfit she'd worn for their first meeting.

But now, Ross thought as they started down the street, he knew that plenty of curves lay just out of sight. Just as he knew, although she again wore it coiled at the nape of her neck, how her dark hair looked flowing down her back. He'd also learned that she could hold her own in a confrontation. He hadn't missed the hint of heat simmering in her gaze when she'd stood up to him after his father had left. She'd been warm around the collar, all right.

And she would be warm in bed, too.

Even through the haze of his own temper, he'd been sure of that. It was one more reason for believing his decision to marry Jenna had been right on target, because he needed some warmth in his life, the kind that only a woman could supply.

Something gut-deep inside him had been cold for too long.

THE BACKYARD of the Hayward home was as neatly kept as everything else about it. That was Jenna's thought on her first sight of a large carpet of deep green grass bordered by well-trimmed rows of low bushes. A pale stone birdbath made of the same material as the chest-high fence enclosing the yard held center stage, a narrow circle of pale pink chrysanthemums growing at its feet.

As at the front of the house, the impression was one of understated good taste. Only a tall swing set standing in a far corner indicated that at least part of the backyard was geared for play rather than quiet contemplation.

Not that the Hayward children made a great deal of noise when they played outdoors. Not today, anyway. Jenna had no trouble noting that in the slanting rays of the late-afternoon sun as she watched Katie swinging to the tune of soft words sung to the doll propped in her lap. Seated beside her on the white wood slats of a twin swing, Caroline again had her nose in a book. Despite the fact that both seemed occupied with their own pursuits, Jenna took their choice to spend some time together after school—rather than retreating to their separate rooms—as another sign of better sisterly relations.

"I'm glad you two decided to spend some time outside," she called as she left the rear porch and approached them.

Caroline glanced up from her book. "It's a nice day," she said, faithfully minding her manners.

Jenna bit back a sigh. She and Ross might have managed to put an end to their recent polite-at-all-costs behavior toward each other during a casual chat over chocolate milkshakes earlier that day, but his eldest daughter showed no signs of following their example.

Giving up on any attempt to change that for the moment, Jenna looked at Katie. "Don't stop singing on my account," she told the little girl, whose voice had drifted to a halt while her enthusiastic swinging slowed to a gentle back-and-forth movement. "I used to sing that same song when I was your age."

Katie blinked. "You did?"

Jenna swallowed a laugh at the child's clear astonishment that any song could be around that long. "Yes, even back in the old days we learned it in school." In a bid to keep the conversation going, she asked, "Does Pandora like to swing?"

"Uh-huh." Katie studied her doll. "I think she likes the way you did her hair, too," she added with a peek up at Jenna.

Pleased by that comment and hoping it was a sign that Katie was on the road to returning to her once chatty self, Jenna said, "I'm glad."

The youngest of the Haywards slid a sidelong glance at her older sister, as if seeking guidance on whether to say anything more, but Caroline was again bent over her book. "Fluffy likes to swing, too," she confided at last, again looking up at Jenna, "but it's hard for me to hold him 'cause he's so big."

Jenna nodded. She doubted that Katie could even see over the top of the large stuffed dog when it was in her lap. "Maybe you need a smaller dog you could hold better."

The little girl gave her head a slow shake. "I don't want another dog, not unless…"

"Unless what?" Jenna prompted when Katie's voice drifted to a halt.

Again Katie aimed a brief glance at her sister, who continued to concentrate on her reading material. "Unless I could have a *real* dog."

That statement won Caroline's attention at last. "Dogs

are messy. Grandmother Arlene said that, and Mom agreed. She didn't want one in the house.''

The corners of Katie's mouth turned down. ''I know. You told me that. I just don't remember her saying it.''

Jenna had to wonder how much Katie recalled at all about her mother and grandmother. Not much, if anything, was probably a good guess. Caroline, however, not only clearly remembered both women, but had plainly looked up to them.

''Well, it's true. She didn't want a dog in the house,'' Caroline told Katie. *And that was that,* her staunch tone implied.

When Katie offered no response, Caroline marked her place in her book and rose to her feet. ''I have to do my homework so Dad can check it after dinner and make sure I did everything right.''

Jenna knew it was useless to offer any help with the homework in question. Caroline had already made it plain that she didn't need her stepmother's assistance—with anything.

As Caroline departed with graceful steps, her small spine held straight, Jenna eased herself down onto the now-empty swing and turned to Katie. Her heart went out to the little girl who looked so wistful. Did Ross know how much his child seemed to want a real-life pet? If so, he hadn't mentioned it.

''What does your father say about a dog?'' she asked softly.

''Caroline says he wouldn't want one around, either.''

''But *you* haven't talked to him about it?''

''Uh-uh.'' Katie raised her gaze to meet Jenna's. ''Do you think he would let me have one?''

''I have no idea,'' Jenna replied with total honesty. ''The only way to find out is to ask him.''

Katie frowned thoughtfully, as though debating the merits of that plan. "Do you like dogs?" she ventured at last.

"Yes. And cats, too," Jenna added. It was hard to recall a time in her own childhood when the Lorenzo family hadn't had a pet, sometimes several at the same time.

All at once Katie's blue eyes widened in a way that seemed to plead her case even before she spoke. "Then can we both ask Daddy if I could have a dog?"

Uh-oh, Jenna told herself. She had no trouble remembering how she'd been the target of that same pleading look right before she'd wound up giving Katie's doll a new hairdo. "I think you can do it on your own," she said.

Katie batted her tiny lashes. "Please?"

Jenna frowned. "You're very good at that, you know."

"At what?" the little girl inquired oh, so innocently, batting her lashes one more time.

Jenna let out a long breath. She knew when she was licked. "Okay, we'll both ask your father about a dog."

Katie smiled then, the first wide, genuine smile she'd aimed Jenna's way since the Hayward girls had learned that they were getting a stepmother. Jenna couldn't hold back a smile in return, not any more than she could help hoping that she and Katie had reached another turning point in their relationship. Maybe things would be better between them from now on. Maybe the smallest member of the family would even come to accept the new woman of the house as a friend. Maybe.

And maybe Ross wouldn't consider it meddling on her part when she and his youngest daughter joined forces to explain Katie's longing to add yet another member to their household—a real, live, canine member.

Again, Jenna could only hope, because the last thing she wanted to do was to lock horns with her husband anytime soon. Not after the last time. As far as she was concerned, no one had come out the winner in that confrontation. She still believed it could only do far more good than harm for Ross to let his father back into his life, and he was clearly still firmly against it. So she was keeping her peace.

"Can we talk to Daddy about a dog tonight?" Katie asked eagerly.

Jenna nodded. "But if he says no, we have to accept that," she warned gently.

"Uh-huh." Despite that quick agreement, Katie looked far from ready to accept the possibility of failure. "One of the girls in Caroline's grade at school has a dog named Jones." She scrunched up her angelically fair face in concentration. "What could I name my dog?"

"If you got one," Jenna didn't hesitate to tack on, then watched as Katie continued to mull the matter over as though that reminder had never been issued.

Oh, Lord, she thought, rolling her eyes heavenward, please let Ross agree to at least consider getting this child a pet. Otherwise, Jenna knew, the Hayward house was going to find itself home to one sadly disappointed little girl.

Chapter Six

The sprawling brick building housing Harmony's animal shelter was located on the outskirts of town just down the road from the Mountain View Drive-In. Ross had passed it many times, but had never been inside.

There'd been a time as a kid when he'd pushed for the idea of adopting a pet, but his mother had firmly vetoed that plan. Arlene Hayward had never been all that fond of animals, other than the canary occupying a small cage in one corner of her kitchen that had sung lilting tunes to its mistress. So her son had settled for playing with some of his friends' pets on occasion.

Now, he was visiting the shelter because his youngest daughter wanted a dog. In fact, as he'd found out earlier that week, she had wanted one for a while.

Why hadn't he at least suspected as much? Ross asked himself as he pulled into a gravel parking lot with Jenna at his side and a clearly thrilled Katie occupying the back seat. He'd always considered himself a concerned father who did his best to keep close tabs on his children, but he had to admit to being more than a little surprised when the two females now in his company had sprung the news on him. In the end, it hadn't taken much to win his agreement, although Caroline had turned her straight little nose up at the whole idea. She'd even chosen to spend her Saturday morning at the home of one of her girlfriends rather than visit the shelter.

But that hadn't dampened Katie's enthusiasm one bit. "How many dogs do you think they have here, Daddy?" she asked as they entered the building.

"Probably quite a few, sunshine."

A stocky man in his fifties seated with his scarred boots propped up on a beige metal reception desk greeted them with a smile that showed a string of slightly crooked but nonetheless gleaming white teeth. "Well, hi there," he said to Ross in an easy drawl.

"Hello, Leon." Ross had no problem recognizing Leon Wiggs, a handyman and jack-of-all-trades who did occasional maintenance jobs at the complex where Hayward Investments kept its office. Leon was, in a word, *distinctive.* "I didn't realize you worked here."

"I volunteer on the weekends," the man who sported a shaved head as round and smooth as a bowling ball told him. "Being an animal lover myself, it just seemed like the thing to do."

"You have any animals of your own?" Katie asked.

"Sure do," Leon replied. He dropped his feet from the desk, sat up straight and looked down at the little girl. "Two dogs, three cats, four rabbits, a horse that eats hay like it was going out of style and a parrot that can squawk out 'The Star-Spangled Banner.'"

"Wow!" Katie's eyes went wide.

Leon chuckled and aimed a brief glance at Jenna before returning his gaze to Ross. "The news going around is that you got married."

And that news had traveled fast. He'd probably have a hard time finding someone who wasn't aware of his recent marriage. Ross introduced Jenna, then Katie, and finally got down to the matter at hand. "We're looking to adopt a dog."

"Well, I sure am glad to see you then," Leon told him. "Having lived on the edge of this town all my life, I can't see anybody thinking a Hayward wouldn't give a pet a good home." He stood up, brushed a hand over his faded Wranglers and came around the desk. "The kennels are back this way. Once we match you up with a dog, it won't take long to fill out the paperwork."

That said, Leon started down a narrow hallway, with Katie skipping along at his side. "It's gonna be my dog," she explained with more than a hint of pride.

"What kind do you like?" Leon asked her.

"I like them all."

"But she's not taking them all," Ross muttered out of the corner to his mouth to the woman walking beside him.

Jenna's lips twitched, as if she more than suspected that Katie could twist her father around a tiny finger on occasion. "I think you made it clear that she was only getting one dog."

He ran his tongue over his teeth as a raucous round of barking reached them. "Maybe I should have said one small dog."

"Hmm." Jenna raised her voice enough to be heard over the growing din. "Well, we can try to steer her in that direction."

"Good idea," Ross said as they turned a corner and found themselves in a high-ceilinged room with a row of large pens standing along one wall. Each pen held several animals, and the first group they came to rushed forward to greet them, some of the dogs still barking to beat the band.

Ross was no expert on members of the canine community, but he nevertheless recognized the short-haired breed standing low to the ground at the front of the pen as a dachshund. A small dachshund. "That's a nice dog," he told Katie, hunkering down beside her for a better look.

Katie grinned. "It's funny-looking."

"Oh, I think it's as cute as a button," Jenna contended with a grin of her own, readily backing up her husband's bid to point out some of the virtues of a small animal.

"Maybe it's funny and cute, too," Katie allowed at last, "but I don't know if it's the kind of dog I want." She studied the dachshund for another moment before another of the pen's occupants captured her attention.

And so it went as they walked down the line, with Ross and Jenna raining praises on the smallest members of the panting, sniffing and sometimes yapping assembly while Katie, although plainly taken with several of the dogs, continued to reserve judgment. It wasn't until they reached the last of the pens that the little girl let out a joyous shout.

"It's Fluffy!"

Startled, it took Ross a second to realize what had produced the shiny gleam of excitement building in Katie's eyes. The cause turned out to be a real, live dog that could have doubled for the stuffed version his daughter kept on her bed—right down to the fact that the animal covered from head to tail in a thick coat of black hair was more than half as tall as she was.

Small—even midsize—by no means applied. Not to this dog. And unless he missed his guess, Ross thought, the animal, as large as it was, hadn't yet grown into the four huge paws that seemed out of proportion to the rest of it.

"I remember when he was brought in a few weeks

ago,'' Leon said in the same friendly drawl he'd used to comment on the other dogs eligible for adoption. "He seems to be part retriever mixed with who knows what else. Someone found him wandering up in the mountains without a collar. The people who run the shelter tried to find the owner, but I guess they came up empty, because he's still here.'' The handyman paused for a beat. "As far as we can make out, he's still mostly a puppy. If you took him, you'd probably have to train him.''

Katie looked up at her father. The gleam in her gaze hadn't dimmed a watt. "We could train him, couldn't we, Daddy?''

A swift study of the "trainee'' nearly had a groan slipping out before he swallowed it. "I don't have much experience in training an animal, sunshine,'' he pointed out with frank honesty.

Far from defeated by that statement, Katie switched her gaze to Jenna. "You said you liked dogs, and cats, too. Did you ever train a puppy?''

"I've helped train a few, yes,'' Jenna acknowledged after a brief hesitation. She slid a glance at her husband. "A smaller puppy, though, might be easier to deal with, because young dogs can be a handful.''

A puzzled frown bloomed on Katie's brow. "A handful?''

Jenna nodded. "That means they sometimes like to play more than they like to learn. They have a lot of energy, and that makes them…well, I suppose *frisky* is a good word for it.''

"So if a dog is frisky it means he likes to play?'' Katie ventured, her frown turning thoughtful.

"That would be one description,'' Jenna agreed.

Ross watched his daughter mull over what she'd just been told while the penned animals continued to bid for the visitors' attention, especially the large black dog in question. It now jumped up and down, its nose an inch from the wire gate, looking as excited as Katie had been a moment before.

And as she was again in the next breath when a wide grin appeared that reached from ear to ear. "I could name this puppy Frisky, and then I'd have twin dogs— Frisky and Fluffy."

Jenna met her husband's gaze over the top of Katie's riot of blond curls. *I think we're on a fast track to adopting a big dog,* it said as clearly as if she'd spoken the words.

A dog that was only going to get bigger. Ross blew out a resigned breath. "Well," he muttered to himself, "how hard can it be to train a dog, even a big one?"

IT WASN'T going to be easy. Jenna had known that even before they'd left the shelter with a bouncing bundle of canine zest for life in the fast lane. Frisky had been aptly named, she thought as she stroked a hand over the puppy's head, even if he wasn't living up to that name at the moment. No, after darkness had set in and the children had gone upstairs to bed, the newest member of the Hayward household had begun to look far more sad than cheery as the house grew quiet. Then the whimpering had started when he'd been penned in the kitchen for the night, a necessity rather than a choice after the discovery that Frisky, while already trained to go outside to do his duty, was still subject to accidents on occasion.

"You just have to get used to your new home," she told the dog in a soft murmur. "In a day or two, you'll be fine." But it hadn't stopped her from tiptoeing through the sitting room of the master suite where her husband lay sleeping and coming downstairs in the middle of the night to check on the new arrival.

After finding Frisky stretched out on the oldest blanket she'd been able to come up with earlier and still whimpering in the soft glow of a night-light left on for him, she'd settled herself on the blanket at his side and done what she could to comfort him. Trouble was, every time she made a move to head back to bed, he looked so mournful at the prospect of being left alone again that she didn't have the heart to do it.

Jenna yawned. "What we both need is to get some more sleep, puppy."

Frisky blew out a long sigh in reply. Then, as though his ears had caught something hers hadn't, he lifted his furry head and looked toward the doorway to the hall.

Jenna followed the dog's gaze and soon caught sight of a bare-chested man dressed only in a pair of pajama bottoms as he stopped before a low mesh gate sealing the kitchen off from the rest of the house.

"I thought I heard someone talking," Ross said as his eyes met hers in the dimness all around them. "At first I thought maybe Katie had snuck down here."

"I decided it might be wise to check on him," Jenna said, continuing her stroking.

"I figured it might be a good idea, too." With his superior height, Ross stepped over the gate in one easy movement, rather than having to slide it open as Jenna had. "How long have you been down here?"

"Awhile," she admitted.

He lowered himself to the tiled floor next to her side of the blanket, bent his legs and clasped his arms around them, a move that put his shoulder scant inches from hers. His broad, bare shoulder, she couldn't help but notice, even though she knew she ought be used to that sight by now. She hadn't seen him wearing no more than a towel since she'd barged into the bathroom, but the fact that they shared a closet had led to her catching glimpses of him in various stages of undress.

And why shouldn't she? They were married, after all. She might feel the need to wrap herself in the same terry-cloth robe she wore at the moment and use the bathroom to dress and undress without fail, but that hardly meant he had to follow the same pattern. She just wished the regular sight of him slipping into a crisp white shirt and buttoning it with strong, well-formed fingers didn't rattle her pulse so much.

Ross issued a low chuckle. "If anyone had predicted just a week ago that I'd be dog-sitting in the near future, I flat out wouldn't have believed them."

"Me, either, I suppose." She'd certainly never envisioned a dog in this particular house until Katie had brought it up.

A few silent seconds passed before he spoke again. "Have you recovered from dinner?"

Her lips curved of their own accord at the reference to a memorable meal. "In hindsight, the last thing I should have made was pasta—at least not with red sauce."

"Well, I've got to admit it made quite an impact when it splashed over half of the kitchen." He shook his head. "You can lay the blame at my door, though, for trying to give Katie a backyard lesson on teaching her new pet to fetch without making sure she understood not to do it in the house."

Which still wouldn't have led to a culinary disaster if the little girl's aim had been better and the wooden spoon she'd thrown hadn't landed in the middle of the table where a large serving bowl heaped with their dinner had just been put out. A small laugh threatened to bubble up from Jenna's throat at the memory of what had happened next. Not that it had been all that funny at the time.

As though he'd also managed to find some humor in the situation, Ross chuckled again. "At least the dog did his best to eat most of what he knocked on the floor. He even gave up trying to get to the spoon after he got a taste of your spaghetti."

"Mmm. I guess I'll take that as a compliment. Too bad he's the only one who got a taste of it, though."

"I'll second that thought," Ross replied without the least hesitation.

Caroline, Jenna recalled, hadn't actually said *I told you so*. Nevertheless, the comment on dogs and their messy habits had rung out loud and clear by means of a pointed glance aimed around the table at the rest of her family when they'd all finally sat down to a meal of cold sandwiches.

"On a positive note," Jenna said, "Frisky didn't get the blueberry tarts we had for dessert."

As though regretting that fact, the puppy snorted out another sigh. And now Jenna had to laugh.

The sound had the man beside her casting a sidelong look. "You know how to take things in stride, don't you?"

"For the most part," she acknowledged. She had no intention of mentioning that what was difficult to take in stride at the moment was his closeness. Maybe if they were seated in the same spot in the middle of the day, it wouldn't have seemed so...intimate. But it was the middle of the night, when they usually slept with a door closed between them.

"Quiet, isn't it?" he remarked, shifting to face her.

"Mmm-hmm." To her, it was *too* quiet. In fact, her senses were on full alert.

Nevertheless, she wasn't prepared for what happened next when the dog suddenly rolled over. The force of the animal's weight as it hit her sideways sent her tumbling in the opposite direction, straight into the long arms that swiftly reached out to stop her upper body from making a hard landing against a solid male chest.

"Sorry," she murmured, glancing up to meet Ross's gaze as he eased her back to a seated position. She waited for him to drop the bolstering hands he'd cupped around her shoulders. Instead, he tightened them another notch and studied her for several hushed seconds ticked off by the kitchen clock.

"No problem," he said at last. "I've been caught off guard a few times myself—including, I'll admit, the first time I kissed you."

"Oh." She swallowed, suddenly recalling in detail, as if it had just happened minutes earlier, how he'd knocked her for a loop that unforgettable evening.

"I suggested then that we take it all the way."

All the way. She took in a steadying breath. "To the altar, yes."

Again he studied her. "I promised I wouldn't push you on this, but I'd be kidding both of us if I didn't say that I want to kiss you again, long and hard and right this minute."

And, right this minute, she wanted him to do exactly that. She'd be the one kidding herself if she denied it. She still couldn't imagine them sharing a bed, especially not the one so suited to his late wife, but... "I suppose I could handle a kiss."

He raised an inquiring brow. "A long and hard one?"

She hesitated a bare moment, then said, "Yes."

The single word was scarcely out when he tugged her closer and covered her mouth with his. Almost instantly, she knew that this wouldn't be like the first time. On that earlier occasion, she could see in hindsight, her escort had been holding back. Now, the man who'd become her husband seemed to hold back nothing as he deepened the kiss with swift effectiveness, using his firm lips and questing tongue to maximum advantage.

And she was responding, couldn't help but respond, to what he could spark inside her. Suddenly feeling became far more important than thinking, so she let herself feel, just feel, as she slanted her mouth for a better fit and issued a low hum of approval in the back of her throat.

Ross heard it, even through the roar of unchecked desire rising to clamor inside him. *Long and hard,* he thought. That's how he was kissing her, how he intended to keep on kissing her. And she was enjoying it.

Nothing could have been guaranteed to test his control more.

Don't let it slip away completely, the brain he usually put to good use warned. This was only a kiss. Trouble was, his body didn't want to listen. No, it had its own agenda, one that had his hand releasing its grip on Jenna's shoulder to inch its way down her arm, then over her waist, and finally up to her breasts. There, it paused at the opening of her belted robe while he continued to kiss her, eagerly and thoroughly. And then, with a will of their own, his fingers slipped inside and stroked themselves over a smooth mound covered by a silky nightgown.

As gentle as his touch was, it had her stiffening in the blink of an eye, and he knew he'd gone too far—even though it wasn't nearly far enough, not for him. Which was just too bad, he thought as he dropped his hand, because the deal had been for a kiss—which he'd gotten, in spades—and now he had to put an end to it before his libido took over and had him trying to convince his clearly reluctant wife to go all the way right this minute…and not to the altar, either.

Pulling back, Ross dragged in a ragged breath. It was only a kiss, he'd been telling himself while savoring the taste of a mouth far softer than his own. And yet, somehow, he'd come to feel as if all that female softness had flexed its muscles and flipped the whole solid length of him to stand him flat on his head. "I think that was long and hard enough," he said, his low voice underscored with a huskiness he couldn't begin to mask.

After a few quick blinks of her dark lashes, Jenna cleared her throat. "I…think you're right."

He raised a hand and ran it through his hair. "Why don't you go to bed? I'll stay with the dog for a while. Sooner or later, he's bound to fall asleep." Which Ross knew wasn't in the cards for him, not anytime soon. Not with some parts of his body still raging at being denied their way.

"All right," Jenna agreed after a brief hesitation. "I'll, uh, see you in the morning." That said, she gave Frisky a last pat and stood, then left man and dog to watch her swift departure, the latter with a mournful whimper.

"Yeah, I know just how you feel," Ross muttered. His mouth twisted in a rueful grimace as he eased himself off the tile floor and onto the blanket. It wasn't long before Katie's new pet snuggled up to him. "I know I'm probably a poor substitute for a woman who smells like a field of wildflowers when you get close enough to get a whiff, but I'm all you've got."

Frisky yawned his opinion of that statement.

"I'll admit she has more experience when it comes to dogs than I do, but I think you and I should get something straight." Ross ran a hand down the animal's back, the fur soft under his palm. "No more knocking food off the table, okay?"

Frisky lifted his head and looked at the man seated beside him, his tongue lolling as he panted a response.

"While you're at it," he told the dog, "do your best to do your duty outside and not have any more accidents, especially not on the carpet." At the sound of more panting, Ross added, "Everything considered, it wouldn't hurt to try to stay out of trouble—period."

But only silence followed that last remark.

IT TOOK HIM the better part of a week to come to terms with the fact that kissing his wife—when he had to stop at kisses—was a bad idea. He had no doubt about having to stop, either, because Jenna hadn't given him one signal indicating otherwise. Instead, although she hadn't said as much, she only seemed to be more wary of taking their relationship to the next stage than before they'd locked lips in a heated kiss in the middle of the night while dog-sitting.

At least things were improving as far as the dog in question was concerned, Ross thought on a cool and windy late Friday afternoon as he headed to the paved parking lot located behind the office complex. There'd been no canine-related accidents, on the carpet or otherwise, for the past few days, and mealtimes had come and gone without any further incidents.

"Hello, Ross," a deep voice called. "Haven't spoken to you for a while."

He halted in his tracks and glanced back to find Warren Bennett walking several steps behind, wearing one of the conservative and always well-tailored three-piece suits the head of Bennett Enterprises favored. "Good to see you, Warren," he said, his easy tone displaying the truth of that.

The Bennetts had first settled in Harmony soon after the Haywards, and the two families had alternately joined forces on community projects and been friendly rivals in the business arena for generations. Both groups had invested heavily in their city's future and had reaped the rewards of success as Harmony continued to prosper over the years.

Warren's thin lips quirked in a smile. He was ten years Ross's senior yet looked younger, with a fit-and-trim body topped by a short mass of thick, dark brown hair that held no hint of gray.

"How does it feel to be a husband again?" Warren asked.

"I think I'm getting a handle on it," Ross replied mildly. He'd be doing a lot better if he could get his hands on the woman he'd married, but he had no intention of saying so.

"Congratulations on the Edmonds deal." Warren's smile didn't falter, despite the fact that Ross's company had beaten Bennett Enterprises to the punch and acquired a prime piece of land on the outskirts of the city from an elderly couple who'd decided to relocate to southern Arizona to be closer to their son and his family.

"Thanks." Ross grinned a satisfied grin. "Since you wound up on top the last time we both had something in our sights, I won't offer condolences."

The older man chuckled. "Always a pleasure to cross swords with you."

"Likewise," Ross told him, and the two men parted with a companionable handshake.

His grandfather would have enjoyed that encounter as much as he had, Ross mused as he left the downtown area behind and drove down neighborhood streets. Thornton Hayward had savored the chance to tangle with a worthy competitor as much as his grandson did. Luckily they'd both had Bennetts who could fill the bill.

And, luckily, he could now look forward to setting aside business for a couple of days and spending a quiet weekend with his family. Or as quiet at it got these days with a new large-pawed bundle of sometimes seemingly endless energy in the house.

At least Katie was happy, he thought, only to have that reflection reconfirmed when he spotted her playing in the backyard with her new pet as he pulled up to the Hayward home. Rather than park the car in the garage, he left it in the driveway, his briefcase propped up in the passenger's seat, and walked around the side of the house. He'd barely opened the steel wire gate when his youngest child came running up to him, the dog hard on her heels.

"Frisky knows how to fetch real good now, Daddy. Watch." Turning, she threw the small stick she'd been holding toward the rear of the yard and the dog wasted no time in bounding after it.

Ross reached down and plucked her up in his arms as a crisp breeze whipped around them. "You're a good teacher, sunshine."

"Uh-huh." She pressed a soft kiss to his cheek, and, as always, it made her father feel like a king. He didn't even want to consider a time when he wouldn't have that to look forward to every day, when he'd have to settle for long-distance phone calls and trips back from college.

"You're getting too big too fast," he said with a mock frown.

"I look bigger in this jacket," she explained, "'cause it's puffy."

He ran his gaze over the quilted jacket shaded a bright peach. "Could be," he allowed, and set her down as the dog made a rapid return, the stick held in his mouth. "Why don't you keep playing while I get some wood from the shed? It'll be nippy enough tonight to have a fire in the fireplace."

"Okay," Katie agreed in her typically easygoing manner. "Can we watch TV, too?"

"We can if there's anything good on and you snuggle in my lap."

She grinned up at him. "Popcorn?"

He pretended to mull that suggestion over. "Only if you let me eat my share."

Her grin widened. "You always eat more than me, Daddy."

"And I will again tonight," he warned with a wink before heading toward a small white shed at the rear of the yard where he'd already stacked a supply of logs in preparation for winter.

Which was good thinking on your part, Hayward, Ross told himself, only to come to that same conclusion a few hours later as he watched small flames spring to life in the family room fireplace after dinnertime had come and gone.

Now he could look forward to a relaxing evening. A little TV, a hefty helping of popcorn, and lots of snuggling with his two girls, because he'd make sure Caroline got her share, even if she did roll her eyes whenever he gave in to temptation and bounced her on his knee like the beautiful baby she'd once been. She might say, "Oh, Dad," with a heartfelt sigh at his antics, but he wasn't letting that stop him anytime soon.

Ross tossed a few more small kindling sticks on top of the flickering flames, then stood, brushed his palms on the casual pants he'd changed into before dinner, and lifted the wrought-iron fireplace screen in place. With that accomplished, his nose took him to the kitchen, where the buttery scent of popcorn filled the air.

Jenna stood at the stove, shaking a large, covered pot over one of the burners. It smelled better than any popcorn he'd ever made in the microwave, Ross had to admit.

He crossed his arms over the front of his navy V-necked sweater and leaned in the doorway. "Where are the kids?"

She glanced at him over a shoulder clad in a long purple top that reached well past her hips. Matching knit pants covered the length of her legs down to the ankles, and black ballerina-style slippers completed her outfit. "They went up to their rooms for a minute," she told him.

He looked around the kitchen. "And the dog?"

"I think he followed Katie upstairs." As she kept shaking the pot, the sound of popping rapidly rose in volume. "This will be ready in a second."

Ross walked over to the refrigerator and reached in for a bottle of beer. "What do you want to drink?"

"I'll have cola with the girls." She emptied the popcorn into a large china bowl. "Want to take this to the family room? I'll bring some napkins and the soda."

"Sure."

Ross left the kitchen with one arm wrapped around

Live the emotion™

Anytime. Anywhere.

send for your 2 FREE ROMANCE BOOKS!

See Details Inside...

We'd like to send you 2 FREE BOOKS

and a surprise gift to introduce you to Harlequin American Romance®. Accept our special offer today and

Live the emotion™

HOW TO QUALIFY:

1. With a coin, carefully scratch off the silver area on the card at right to see what we have for you—**2 FREE BOOKS** and a **FREE GIFT**—ALL YOURS! ALL **FREE!**

2. Send back the card and you'll receive two brand-new Harlequin American Romance® novels. These books have a cover price of $4.75 each in the U.S. and $5.75 each in Canada, but they are yours to keep absolutely free!

3. There's no catch. You're under no obligation to buy anything. We charge nothing—ZERO—for your first shipment and you don't have to make any minimum number of purchases—not even one!

4. The fact is, thousands of readers enjoy receiving books by mail from the Harlequin Reader Service® Program. They enjoy the convenience of home delivery…they like getting the best new novels at discount prices, BEFORE they're available in stores…and they love their *Heart to Heart* subscriber newsletter featuring author news, horoscopes, recipes, book reviews and much more!

5. We hope that after receiving your free books you'll want to remain a subscriber. But the choice is yours—to continue or cancel, any time at all. So why not take us up on our invitation with no risk of any kind. You'll be glad you did!

GET A *Free* MYSTERY GIFT…

We can't tell you what it is…but we're sure you'll like it! A FREE gift just for giving the Harlequin Reader Service® Program a try!

Visit us online at
www.eHarlequin.com

Your FREE Gifts include:

- 2 Harlequin American Romance® books!
- An exciting mystery gift!

HARLEQUIN®
Live the emotion™

Scratch off········
the silver area to see what the
Harlequin Reader Service®
Program has for you.

YES! I have scratched off the silver area above. Please send me the 2 FREE BOOKS and gift for which I qualify. I understand I am under no obligation to purchase any books, as explained on the back and on the opposite page.

354 HDL DU39   154 HDL DU4Q

FIRST NAME   LAST NAME

ADDRESS

APT.#   CITY

STATE/PROV.   ZIP/POSTAL CODE

(H-AR-08/03)

THE HARLEQUIN READER SERVICE® PROGRAM—Here's how it works:

Accepting your 2 free books and mystery gift places you under no obligation to buy anything. You may keep the books and gift and return the shipping statement marked "cancel." If you do not cancel, about a month later we'll send you 4 additional books and bill you just $3.99 each in the U.S., or $4.74 each in Canada, plus 25¢ shipping and handling per book and applicable taxes if any.* That's the complete price and — compared to cover prices of $4.75 in the U.S. and $5.75 in Canada — it's quite a bargain! You may cancel at any time, but if you choose to continue, every month we'll send you 4 more books, which you may either purchase at the discount price or return to us and cancel your subscription.

*Terms and prices subject to change without notice. Sales tax applicable in N.Y. Canadian residents will be charged applicable provincial taxes and GST.

If offer card is missing write to: Harlequin Reader Service, 3010 Walden Ave., P.O. Box 1867, Buffalo NY 14240-1867

DETACH AND MAIL CARD TODAY!

BUSINESS REPLY MAIL
FIRST-CLASS MAIL   PERMIT NO. 717-003   BUFFALO, NY

POSTAGE WILL BE PAID BY ADDRESSEE

HARLEQUIN READER SERVICE
3010 WALDEN AVE
PO BOX 1867
BUFFALO NY 14240-9952

NO POSTAGE
NECESSARY
IF MAILED
IN THE
UNITED STATES

the bowl and the beer held in one hand. He was two steps down the hall when the sound of a soft crash came from the direction of the family room, as though something had hit the carpet.

His first thought was that the dog Jenna had assumed was with Katie had knocked something over, probably a lamp. And he was at least partially right, he found when he entered the large family room at a fast clip.

The dog had knocked something over, but it wasn't a lamp.

It was the fire screen, and now Katie's new pet was doing his best to "fetch" one of the smaller pieces of wood meant to fuel the larger logs.

"No, Frisky!" he shouted in a sharp command, swiftly setting the popcorn and beer bottle down near the doorway before he rushed forward.

But it was too late.

The dog had already pulled a thin length of kindling wood from the bottom edge of the burning logs, sending them tumbling past the narrow stone hearth and onto the snowy-white carpet. Hot embers flew into the air, plainly startling the dog enough to drop the stick he'd been holding.

"Get away from there!" Ross ordered.

This time Frisky didn't hesitate to obey, and when Ross raced out of the room, the dog already had a head start, issuing a series of excited yelps as he ran toward the front of the house.

Jenna met her husband at the kitchen doorway, a tray with three tall glasses filled with cola held in her hands. "What in the world is going on?"

He swept past her and reached the sink an instant later, where he explained the situation in a few succinct words aimed over his shoulder as he retrieved a portable extinguisher from a bottom cupboard. Jenna had already set the tray down and was reaching for the cordless phone on the counter by the time he turned back to her.

"Go upstairs and get the girls first," he said. "Then call the fire department from outside. Hopefully I'll be able to handle it with this." He lifted the extinguisher. "If not…"

Her gaze, widening with concern even as he let those last words hang, met his for a stark second. "Be careful."

"I will," he assured her.

Then she was gone and he was racing back to the family room. For a stunned moment he couldn't believe what he found there, how things had gone from bad to much, much worse in the brief time he'd been away. Now flames weren't only licking up from the carpet, most of the furniture near the fireplace was burning, as well. Even the long white drapes covering a nearby window were rapidly disappearing, sacrificed to the growing blaze as if the thick fabric were no more than paper.

Nevertheless, no matter how bad things looked, it didn't stop him from attempting to put out the fire to the tune of a smoke alarm now jangling in the background, the handheld extinguisher his only weapon in an uphill battle to make headway against a rising tide of heat.

A Hayward didn't concede defeat easily, he told himself. And he kept telling himself exactly that as the flames continued their relentless march forward, pushing him from the family room, then down the hall, inch by inch, until the extinguisher gave out with a final spurt.

Still, only the knowledge that everything he really cared about was safe and waiting for him outside made him give up the stubborn fight at last. Sirens wailed in the distance as he headed for the front door, and he had to hope that the fire department could do what he'd failed to do despite all of his efforts.

Yes, he had to hope they could get things under control, he thought, aiming a last look back at a wall of flames.

Chapter Seven

The house went up in smoke. Standing at a safe distance
across the street, Jenna watched it happen. Despite all
the efforts to contain it, the fire gained the upper hand
as it moved from the first floor to the second, and then
to the rooftop, where it was whipped to new heights by
a steady wind swirling down from the mountains surrounding the city.

Eventually, it had its way.

Now the air was acrid, a smoky legacy of a serenely
elegant home's destruction that was all but total. The
once dove-gray bricks were scorched a muddy black, the
wide windows broken, the stylish furnishings no more
than a heap of charred rubble.

"Why did our house burn, Daddy?" Katie asked in a
small voice.

Ross kept a reassuring hand on the shoulders of both
of his daughters as they stood on opposite sides of him.
His eyes met Jenna's over the top of Katie's head.
"There was an accident with the fireplace," he said.
And that was all he said.

She got the message. He didn't plan on mentioning to
the children that the new pet his youngest child had already grown to love by leaps and bounds had unwit-

tingly started the fire, and Jenna could certainly understand why. She wouldn't have had the heart to do it,
either.

Glancing down, she studied the puppy stretched out
on the sidewalk beside her, as though exhausted at last
from all the commotion he'd not only witnessed but
done his best to add to by his repeated attempts to cross
the street, tail wagging up a storm in his eagerness to
play with the firefighters. She could only be grateful that
she'd been able to get a leash hooked to his collar and
get him out of the house safely after wasting no time in
herding Caroline and Katie downstairs, their shoes hastily donned, their coats slung over their shoulders and a
few of their most prized possessions in hand.

Now Katie held her doll, the auburn-haired Pandora,
while Fluffy, her large stuffed dog and the real-life
Frisky's twin, stood propped up against her short legs.
Meanwhile, Caroline held the silver-framed photograph
of her mother together with a favorite book that had been
resting next to it on her bedroom dresser.

That was all they'd managed to save. And as little as
it was, none of Jenna's personal belongings had been as
lucky. She'd only taken the time to grab her shoulder
bag, long beige raincoat and some flat-heeled shoes from
the front hall closet, and Ross wouldn't even have had
that much clothing to his name if she hadn't also thought
to snatch up his short leather jacket and a pair of brown
loafers before leaving the house with the wide-eyed children and happily prancing dog in tow.

For his part, her husband had had the presence of
mind to get both of their cars away from the house before the fire department's equipment blocked the driveway, otherwise the cars would have been reduced to little
more than burnt rubble right along with the garage.

"Lord, I'm sorry this happened, folks." Tom Kennedy, who had arrived shortly after the firefighters to deal with traffic control in his role of police chief, gave his head a slow shake as he approached the Hayward family, his boot heels tapping on the pavement. When he reached up to thumb back the wide brim of his well-worn tan hat, the grim set of his expression was more than apparent in the soft light of a nearby street lamp. It was plain that his sympathy was genuine.

"Thanks for the thought, Tom," Ross replied in an even tone that displayed little emotion, as though he were keeping a tight grip on his feelings. Either that or he was still stunned by what had happened.

Jenna had no trouble believing the latter. Although she'd done her best to maintain a calm front, she still felt shocked down to her toes by the suddenness of the whole thing, and she'd only been living in the now destroyed home for a matter of weeks.

"Everything's gone," Caroline said in a hollow voice. It was the first time the older girl had spoken since Jenna had hurried the children out of the house.

Katie sniffed. "We got no place to sleep now, Daddy."

"We'll find somewhere, sunshine, don't worry." Ross ran a hand over her blond curls. "Everything's going to be fine."

"That it will," Tom agreed, mustering a heartier tone. "For tonight, at least, I suggest you all stay at my place. Being a longtime bachelor, I've got a house with plenty of room to spare."

Ross looked at the older man. "I appreciate the offer, but—"

"Don't even think about turning me down," Tom said, breaking in. "I know you could stay at one of the bed-and-breakfasts in town or a motel along the highway. But with the dog, that might be tricky, and he won't be a problem at my place.''

Ross shifted his gaze to Jenna and lifted an inquiring brow. ''What do you say?'' When she slanted her head in a nod of agreement, he continued. ''Okay, Tom, we'll take you up on that offer. And thank you again.''

''No further thanks necessary. I spoke up first, but your neighbors would do the same thing.'' The chief glanced at the people who had gathered on the sidewalk, their expressions grave. ''Right from the day this town was named, Harmony has been about folks looking out for each other.''

''Can't argue with you on that score,'' Ross allowed.

''Good.'' Tom turned his head to watch the last of the fire trucks pull away. ''I'll post a man here to keep an eye on things for the rest of the night and then head back home. I know I don't have to give you directions. Just come over when you're ready and we'll get these tired kids put to bed.''

With that, the chief departed, and again Ross looked at Jenna. ''I don't think there's much to stick around for.''

She could only agree. There was nothing to be done, not here. As if they concurred with that judgment, the crowd began to disperse. ''Do you want to take the girls with you in your car, and I'll take the dog in mine and follow you?''

''Sounds like a plan,'' Ross told her in that same even tone, still displaying little of his feelings. He reached down to retrieve Katie's stuffed dog from the sidewalk, then tucked it under one long arm and urged his daughters down the street toward his car, again placing a steadying hand on their shoulders.

"Things will look better in the morning," he assured his girls as they walked off.

Jenna had to hope it was true.

"Come on, Frisky," she said, giving a slight tug on the leash.

The puppy hopped to his feet and issued an eager bark, as though ready to start on his next adventure.

"You don't have to look so chipper," she told him with a wry curve of her lips. "We'll have a roof over us, thanks to Tom Kennedy, but who knows exactly where we'll all be sleeping."

And who they'd be sleeping with, she thought. How much sleeping space would be available, after all, despite Tom's having a whole house to himself? Then again, what did it matter? He'd never consider giving a newly married couple separate bedrooms, even if he had a dozen extra.

She and Ross would be sharing a room tonight.

And they might well be sharing one for the foreseeable future, she knew, no matter where they wound up living. Most homes in Harmony, assuming they could even find one to rent on an emergency basis, didn't come with large master suites that ensured two parties their privacy while giving the appearance of a far-more-intimate relationship. An outward appearance that still had to be maintained, she was sure Ross would contend. Unfortunately she could only agree, because it remained important not to give the children any cause to wonder about the state of their father's new marriage, especially Caroline.

There was no getting around it, Jenna reflected with a lengthy sigh. Her relationship with the man she'd married was about to take an intimate turn—at least considerably more intimate than it had been—whether she was ready or not.

And she wasn't ready.

HE WASN'T READY, either.

Hell, Ross thought, at the moment he was a long way from prepared to sleep in the same room—in the same bed!—as his wife and convince his body to ignore the situation. Now that he'd dealt with his first concern and seen his children settled for the night, he'd at least have to have a little time to gear himself up for the prospect of lying beside Jenna and pretending that he was too worn out to care.

The pure truth was that the adrenaline rush he'd experienced earlier when he'd fought a futile battle against the fire had gradually seeped away and left him at least marginally more relaxed than tense. But not *that* relaxed.

"Tired?" he asked as he watched Jenna aim her gaze around the bedroom Tom had assigned to them. There was nothing fancy about it, but everything was clean— a circumstance, Tom had readily admitted, owing a lot more to the efforts of the cleaning service that came in once a week than any inclination on his part to wave a dust cloth around.

"Tired, yes," Jenna acknowledged, "but not sleepy."

"Sorry about the arrangements," he said, and left it at that. He meant the sleeping arrangements, but he doubted there was any need to spell it out.

As if to confirm the truth of that, she slid a look at the spindled oak bed covered with a simple chenille spread. "I suppose we'll manage."

"Uh-huh," he muttered. What else could he say? They'd have to manage…but not just yet. "I'm going to take Tom up on that offer of a beer."

She sighed. "I wouldn't mind a glass of wine myself. I'm just not sure I should risk the homemade version he mentioned."

That had a faint smile curving his lips, despite everything. "Desperate times call for desperate measures," he said dryly.

She mulled that over for a moment, then squared her shoulders. "You're right. Let's go find our host."

They found him in the kitchen at the back of the house, nursing a bottle of the beer he'd offered. In a matter of minutes the three of them were seated around a beige Formica-topped table with their drinks in hand and the dog responsible for so much of the evening's momentous events stretched out and snoring on the brown-and-cream, checker-tiled floor.

Jenna took a sip of her wine, swallowed quickly, and sucked in a sharp breath. "Goodness gracious," she said, eyes widening. "That's…potent."

Tom's gaze glinted with amusement. "Good for what ails you. That's what my next-door neighbor contends every spring when she makes a batch and hands it out. Since she's over ninety and still going strong, I'm not inclined to argue the point."

Jenna studied the ruby-red contents of her small, footed glass in the bright fluorescent light beaming down from the kitchen ceiling. "Well, it certainly clears the sinuses."

Ross lifted his beer bottle and took a long swallow. At the moment he would have preferred a stiff shot of something else. But the twelve-year-old Scotch he'd received as a Christmas present last year from his employees was history. As were the rest of the contents of the house that had been built on a spacious lot in one of

Harmony's more fashionable neighborhoods shortly after he'd become a husband for the first time.

Tom's expression settled into more serious lines as he switched his gaze to Ross. "What will you do now?" he asked after a moment.

Ross didn't have to think about it twice. His children needed more than a temporary roof over their heads. "Finding a place to live has to be the first priority."

Tom raised a broad hand and ran it through dark auburn hair tinged with gray. His brow furrowed under his steadily receding hairline. "Could be you already have a place. Not nearly as new as the home you lost, but it seems to be in pretty good shape for its age, at least from the outside."

A short moment passed before Ross caught Tom's drift. "You mean, my grandparents' house."

"Yep."

Jenna set her glass down. "The blue Victorian just north of Harmony Park?"

"Yep," the police chief offered for a second time.

She looked at Ross. "I remember walking by that house whenever my sisters and I went to the park to play. Is it still owned by the family?"

He nodded. "As it happens, I inherited it from my grandfather." Which hadn't come as much of a surprise to anyone at the time, Ross recalled from the reading of the will. Since Thornton Hayward's wife of many years had predeceased him, his considerable estate had been divided several ways after his death, but the house had gone to the grandson with whom he had formed close bonds in the latter part of his life.

"The old man wanted you to have it," Tom said softly. "Might be it's been waiting for a new crop of Haywards to move in."

Ross mulled that over for a second, trying to remember the last time he'd actually been inside the home that had once been almost as familiar to him as the one he'd shared with his parents. He'd sold that far more modern house after his mother was gone, but he'd never so much as considered selling the aging Victorian. His grandfather hadn't been the first Hayward to live there, even though he had been the last.

"I'm a long way from sure how livable it is at the moment," he had to admit. "The place has been empty for quite a while."

"Still, it wouldn't hurt to take a look at it," Jenna pointed out. She took another sip of her wine. "The house may just need a little fixing up."

"A lot of fixing up could well be more accurate," Ross countered with blunt honesty as he leaned back in his chair. "Wouldn't you rather move into something newer if that turns out to be an option?"

"Not especially," she replied, looking as though she fully meant it. "I like old houses."

His mother hadn't. Neither had his first wife, who'd worked with a contractor to produce the home of her dreams.

But Jenna Lorenzo Hayward seemed to be another sort of person entirely—one he was just beginning to truly get to know. Every day he was learning more about her. Earlier that evening, the fact that she didn't panic in a crisis had come to light. She'd done what she'd had to do without so much as a whiff of hysterics. Now, although the aftermath of the fire had left her weary— he could tell as much from the slight slump of her shoulders—her chin was still held high.

No doubt about it, Jenna had "sticking power," as

his grandfather would have said. It would have sparked admiration on the part of his ancestor, Ross was sure.

And what if Harmony's former mayor had lived long enough to watch her walk down the aisle wearing the antique wedding gown that had once belonged to his own bride? Would it have left Thornton Hayward a little misty-eyed?

Not hardly, Ross told himself. His grandfather had always put up a tough-as-nails front in public. Which was precisely why he would no doubt have approved of the fact that Jenna seemed far from intimidated at the prospect of calling one of the oldest houses in Harmony home.

"Why am I getting the feeling you thrive on challenges?" Ross asked his wife dryly.

The question won him a faint smile. "The Lorenzos are a tough bunch," she said.

"More power to 'em" was Tom's staunch judgment.

"As I understand it," Jenna continued, "my great-grandfather came over on a boat from Europe, took one look at New York harbor and concluded that a skilled carpenter could do well in all the hustle and bustle of continuous construction going on in those days. Ultimately one of his many sons decided to try his own luck farther west, and a branch of the family tree eventually wound up in Arizona."

"I remember that more than a few people were mighty disappointed to see the Lorenzos move away from Harmony," Tom told Jenna, "although they understood the building boom in Nevada was a good opportunity for your folks."

Jenna polished off her wine. "Yes, it all turned out for the best," she said after a moment.

Nevertheless, Ross had little doubt that she'd been

sorry to see her family leave after the wedding. The Lorenzos seemed to be a close-knit bunch. Closer than some of the Hayward clan, he had to admit.

"Well, I can only be grateful for the fortitude we both inherited from our ancestors," he said, "because no matter where we wind up settling down, the next few weeks are bound have their rough spots."

Jenna met that statement with a brief nod followed by a small yawn. "Sorry," she murmured, "I didn't think I was sleepy, but now I'm fading fast." She dropped a look down at her empty glass and then raised her gaze to fix it on her host. "Probably because of your take-no-prisoners brand of wine."

Tom grinned. "Mrs. Honeycutt will be happy to know she hasn't lost her flair."

Jenna raised a brow. "Does that mean you haven't tried it?"

Tom chuckled then. "I'm strictly a beer man, myself. I save Mrs. Honeycutt's stuff for my guests."

Jenna's eyes drooped to half mast. "I think I have to go to bed now."

"Good idea," Ross said, thinking that with any luck she'd be fast asleep before he had to follow. Maybe he should have some of that wine and try to knock himself out. On the other hand, probably the last thing he needed was to down too much alcohol. For all that he could usually keep a grip on his control, it just might get away from him with a good dose of an elderly woman's potent brew after the day he'd had.

God, he'd lost what had been his home for ten years and everything in it. The blunt reality of that was just setting in.

"Don't let me keep you up," Tom told him moments later when Jenna had departed and left the two men seated across from each other at the table with the dog still snoring softly on the floor beside them.

"I'm not really ready to call it a night yet," Ross said with complete honesty. He lifted his beer bottle for another swallow. He knew a shower was next on his agenda. His hair and skin, not to mention most of the clothes he had to his name, smelled of smoke from his earlier attempt at fire fighting. But he wasn't ready to do that, either.

Tom slapped his hands on his knees and got up. "Then let's raid the refrigerator and make ourselves a sandwich." He patted a silver, Western-style buckle that cinched his slightly rounded waistline. "My motto is that you can't go wrong with food."

As though he'd heard the magic word, Frisky snapped his head up to look at both of his companions. By the time Tom headed across the room, he was on his four feet and only a short step behind.

"Guess you feel the same way," Tom drawled, dropping a glance down at the dog.

Frisky offered a soft whine in response and wagged his tail with enthusiasm.

Ross shook his head. "Hell, we might as well make him a sandwich, too. He's had a busy evening."

THE FOLLOWING DAY Jenna stared up at the old, two-story Victorian frame house painted a traditional slate blue and found it looking much the same. At least, that was her judgment. To her eyes, even now, it still had its share of the dignified charm that had once drawn her gaze as a child.

Somehow it didn't matter that the clapboard trim needed a fresh coat of creamy white and that the trio of narrow wood steps leading up to the wraparound front porch—or veranda, as it had probably been called in earlier days—sagged slightly in the middle.

Standing on the sidewalk and gazing down a wide flagstone walkway, she could almost see the home decked out in its Christmas best, with snow dusting the tall evergreens decorating the front lawn, and each and every window lining both floors of the house sporting a cheery wreath. Even the attic high overhead, with its own small row of windows and steeply pitched roof, would beam out a merry welcome with a string of tiny lights twinkling in the night.

"This would be a good place to live," Jenna said. She didn't know how she could be so sure of that. She only knew she was. Just as she knew the man standing beside her remained far more skeptical about the matter.

"You haven't seen the inside yet," Ross reminded his wife as he shoved his hands into the front pockets of the short leather jacket he wore with the casual slacks and sweater he'd purchased that morning. Despite the need for housing, shopping for a small supply of new clothing and other personal necessities for all of the Hayward family had been even more important.

Now, with that accomplished and the girls spending a few hours at the home of one of Caroline's friends while Katie's new pet remained at Tom Kennedy's place, Jenna and her husband were free to check out possible options for putting a roof over everyone's head. And as far as Jenna was concerned, she already liked this particular one.

"Then let's see the inside," she urged, keeping her tone upbeat. "Everything may be fine."

Ross looked a lot less than convinced of that as they started down the path to a dark mahogany door topped by a narrow length of stained glass displaying a capital

H at its center. "I did say that no one had lived here for quite a while," he pointed out, producing an old key and inserting it into the brass lock. "Some neighbors down the street have been keeping an eye on the place. They have a teenage son who was happy to earn extra money by cutting the grass and watering the outdoor plants. But I don't think I could have paid him enough to act as housekeeper around here."

"Probably not," Jenna had to agree. Teenagers weren't known for their dedication to wielding a mop and broom. Entering as Ross pushed the door open with a quiet squeak of the hinges, she tossed a look back over her shoulder. "Luckily you now have an experienced housekeeper on hand."

With quiet steps, she walked into a small entryway that featured a thick Oriental rug stretched across most of the planked wood flooring. She then made her way past a steep staircase that led up to the second floor and was soon glancing through a wide, arched doorway into a spacious room filled with furniture topped by cotton dustcovers.

"This is the front parlor," Ross explained. "At least, that's the way my grandparents always referred to it. A combination library and study is across the hall. Then comes the formal dining room, and finally the kitchen and a screened-in sunporch at the rear of the house."

Jenna aimed an assessing glance around the parlor. She decided that its furnishings, having been protected, would probably be at least in reasonably decent shape despite the house having been locked up for some time. The rug, again one sporting an Oriental design, needed a thorough vacuuming, and the wood floor visible around the edges of the room a good cleaning—which also applied to the heavy brocade draperies lining the windows and the windows themselves. But all of that, she knew, could be handled with fairly little trouble.

The walls, however, were another matter. One look at the floral-print paper pealing in several places not covered by a variety of black-and-white photographs mingled with several vivid oil paintings told Jenna that some real work needed to be done there.

As if his thoughts ran along the same lines, Ross said, "We'll be lucky if pealing wallpaper is the biggest problem we run into."

And by the end of their tour of the first floor, Jenna couldn't deny that several more problems had come to light. Chief of which was a rear porch that looked in need of some major repairs to bolster one side of a weathered wood floor sloping at an obvious slant.

"One plus," she said as they climbed the stairs to the second floor, "is that you were able to get the electric company to turn on the power this morning, so we know the kitchen appliances still work." A tribute to the quality manufacturing methods of a prior age, she reflected to herself, because nothing in the large, old-fashioned kitchen was anywhere close to state-of-the-art.

"I suppose we'll count that as a blessing." Ross reached the landing and started down a narrow hall featuring more peeling flower-strewn wallpaper. They opened doors as they went and found that two of the rooms closest to the staircase held bedroom furniture again protected by dustcovers, while a third had been turned into a small domain once ruled over by the lady of the house.

"Some long ago Hayward woman furnished this place to suit herself," Ross said. He lifted dustcovers to reveal an antique sewing machine complete with manual foot pedal, and a chaise longue draped in dark gold velvet.

"My grandmother liked it and decided not to make any changes, although I gather she didn't use it much herself. She wasn't a Hayward by birth, but she fell right in with the family work ethic. After her children were grown, she spent a lot of time in community service."

Jenna tried out the chaise longue. Leaning against its well-padded back, she put her feet up and crossed her arms over the front of her raincoat. "I wonder if this could be considered what was once referred to as a 'fainting couch.'"

Ross's mouth quirked up at the tips. "I have no idea, but I guess if you have to faint, it would be as good a place as any."

Her lips took a wry slant of their own. "How many of those ladies from another era actually ever fainted, do you suppose? It seems to me they would have been too busy coping with the large families a lot of people had back then."

"No time for smelling salts, huh?"

"I wouldn't think so."

"You could be right." He lifted a hand and rubbed a finger over a small nick on his jaw, the result of an unfamiliar razor borrowed from their temporary host that morning. "If we decide to stay here," he added after a beat, "the two bedrooms we've seen so far would probably work for Caroline and Katie."

"Mmm-hmm." *And what about us?* That question suddenly became foremost in Jenna's thoughts. During their just-completed trip down the second-floor hall, they'd discovered a linen closet filled with clean, if somewhat musty, bedding and a good-size bath that, like the kitchen, held fully functional if by no means state-of-the-art equipment. Only one door at the far end of the hall remained to be opened.

She cleared her throat. "I take it there's another bed-room."

"Yes, the one my grandparents used." His gaze met hers. "It's the biggest bedroom in the house and has the added advantage of an adjoining bath due to some re-modeling done a while back."

And now it would be their room if they moved in. Jenna knew that was a given. She got to her feet. "I suppose we should take a look at it next."

They looked, with Jenna noting, not much to her sur-prise, that the biggest bedroom in the house was still small by modern standards. Ross lifted more dustcovers to reveal a brass bed that seemed old enough to have served as a sleeping spot for generations of his family, and it was far from the largest Jenna had ever seen. In fact, the double bed matched the size of the one she and her husband had slept in the night before.

Or she assumed he had slept there. She'd been dead to the world—thanks to that killer homemade wine—by the time he'd retired for the night. When she'd awakened that morning, all she'd found to indicate he had stretched out beside her at some point was the imprint of his head on the pillow next to hers.

Certainly he didn't look as if he had gotten much sleep. Or any. Not that he wasn't every bit as attractive as always, even with a hint of dark circles underscoring his navy eyes. At least he was to her.

"What do you think?" he asked from her side.

That we need some space we obviously won't get. Jenna resisted the urge to sigh. Hadn't she already more than suspected that sharing a room with this man for the foreseeable future would be far less of a choice than a necessity? It would either be here or at the only other house in town—a smaller house than this one—currently for rent.

She tilted her chin and looked up at her companion. ''I think we'll make do.''

''Because we have to,'' he added.

''Yes.'' Jenna ran her tongue over her lips, thinking that the bedroom itself might be a lot less than ideal under the circumstances, but the house...

''I haven't changed my mind,'' she said. ''I still believe this would be a good place to live.''

He lifted a brow. ''In spite of all the repairs that will have to be made?''

''In spite of everything.'' And she knew she meant exactly that. Something about the old Victorian, even in the state it was in, continued to appeal to her.

He mulled that over for a minute. ''Then I suppose we can move in later this afternoon,'' he said at last.

Jenna nodded. Although Tom Kennedy had gone out of his way to assure them that they were welcome to stay with him as long as they liked, Ross obviously felt as she did. It would be better for everyone, especially the children, to get settled as soon as possible.

She squared her shoulders. ''If you'll drop me off at the supermarket, I'll get some cleaning supplies and a few groceries while you pick up Caroline and Katie. We can give the house a fast once-over to get it into a little better shape and worry about the rest later.''

''All right.'' He ran a hand through his hair, brushing back a stray strand that had fallen over his forehead. ''Don't bother with buying anything for dinner. We'll go out to eat and drop by Tom's place to get the dog on the way back.''

''And then we'll have a quiet evening.''

''It should be quiet, all right,'' he agreed. ''I doubt

that the girls will have much interest in watching the old TV downstairs in the library when there's no cable. It'll probably take a while to get that set up.''

''We'll manage,'' Jenna told him.

''Uh-huh.'' He blew out a gusty breath as his gaze drifted back to the ornate brass bed currently stripped of its bed coverings. It lingered there for a long moment before he switched it back to her. In the next breath she found herself pinned by a steady and sober stare. ''After the girls are settled for the night, you and I need to talk.''

She could have asked about what but didn't. Something told her even as her heart picked up a rapid beat that the discussion he had in mind was personal. Very personal.

Far too personal to put it out of her thoughts in favor of more immediate considerations, even after she agreed to that talk with a quick dip of her head and turned to leave the room.

Chapter Eight

He would have to be blunt about it. Ross knew there was no point in beating around the bush. Once he and Jenna were alone for the night, he had to make something plain.

But first they all had to get through this evening.

It didn't help that his daughters had failed to work up much enthusiasm for moving into their great-grandparents' home. Then again, it didn't hold the memories for them it did for him. Memories that had slowly stirred to life as he and his children did their share to strip a thick layer of dust from surfaces left to gather for years while his wife tackled the bathrooms and made up the beds.

His grandparents had been hard taskmasters in many ways, but they'd also taken pride in his childhood accomplishments and encouraged him to do his best. That's what he remembered most.

And maybe it would be worth the effort to restore the house that had once been theirs. However, considering the amount of repairs needed, he was still reserving judgment on that score.

"We're not gonna light a fire, are we?" Katie asked with a tiny frown. She was sitting at a leather-topped card table in the library. A board game they'd found in a small cabinet was spread out in front of her.

Ross aimed a glance at the elaborately carved mahogany fireplace, one of several built into the outside walls of the house. "No open fires for a long time, sunshine," he assured her in an effort to put her worries to rest.

Even once the chimneys had been given a good cleaning, he had no intention of putting a match to a log until the dog stretched out beside Katie's chair was long past the puppy stage. Luckily, the old furnace in the basement still seemed up to the task of heating the place. With the nights now regularly sporting temperatures more brisk than balmy, they all had to be thankful for that much.

"Now that we've divided into sides, it's time to start the game," Jenna said.

"I never played Monopoly before," Katie reminded her.

Jenna nodded. "So you said. That's why we're going to be a team and try to beat your father and sister. Now, each side rolls the dice to see who gets to go first."

"That means you have to count the spots on the top when they stop to find out who got the most."

"You're absolutely right," Jenna told Katie. She handed her the white dice. "You get to roll for our side."

Katie nibbled at her bottom lip. "Do I get to count the spots, too?"

"That'll be your job," Jenna agreed. "Your father's going to be banker. That's why he passed out starting money to both sides. Now whenever we land on one of the little squares, we have some choices to make, depending on what square we land on."

"What you want to try not to do is land on the one that says 'go to jail,'" Ross offered with mock gravity.

Katie dipped her head in agreement. "That would be bad." She proceeded to toss the dice. As they clattered across the board, Frisky jumped to his feet and put his nose over the rim of the table. She counted six spots before Ross picked up the dice and gave them to Caroline, who sat next to him with her chin cupped in the palm of one hand.

"Go for it, princess," he said with a light tug on a few straight strands of her shoulder-length hair. Usually the gesture won him at least a brief curve of her mouth. Tonight, however, he neither expected, nor got, more than a softly resigned sigh. Still, although her heart obviously wasn't in the game, no hint of a pout marred her delicate features. When push came to shove, his eldest child had backbone. Even as Ross had to admire that, he couldn't help wishing for a return to the days when she didn't sometimes seem to be ten going on thirty.

Caroline rolled the dice, and this time the dog made a quick run around the table at the sound.

"I think Frisky thinks he's playing, too," Katie said as her own smile bloomed, the first wide, genuine one Ross had seen from either of his daughters since their home's total destruction. Of the two sisters, Katie seemed to be making the faster recovery after an eventful night probably neither would ever completely forget.

Ross allowed himself a small grin of gratitude for the resiliency of the very young as his team started first and the game began in earnest. Both sides mapped out their strategy as they went along, with Frisky making a beeline around the table at every roll of the dice.

"Are we winning?" Katie asked Jenna sometime later, her brow furrowed in concentration as she studied the board.

"We've got one more hotel on our properties than

they do and haven't gone to jail so far, but we can't drop our guard,'' Jenna warned with an amused gleam in her eye.

"Okay." Katie warmed the dice in her hands and let them go with another clatter. This time, however, her growing enthusiasm sent them skidding off the table and launched the dog into a headlong pursuit. In the process, he jarred one of the table's thin legs with a sharp bump that threatened to upend it until Ross reached out and set it upright again. Unfortunately, he wasn't able to act in time to stop the board and everything else the table held from sliding off and crashing to the floor. Fake money went flying, along with playing cards and game pieces.

To make matters worse the dog had started to paw and sniff his way through the floor's contents with an eagerness usually reserved for anything in the food department. "Good grief," Ross said, "I think he's going to try to eat the stuff."

"Oh, Frisky. No!" Jenna commanded as they both pushed back their chairs and rushed forward. Ross was the first to drop to his knees and extend a long arm out to grab the dog's collar. Jenna came down close beside him a split second later.

Too close, as it turned out. Before he could get his balance, she sent them both sliding sideways. In a matter of instants, Ross was flat on his back with one arm still extended to hold the dog and Jenna stretched out half over him.

Their gazes locked for a humming moment. Feeling the fit of her soft body pressed to his far-more-solid form, every ounce of blood in his head promised to take a fast drop below his waist if she didn't move and be quick about it.

Just then, Katie ran up to them. A small giggle escaped as she stared down at both adults. "You look funny, Daddy."

But what he felt was… Hell. "We damn well need to talk—and soon," Ross muttered just loud enough for his wife's ears before she scrambled off of him.

The game, as far as he was concerned, was over.

JENNA TIED THE SASH of her new terry-cloth robe and viewed her reflection in the long mirror of the bathroom she had scrubbed bright that afternoon. The yellow robe had been the brightest and most cozy replacement she could find for the one destroyed in the fire, and now she welcomed both its soft feel and cheery color.

She could, she thought, use some cheering up.

She and Ross were about to have the "talk" he'd mentioned twice, the last time just over an hour earlier with a determined set of his jaw. They'd already said their good-nights to the girls and checked back to see that both had drifted off to sleep in short order—Katie with her new pet stretched out on a colorful braid rug beside her delicately carved rosewood bed.

Now nothing remained to delay the discussion the man of the house was plainly set on having. Jenna just wished that he hadn't looked quite so grim when he'd said he'd see her in their room before heading off to turn out the lights downstairs and make sure that everything was secure for the night.

Knowing there was little to do but get on with it, Jenna quietly opened the bathroom door and found Ross sitting in the bedroom chair, an overstuffed version shaded a rich garnet red to match both the long drapes and fringed bedspread. His eyes were closed, his expression weary. Then, as if he sensed her presence, his eyes drifted open and he shifted to look her way.

"You look tired," she told him, keeping her voice low.

"I am," he replied, matching her tone.

But, despite his relaxed posture as he lounged in the chair with one ankle propped on a knee, he also still looked determined. And even fully dressed, with the lines around his firm mouth deeper than she'd ever seen them, he looked formidably male, as well.

She squared her shoulders, took a few quiet steps forward in her new ivory satin slippers and sat across from him on an edge of the bedspread. "Then we'd better talk so you can get some sleep."

Suddenly he pinned her with a steady stare, as he had that morning, and once again it jump-started her heartbeat. "That's just it," he said after a second of stark silence. "As things stand, I'm going to have a devil of a time getting any sleep—tonight and who knows how many nights down the road."

All at once she was sure where the conversation was headed. There was no point in pretending otherwise. "Because we'll be sleeping next to each other," she finished in the next breath.

His gaze didn't waver. "You're right on target. I know I told you I wouldn't push you on making this a real marriage in every sense of the word, but I wasn't counting on the house burning down." He paused for a beat. "The blunt fact of the matter is, the situation has changed, and dealing with it will be a long way from easy for me, unless…"

Unless I'm willing to accept another major change, Jenna added to herself when his voice trailed off and he arched a meaningful eyebrow. Her husband had laid it on the line, she had no trouble concluding, and now it was up to her to make a decision.

Jenna frowned in thought, wondering if a willingness to take their relationship to the next stage was totally beyond her at the moment. But that quandary had no sooner formed in her mind when another one—the real one, she recognized with sudden insight—rose to take its place.

It was less a matter of being willing than one of being able, she realized. Could she, after finding herself a bride only weeks earlier, agree to be a wife in every sense of the word to this man who had once—not just in her judgment, but in the eyes of so many Harmony residents—had the ideal marriage?

You couldn't, something told her, *if the bed you were sitting on right this minute was the one so suited to another woman—the bed lost in the fire.* But this was a far different bed in a far different room in a far different house. And that made all the difference, Jenna was beginning to see.

Now she…could.

"I think," she told Ross with the same soft yet frank directness he'd used only moments ago, "that it's time to make this a real marriage."

He went stock-still for an instant, every muscle in his face tight. "Do you really mean that?"

"Yes."

"Remind me to get down on my knees in sheer thankfulness later," he said as he surged to his feet.

Despite nerves that were far from calm, it made her smile. "I'll try to remember."

"You do that." Two swift steps across the well-padded surface of yet another of the home's thick Oriental rugs took him to her. Once there, he bent to catch her hands in his and pull her up beside him. Then his mouth came down on hers.

So far they'd shared three kisses and he had lingered over all to some degree. This one, although hard and deep, was over almost before it began, and in the blink of an eye he was pulling her robe off to leave her standing in her long ivory nightgown.

Watching his hand's progress, he ran a palm down the satin garment, from its high neck to its flowing waist. "For more than a few nights after our wedding I kept seeing you in that little black number your friend bought you," he said.

She had no problem recalling the skimpy teddy. "Maybe I had a few late-night thoughts of my own about those silky boxer shorts you got," she told him.

He leaned in and whispered in her ear. "Just maybe?"

"Okay, so I did," she confessed.

"I've got cotton briefs on now."

A vivid image bloomed in her mind, one in which he wore not briefs but only a towel hitched at his narrow hips. "I don't think I'm going to be disappointed." And she certainly wasn't when he took a small step back, fisted his hands on the hem of his lightweight sweater and pulled it over his head.

Much to her delight, she got another look at his leanly muscled chest. Only this time she also got the chance to reach out and rub her palms over the crisp hair there.

In response, he exhaled a shuddering breath. After that, things happened at an increasingly rapid pace, as more clothing made a hasty slide to the floor. True to her expectations, Jenna was far from disappointed when his cotton underwear was soon revealed, and disappointment was inconceivable at her first sight of what lay under it. She was, in fact, so busy being fascinated with the all-male body on full display that she scarcely noticed when avid hands removed her nightgown. Soon they were stretched out on a floral-print sheet with the bedspread thrown to the foot of the bed and nothing to stop them from meeting skin-to-skin.

Jenna, now flat on her back with her long hair fanned out on the pillow and Ross poised above her, swallowed a gasp as he dropped his head and gave her chest some attention—very special attention—as his mouth first sought and then nibbled on the pebbled tips of her full breasts.

"I figured these were there all the time under the loose clothing you favor," he offered in a rough murmur, "but it's damn nice to have my suspicions confirmed."

Her hands moved with a will of their own to cup the back of his head and hold him to her. Before long her hips were also moving of their own accord in an intimate invitation for more. She knew it wasn't because she had been without a man in her life for some time before her marriage, but rather that she couldn't deny her body's growing need to join with *this* man.

She, the same person who'd once been a wide-eyed girl watching a boy several years her senior cut a dashing path through his teenage years, now found herself on the brink of something she couldn't even have imagined back then.

Jenna Lorenzo and Ross Hayward were about to make love.

All at once he raised himself up enough to look down at her, his eyes boring into hers. "Do I need to wear protection?" he asked. "I bought some this morning when we stopped at the drugstore."

She knew what he was really asking. Was she ready to risk having another member added to their family?

For all her earlier hesitation about coming this far, she discovered that there was little need to think twice about her answer. "No protection. Whether it happens soon or sometime later, I want your child."

That's all it took to have him positioning himself and surging inside. The feel of him captured her breath and soon robbed her of her ability to string two thoughts together as he established a steady rhythm. Oh, but it did feel good...

Inches above her, Ross braced his upper body on his forearms and watched as Jenna's eyes drifted closed. The knowledge that she saw no need to wait to have a child—his child—had threatened to break the already shaky grip he had on his control. He'd won that contest. Barely. But he wouldn't hold out for the long haul, he knew.

Luckily, she was matching him thrust for thrust, and unless he was badly mistaken, they were both on their way to finding satisfaction. *Just don't find it before she does, Hayward.*

Yes, he had to remember that.

He heightened the rhythm and tried to think about something—anything—else. And came up empty.

Again and again, his thoughts seemed determined to center themselves on images of the woman under him. Her face, first wary while she'd heard him out, had become surprisingly calm when she'd agreed to make their marriage as real as it gets. Her body, well-curved and smooth as cream, when he'd removed the last scrap of clothing that hid her from his sight. Her voice, soft yet sure, when she'd told him no protection was necessary.

And her warmth that had seemed to rise up and surround him when he'd joined his body with hers.

Yes, he'd been right about that. Jenna Lorenzo Hayward was a warm woman.

Now he had to make sure she was a satisfied one.

"Ready for more?" he asked, lowering his head to whisper near her ear.

"Hmm."

So he gave her more, then more still, pushing them both to an invisible edge as tension wound tight, then tighter still. But he couldn't go over. Couldn't give in. Not yet, he told himself.

And then she came apart with a soft cry, shuddering in his arms, and he knew that his wait had been worth it. Satisfaction of another sort filled him even as he continued to move with rapid strokes. What happened in the next few seconds might give him another child—maybe even a son—but that wasn't what drove him now. Now, he simply needed release, one he hadn't felt in what seemed like far too long. When it hit, he had to drop his head and bury his mouth against a plump pillow laced with his wife's silky hair to smother a shout.

Finally, he'd gotten what had been denied him on his wedding night, he thought as he drifted toward oblivion

JENNA SLOWLY OPENED her eyes and found a long length of solid male stretched out over her. It felt wonderful, was her first thought. *He* felt wonderful. She allowed herself a moment to just relish the sensation, then blinked her way back to full reality and regained a sense of her surroundings.

The short brass lamp set on a sturdy mahogany nightstand beside the bed was still on, she noted. Its soft glow provided the only break in the darkness blanketing the room, with no hint of backlight showing through the closed drapes to indicate that dawn had arrived. Obviously she'd woken up somewhere in the middle of the night.

A night she knew she would never forget.

The lengthy sigh she couldn't hold back brought a muttered response from the man whose head rested next to hers. "Is it morning yet?" he asked, his lips a breath away from her temple.

"No."

"Good."

Ross raised his head and rolled slightly to one side. Even though it allowed her to breathe more freely, she missed the full weight of him flattened against her as soon as it was gone. Still, their legs remained tangled together, his hair-roughened skin so different from hers.

"I think we may have slept a couple of hours," she said, her voice quiet in the silence all around them.

His eyes remained steady on hers as he nodded. "I could use some more. I didn't sleep a wink last night."

That news came as no surprise, not after the "talk" they'd had earlier. "I never heard you come to bed," she said.

His lips quirked up at the tips. "I came, all right. And wound up stretched out and staring at the ceiling, half afraid that if I did manage to drift off, I just might jump my wife before I was fully awake again."

He had wanted her that much. It was all Jenna could think about…and wonder at.

Then again, according to everything she had heard since her return to Harmony, he hadn't been involved in a physical relationship for some time. As a healthy male in his prime, he had needs. Needs that she had just been able to ease. She hadn't been the only one to find pleasure in their earlier lovemaking. She was certain of that.

Yes, but did he once find far more pleasure with the

woman he married first? Even as the question formed, Jenna made a determined effort to oust it from her mind. She couldn't—and wouldn't, she vowed—start comparing herself with anyone else, not on this very private and personal level. She was who she was, and right now she was the one who had Ross Hayward, in all of his bare and breathtaking glory, lying half over her.

It would be beyond foolish, she thought, not to enjoy it to the fullest.

As though enjoyment was a concept he could well agree with, the faint curve of Ross's mouth widened when he pulled his gaze away from hers and let it drift down over her. Jenna felt the impact of his eyes' lingering journey and resisted a sudden urge to give her bottom lip a quick, and undeniably edgy, nibble in response.

Once, as a very young woman, she'd had few reservations about wearing clothes that showed her figure to advantage. It was only later that her wardrobe had taken a much more conservative turn. She knew that change, both an inward and outward one, was a good part of why she was far less than comfortable at the moment with her husband's avid study.

But, despite that, she wasn't going to blush, she told herself.

"You don't look all that sleepy anymore," she said in the most casual tone she could muster.

He brushed a large palm over her breasts, his touch gentle yet thorough. "I'm waking up in a hurry."

She felt the clear evidence of the truth of that growing against her thigh. "Well, certain parts of you are, in any event," she murmured under her breath.

Still stroking a slow path over her flesh, he inched his gaze up to meet hers. "How tired are you?"

I'm wide awake and starting to hum all over. "Not very," she told him with hard-won calm.

He lowered his head and dropped a brief kiss on her lips. "Could be we need some more exercise."

She knew he wasn't talking about giving the house another cleaning. "Could be."

"Want to give it a try?"

She reached up and wrapped her arms around his neck. "Why not?"

He kissed her again. This time, it was long and deep and had them both struggling to take in air when it ended. For several seconds only the sound of their mingled breathing filled the room. Then bedsprings squeaked a protest as he settled himself above her for a second time.

"I didn't hear any springs squeak before," Jenna managed to get out while still trying to catch her breath.

"Neither did I," Ross admitted, his vocal chords roughening with his renewed interest in more…exercise. "If they did," he added, "I was probably too occupied to notice."

"They would have squeaked." Jenna had little doubt about that. The bed had rocked at one point with the force of their first effort. She remembered that much. Vaguely, in any event.

"I'd say you're right." He rubbed his body against hers from shoulder to knee. "I vote that we get too occupied to notice this time, too."

"Okay," she said, wasting scant time in agreeing.

And so they did.

ROSS WOKE UP with a smile on his face the following morning. Even the fact that he found himself alone in bed when he stretched his long arms out and slanted his eyes open didn't wipe it off. No matter how many problems had to be tackled, and soon, in an effort to get his family's life back in order after everything they'd lost, right this minute he felt good.

"Damn good," he muttered, tossing back the top sheet. Bedsprings squealed softly as he slid to the edge of the mattress and sat up. The sound only had his smile widening. After last night, it was music to his ears.

Nevertheless, he supposed he would have to do something about the noise. What, exactly, he wasn't sure. He'd never had to deal with squeaky springs or anything else that came with living in a house filled with furnishings from an earlier era. But if he could run a successful business, he imagined he could learn quick enough.

He stood and looked around for the clothes he'd worn the day before—the first of his clothing, as far as he could recall, that had ever spent a night on the floor—but they had disappeared someplace. He knew where his new pajamas were, though. They were still in the bottom drawer of the old mahogany dresser he and Jenna now shared. He'd never given a thought to putting them on. There'd been no need to, not last night.

And if he had his way, he vowed, there'd never be a need.

Wearing nothing but skin and glad of it, Ross headed to the adjoining bathroom. He showered and shaved in short order, then dressed in another of the sweaters and casual pants he'd picked up during yesterday's hasty shopping trip. By the time he got downstairs and made his way to the kitchen, his stomach was urging him to put something in it.

Which looked promising, he told himself as he found his daughters seated at an old oak table placed under a tall window. Several steps away stood a stove that had

probably once been top of the line but was now a far
cry from the modern version he was used to using—
when he used one at all, he had to admit. In a pinch, he
could scramble eggs or make a grilled-cheese sandwich.
None of his efforts, though, had ever smelled near as
good as whatever his wife currently had sizzling in a
heavy iron skillet.

"What's for breakfast?" he asked, leaning in the
doorway.

Jenna aimed a look at him over her shoulder. Their
eyes met and held, and even as he watched hers dark-
ened to a deeper brown with what he had to hope were
fond memories of the prior night. He had more than a
few memories of his own—and he was fond of every
one of them.

"Denver omelets," she said at last. "I bought some
onions, peppers and sliced ham at the grocery yesterday,
along with eggs." She pushed up a sleeve of her terry-
cloth robe. "Since we all slept later than usual, I think
this almost qualifies as brunch."

Ross nodded and finally broke eye contact. His fingers
itched to run themselves through the long hair Jenna had
secured with a shiny gold clip at the nape of her neck.
His lips wouldn't have objected to another taste of hers,
either, and not a brief good-morning peck. Not hardly.
Instead, mindful that he'd have an audience for whatever
he did, he crossed the room, pulled out a ladder-back
chair and took a seat beside Caroline at the table. She
was wearing a light blue nightgown trimmed in white
lace, a near duplicate of a favorite she'd lost in the fire.

A sidelong glance revealed the fact that his eldest
child looked, if not exactly happy, then at least well
rested. "How are you doing, princess?"

With typical calm, she folded her small hands on the table. "I'm okay, Dad."

He would have liked more than an "okay," but everything considered, he decided to gladly settle for that at the moment. He turned to Katie. "How about you, sunshine?"

Her round cheeks blooming with a healthy flush nearly as pink as her new pajamas, Katie said, "I slept real good until Frisky licked my face and woke me up."

"Ugh," Caroline said with a small grimace.

Katie ignored her sister's comment and dropped a look down at the dog stretched out beside her chair. At the mention of his name, his tail had started to wag in a steady thump against the braid rug covering a large circle of wood floor under the round table. Katie smiled. "I got up and let Frisky out so he could do his business in the backyard," she said with a proud lift of her little chin. "Then I fed him some of his dog food and gave him fresh water."

Ross couldn't help but be proud of her, too. His youngest daughter was quickly learning to be a responsible pet owner. He studied the coal-black dog now panting up a storm, red tongue lolling out of a mouth that never seemed to turn down the chance to eat something. Anything. Even Monopoly pieces.

Surely, Ross thought, the day was bound to come when canine-produced disasters were no longer a regular possibility. Puppies, even large ones with a knack for getting into trouble, grew up and mended their ways... didn't they?

A keen glint in the dark eyes staring straight back at him seemed to silently reply, *Not anytime soon, pal.*

"Terrific," Ross muttered under his breath.

Jenna set a brown stoneware mug filled with freshly

brewed coffee in front of him. He thanked her and took a long sip while the old-fashioned toaster on the wide counter next to the stove popped up a helping of toast. It wasn't long before their meal was in full swing.

"Do we have to go to school tomorrow, Daddy?" Katie asked.

"Yes," he said without hesitation, certain that it would be better for things to get back to normal—or as normal possible.

Caroline looked at him with a worried frown. "But you have to explain why we don't have our homework."

He doubted any explanation would be necessary. By now, most everyone in town probably knew that the Haywards had lost their home and nearly everything in it. More than a few would no doubt also have heard that the family was staying at his grandparents' place. In fact, if he'd taken the time to restore telephone service as well as electricity the day before, the phone might well be ringing off the hook this Sunday morning.

But none of that stopped him from reassuring his conscientious daughter that showing up without her homework this particular time wouldn't be held against her. "I'll take you to school and make sure your teacher understands. We'll get you some new schoolbooks, too, to replace any you brought home."

Her frown faded. "All right."

"Are you going back to work tomorrow?" Jenna asked him after a moment.

Ross considered what would have to be accomplished in the days ahead. Insurance matters. Address changes. More new clothes and other personal items for everyone, including a new cell phone, a briefcase and a few business suits for himself. "I probably should take some time off," he told her, knowing it could be done with little problem. He had a competent staff to fill in for him. "There's a lot to do, including lining up someone to make all the repairs needed around here."

Plus there was the fact that private parts of him only encouraged by recent activity were urging him to take every opportunity in the next couple of days to make love to his wife. Fast and furiously. Slowly and thoroughly. Yes, indeed.

Jenna forked up a helping of her omelet. "I've been thinking about that."

A startled second passed before he realized she must be referring to the repairs on the house, not to the intimate images that had formed in his mind and had his blood stirring in his veins. Ordering himself to get back to the matter at hand, he cleared his throat and reached for his coffee mug. "It probably won't be too hard to find someone."

She met his gaze. "I've been mulling over the idea that we could do most of the work ourselves."

His felt his brows take a quick climb. His hand stilled with the mug poised halfway to his lips. "You and I?"

"Uh-huh."

"Have you had any experience along the lines of home improvement?"

Her gaze didn't waver. "Not really."

"Neither have I," he didn't hesitate to inform her. He might be able to handle squeaky bedsprings, but... "Why in the world would you want to tackle putting this place back into shape when we can hire a professional?"

Her lips curved up at the tips. "I think it could be fun."

Fun? He set the mug down with a soft thud. "Are you serious?"

"Yes." She rested her fork on her plate and propped her chin on an upraised palm. "I'm not talking about the back porch. Obviously a person would have to have some real expertise to deal with a sagging floor. But most of the rest of it we could probably learn to do with little trouble." She lifted one shoulder in a slight shrug. "After all, how hard can it be?"

Ross recognized that question as the same one he'd asked when they'd discussed the difficulties involved in training Katie's new pet. He had no problem recalling how that project had turned out.

Something told him that a stab at home improvement wasn't going to be a piece of cake, either.

"I don't think tackling it ourselves is the best answer," he said, his frank tone making no bones about how he felt. "And it won't be easy to change my mind."

Jenna studied him for a long moment. "Okay," she said at last. "I'll see what I can do about that."

Chapter Nine

She talked him into it. As he'd predicted, it hadn't been easy, but she'd done it. She'd convinced a stubborn male to try something they'd both never done before. And now, with that goal achieved, she found herself enjoying every minute of their joint project to get the old Victorian in better shape.

Or almost every minute.

Watching her husband's deep frown as he stared down at a narrow strip of new wallpaper wasn't the most uplifting of sights. Then again, it also gave her the chance to get another approving look at him wearing the Levi's and denim shirt he'd bought to work around the house. The blue, snug-fitting fabric flattered not only his navy eyes but the whole long length of him. Yes, even watching him view the rose-dotted paper—a close match for what they'd stripped off—as though it were an enemy had its compensations, she decided.

"I'm sure we can do this with little trouble," she said, her tone ringing with a bit more confidence than she felt. Not that she planned on admitting to any shred of doubt. So what if stripping off the old paper in the upstairs hallway hadn't been a walk in the park? The worst might well be behind them.

"That's it," he told her dryly. "Keep a good thought."

"I will." Jenna took one end of the long strip and followed as he led the way to a tall ladder. "At least we were able to get prepasted paper. No muss or fuss. That's what the man at the store said."

"Uh-huh." Ross climbed the ladder and lined up the top of the strip at the ceiling. "Why didn't I believe him?"

"Grumble, grumble," she muttered.

He used the plastic tool the storeowner had also sold them to smooth out the paper. "Did you say something?"

"Nothing much," she said lightly, paying as much attention to the roll of his strong shoulders as to what he was accomplishing. During the past few nights she'd clutched those same shoulders as they'd made love. Fast and furiously at times. Slowly and thoroughly at others.

The intimacy they'd shared had threatened more than once to have her heart yearning for a deeper connection beyond the physical. So far, however, she'd kept those feelings in check, telling herself that while Ross wanted her, something he'd shown no reluctance to demonstrate, wanting didn't always translate into caring. Once, as a starry-eyed girl, she might have believed otherwise. Now she knew it wasn't necessarily so.

She'd agreed to their marriage with the hope that they could have a mutually caring relationship someday. And she was still hoping. More so than ever, in fact. Yet, in spite of that, at the moment she remained far from sure how soon, or how much, Ross Hayward would be able to truly care for a woman again after losing the one who'd been his first choice for wife. It wouldn't do, she knew, to let her growing hopes blind her to the reality of the situation.

No, it wouldn't do at all.

"See, that was easy enough," she told him, summoning a smile as she took the tool from him to smooth it down the bottom of the paper. "No muss or fuss."

His lips quirked up at the tips. "It's only the first strip. We've got a long way to go."

She brushed her palms on the jeans she'd bought at the same time he'd purchased his. Rather than a denim shirt, however, she'd opted for a blue-and-white-striped cotton blouse that fitted loosely enough over her breasts to be comfortable. "If we can do one with no problem, we'll probably just get better at it as time goes on," she said.

Fortunately, that prediction proved to be true as they papered one full side of the narrow hall. It was only as they started on the opposite side that the wallpaper slipped from Ross's grip as he lined it up with the ceiling.

"Watch out!" he called down in warning.

But it was too late. Jenna, who'd been bent over and concentrating on the bottom half of the paper, never saw the upper portion drop. Before she knew it, the top half, sticky side down, was plastered to the back of her blouse.

"Yuck!" She tried to reach around and only succeeded in getting tangled in the lower half of the paper, as well.

"Let me do it," Ross said. He climbed down, twisted her around so that her back faced him and began to peel the runaway strip of wallpaper off her blouse. It made a sucking sound that soon mingled with a wry chuckle.

"For once, I'm grateful that you're wearing your hair up. This is a mess."

She could feel just how much of a mess it was. A gooey, sticky, yucky mess. But none of that foiled the laugh that suddenly broke from her throat as she aimed a look over her shoulder and saw that her companion hadn't come through unscathed. An edge of the paper must have caught him on its way down, leaving a wet slash of pasty glue across the front of his shirt.

For some reason, she found that hilarious enough to have yet another laugh sputtering out, then another.

He turned her to face him, tangling the paper even tighter around her legs so that she had to lean on him for support. "Are you by any chance laughing at me?" he asked with a mock scowl.

That only made her laugh harder. "Yes," she managed to get out between whoops. "I'm laughing…at the…both of us."

For a moment he simply studied her. Then a faint smile appeared, one that soon transformed into an out-and-out grin, and in the next breath he threw back his head and joined her.

Before long they were holding each other up, crushing the jumbled piece of wallpaper between them. Their laughter rang out in the quiet house, with no one to hear it but them. Caroline and Katie were in school and the dog had been banished to the backyard before they started on their project.

"Even Frisky would have had a hard time making this much of a mess," Jenna said, finally gaining control of herself.

Ross issued one last chuckle as he loosened the steadying arm he'd had around her. "I think the only way we're going to get a handle on this is to rip up the wallpaper and take it off in pieces. Then we take off our clothes next and head for the shower.''

Jenna had to blink at that suggestion. ''Together?'' she asked after a beat. For all their recent intimacy, they hadn't shared a shower. Not yet.

''You bet,'' he told her with a distinct gleam in his eye. ''I propose that we start for the bathroom right now and deal with things there.''

''That's going to be tricky,'' she said. ''I don't think I can walk with this paper wrapped around me.''

''No problem,'' he replied. And with that, he picked her up in one fast and fluid movement and carried her down the hall.

IT COULD STILL MAKE HIM chuckle the next day. Maybe the thought of wallpapering anything always would, Ross reflected to himself. He shouldered open the glass-paned door to the back porch, two cans of cold cola in hand, and found Leon Wiggs still conducting an inspection of a weathered oak floor.

''Any verdict yet, Leon?'' he asked, offering one of the soda cans to the handyman, animal-shelter volunteer and first person who'd come to mind as someone knowledgeable enough to handle the porch repairs.

The midday sun slanting through the screened-in windows bounced off Leon's bald-as-an-egg head as he offered a brisk nod. ''Yep. I'm thinking that it won't be too hard to shore it up where it needs it.''

''Good.'' Ross shoved one hand into a front pocket of his Levi's. The denim fabric was softer now after another washing, although still far from as faded as the old overalls his companion wore with a long-sleeved work shirt. ''When can you get started?''

''Day after tomorrow should work out for me.'' Leon

took a lengthy swallow of cola. "That way it'll be done before colder weather settles in."

Which wouldn't be long, Ross knew. Some of the trees in town were already well on their way to turning rich shades of gold and orange. While Harmony didn't have an extended winter, nighttime lows often dipped below freezing during the few months that made up the coldest time of the year. With the end of October fast approaching, it could only be wise to put the large porch where his grandparents had entertained small groups of friends in better shape to withstand any more damage.

"Once I get this done, do you think you'll need any help with the rest of the house?" Leon asked.

Ross had to grin. "Not if my wife has anything to say about it. We've already had a crash course in home improvement, and while things didn't always go smoothly, it doesn't seem to have dampened her enthusiasm one bit. Tackling something neither of us had a scrap of prior experience in accomplishing apparently agrees with her."

Leon studied him for a moment. "Have to say it looks as if it agrees with you, too."

That comment caught Ross off guard. Did it agree with him? he wondered. Although he'd sometimes grumbled at the idea of doing what he could afford to pay someone with a lot more expertise to do, he had to concede the past several days hadn't been all that much of an ordeal. Hell, he might have to go so far as to admit to enjoying what he'd managed to accomplish some of the time—maybe most of the time.

"I guess it does agree with me," he said.

Leon dipped his broad chin in another nod. "As long as he had the time to do it, I wouldn't have expected a

Hayward man to shy away from what I know can be danged hard work.''

Not at all surprised by that statement, Ross raised his soda can and quenched his thirst. Harmony's well-documented history showed that hard work was no stranger to the men on his family tree, going all the way back to when the first settlers had erected cabins from the pines around them. Only one of a long line of Hayward males had ever failed to be a man who met his obligations no matter what, both family-wise and in every other way that counted.

But there was no point in thinking about his father, Ross told himself with a fleeting frown. As far as he was concerned, that subject was closed.

"How are your animals doing?" he asked, referring to the large, and varied, group of pets he recalled Leon mentioning at the shelter.

"Fine and dandy," the handyman replied with an easy smile. "What family I have around here has been telling me for thirty years that I should find a good woman and get hitched, but I don't know where I'd put a wife, and that's the God's truth. The place is already crowded."

"Humph." Ross blew out a breath. "Even one pet can be a handful, I've found."

As though he sensed a wealth of meaning behind that remark, Leon's smile took a wry slant. "Where is the little fella?"

"Probably doing his damnedest to get into some kind of trouble or other inside the house," Ross acknowledged. "And, as you'll no doubt remember, there's nothing little about him."

"I've had a dog or two that could get up to more than a bit of mischief on occasion," Leon told him with an amused twinkle in his eye.

But I bet none of them ever burned down a house,
Ross thought but didn't say. He polished off his drink,
then set the can on a natural wicker end table that
matched a small sofa and several high-backed chairs
grouped around the porch.

"How do you intend to shore up the floor?" he asked,
and listened while Leon offered a detailed explanation.
He supposed that Jenna, with skilled carpenters on her
own family tree, might understand it better than he did,
but the logic behind Leon's methods sounded reasonable
enough.

He said as much, and then it was Leon's turn to ask
a question. "What do you folks plan on doing next
around here?"

"Paint the outside trim on the house."

"Hmm." Another twinkle sparked to life in the
handyman's gaze. "Ever done any painting?"

"No." But the potential for producing a mess had to
be less than wallpapering, Ross reflected. And if that
turned out to be wrong? Well, who knew? He just might
enjoy it, anyway.

Strange what he was discovering about himself.

THE PAINTING PROJECT, while not without its problems,
managed to go fairly smoothly. The good weather held,
which proved to be the most important factor in getting
it accomplished quickly, and no one wound up with
more paint on themselves than where it was intended to
go once the first tentative attempts to wield a brush with
confidence were behind them.

All things considered, Jenna thought, casting a critical
eye over the house from the front yard early on a cloudy
morning, she and Ross had done what could well be
considered a more than respectable job of sprucing the

outside of the place up. Certainly it no longer looked as though it hadn't been occupied for some time.

Now, if no rain followed the clouds today, she would make some strides on getting the garden in better shape. The grass around the home had been cut regularly, but the plants bordering the backyard on three sides had been allowed to run wild. Not that she intended to tame them too much. The way a riot of roses clung to the slatted-wood fence held definite appeal. At least, it did to her.

"Do whatever suits you," Ross had told her when she'd mentioned her plans before he'd headed off to the office. "Just remember to wear those gardening gloves you bought," he'd added as she'd walked with him to the old garage at one side of the house.

Then he'd kissed her soundly, got in his car and driven off with a wave for his first day back at Hayward Investments. As always, he'd looked all too attractive dressed in a well-tailored suit, one of several new ones he'd recently ordered to add to his wardrobe. Still, she missed seeing him in his casual work clothes.

In fact, she just missed him. Period.

"Get over it," she huffed under her breath. And with that firm command, she crossed her arms over the front of the long red sweater she'd thrown on over her own work clothes and strode back up the flagstone walkway. "You can't spend all day every day with him."

He had a company to run—one he liked running. And she had, indeed, plenty to do herself, she acknowledged as she climbed the newly painted porch stairs. A fat orange pumpkin in the form of a bright plastic bag filled with crumpled-up newspaper stood to one side of the front door. The tall black outline of a cardboard witch complete with broomstick stood at the other.

Today, Jenna reminded herself, was Halloween. And with that reminder came a smile. As a child, it had run a close second to Christmas as her favorite holiday. The thought of hearing a string of eager young trick-or-treaters ring the antique brass doorbell that evening put a spring in her step as she opened the door and entered the house.

She wasn't surprised when nothing but quiet greeted her. With breakfast finished, Caroline and Katie would be upstairs getting ready for school.

Jenna decided to toss a handful of the candy she'd bought to give out tonight in their lunch packs as a special treat. Although Caroline hid it better than Katie, she knew both were excited about getting into their costumes later, first to attend a children's Halloween party that the town hosted every year at the Community Center downtown, and then to go trick-or-treating around the neighborhood with their father. Neither girl had voiced any disappointment over the fact that Jenna wouldn't be going with them, though Katie had issued an eager promise to tell her stepmother all about her adventures when she returned.

Little by little, she was building a closer relationship with Ross's youngest daughter. Unfortunately she couldn't say the same thing about his eldest child, who continued to keep a steadfast, if always polite, distance.

Jenna sighed softly into the silence all around her. Then the sound of her quick footsteps broke the quiet as she started down the hall toward the rear of the house. She was halfway to the kitchen when something dawned on her and had her stopping in her tracks.

"Shoes," she murmured, dropping a swift glance at her leather-shod feet.

She'd been able to hear her footsteps because she

wore shoes. Shoes inside the house. And she wasn't the only one who'd taken to doing that, she realized on further consideration. None of the Haywards seemed to feel any need to walk around in stockings or slippers since they'd found themselves living in the house Ross's grandfather had passed down to him.

At first, the floor and rugs had simply been too much in need of a good cleaning to offer an alternative. But even with the rugs scattered throughout the house now once again displaying the full range of their vivid colors and the hardwood floor holding a polished sheen, shoes were no longer removed at the door.

No one had to worry about leaving footprints on a pristine-white carpet. Nothing, in fact, was pristine enough to give anyone second thoughts about putting comfort before a spotless image, because the old Victorian wasn't a showplace…it was a home. Their home.

"And you love every old and far-from-elegant inch of it," Jenna told herself with sudden insight as she aimed a long look around her.

It was true. She wouldn't have traded living here for the chance to occupy the biggest and newest house in Harmony. Here, in a place that might well be considered a town landmark yet would never win any glossy magazine spreads, she could relax at the end of a busy day and take pleasure in her surroundings.

Here, she could be happy.

With that last thought, the beginnings of a wide smile curved Jenna's mouth. And that was the very moment when a piercing scream of what seemed to be pure anguish reached her, coming from the second floor.

The children!

Jenna rushed to the stairs and took them two at a time. She hit the landing and raced into Katie's room, only to find it empty. Without so much as a break in motion, she whirled around and checked Caroline's room next, then the hall bathroom, but there was no sign of the girls.

Don't panic. Those words repeated in her mind even as her heart began to pound. She was barely out of the bathroom when a low bark called her to the upstairs sitting room. There she found a scene that, while far from cheerful, immediately had her breathing easier.

The good news was that the girls were perfectly safe. The bad news was that the rented Halloween costumes she'd carefully draped over the chaise longue to keep from wrinkling now lay strewn over the floor—and wrinkles were a minor concern compared to the damage both had suffered.

"What happened?" she asked, shifting her gaze to a clearly stricken Caroline. After a swift study of a pale face drained of most of its color, she had little doubt that the elder girl was the one who had issued that anguished cry.

"The dog ruined everything," Caroline told her, her voice scarcely more than a whisper now as she continued to stare down at the costumes.

"He didn't mean to do it," Katie added with a tremble in her own voice, dragging Jenna's gaze to both her and the dog who stood behind the little girl, peeking his furry black head out and cocking it at a puzzled angle, as though he knew he was in trouble but wasn't sure why.

Katie looked at Jenna. "You know how we sometimes play tug-of-war with one of the old kitchen towels you said we could use?"

Jenna nodded, recalling what had turned out to be a frequent game, one every puppy she'd known had relished. She'd never considered that any real harm could come from encouraging a young pet owner to engage in an activity that usually produce girlish giggles on one side and eager yelps on the other.

It seemed, however, that she'd been wrong—an assumption soon confirmed as Katie continued her story. "I was all ready for school, but Caroline wasn't yet, so I came in here to..."

"To get another peek at your costume?" Jenna prompted gently at the hesitation. To her, it seemed only natural that Katie might want a last look at the merry clown costume she'd chosen before heading out for the day.

"Uh-huh. A peek." Katie clasped her hands behind her back. "Except I didn't only peek," she confessed. "I picked it up and waved it around, 'cause the colors looked so pretty in the sun shining through the window." Again she hesitated before continuing. "And then Frisky ran in and thought I was waving it at him like I wanted to play, and he grabbed it and it tore." She gave her head a mournful shake. "I pulled it away and tried to put it back next to Caroline's Cinderella dress, but he kept on grabbing for it until Caroline's dress fell on the floor. Then he thought that was part of the game and..."

"And then he tore my costume, too," Caroline finished in a hollow tone when her sister came to a halting stop. "I came out of my bedroom and heard Katie telling the dog to let go, but he didn't until I got here, and everything was already ruined."

"Oh, dear." Jenna could well believe that Caroline's scream had put a swift halt to the destruction.

"He didn't mean to do it," Katie said for a second time with a forlorn look.

Jenna dropped another brief glance at the still half-hidden dog. "Well, it's at least pretty clear that he now knows he's upset both of you girls."

"But that doesn't make it right." That was Caroline's soft yet staunch contention as her gaze remained on the torn costumes.

"No, it doesn't," Jenna allowed, thinking that Caroline's opinion of the canine population was probably dropping rapidly.

At last the ten-year-old looked up and met her stepmother's gaze. "I won't be able to go to the Halloween party or trick-or-treating tonight—not as Cinderella."

And she always went as Cinderella at the ball. While Katie's choices had been more varied, Caroline had opted to portray that fairy-tale character year after year. Jenna had learned as much during their earlier trip to the town's only costume rental store—a store probably in short supply of any costumes at this late date, she reflected to herself. Still, she didn't let that stop her from making a firm—and somewhat rash, the more reasonable parts of her had to admit—promise.

"You'll be going as Cinderella tonight," she told Caroline. "I'll make sure of it."

The confidence ringing in her tone had Caroline blinking. Jenna knew that Ross's eldest daughter was both old enough and intelligent enough to at least have some idea of the difficulties that might very well be involved in making that vow come true.

"How will you do that?" Caroline asked after a moment.

"I don't know exactly how," Jenna conceded, realizing there was no way the costumes with their jagged rips could be returned to their former condition—even by a skilled seamstress, which she wasn't. "But I'll think of something," she added as she switched her gaze to Katie. "Still want to be a clown?"

"Uh-huh," Katie replied without hesitation.

"Then you will be," Jenna said in another promise. "When you girls get back from school, you'll be able to change and start celebrating Halloween. Everything will be ready."

With any luck at all, she thought.

ROSS HEARD ABOUT the latest crisis from his daughters when he picked them up at the largest of Harmony's growing network of elementary schools that afternoon. Normally they took the school bus back and forth, but with his workday cut short so he could take them to the town's annual Ghost Fest where children's costumes would be judged and prizes awarded, it had seemed just as convenient to make a brief detour to drive his girls home.

He had to hope they'd have costumes to put on once they got there.

Jenna met them at the door. He took her welcoming smile as a good sign, although he didn't miss the fact that she looked as though she'd already put in a memorable—maybe even frantic—day. Even when they'd been knee-deep in household repairs, she'd never seemed as frazzled around the edges as she did now.

There was no denying that he'd had an eventful day himself. Eventful enough, at any rate, to give him something important to talk over with his wife. Still, it wasn't an emergency. It could wait until they were alone tonight.

"Your costumes are ready," Jenna told the girls, brushing back stray strands of hair that had escaped the usual neat coil.

"Am I going to be Cinderella?" Carolina asked hesitantly, as though half afraid to hear the answer.

Jenna's smile widened. "Yes, and Katie's still going to be a clown. Let's head upstairs and see what I came up with."

"Okay!" Katie said in eager anticipation.

The girls climbed the stairs with Jenna following a step behind and Ross bringing up the rear. "Were you able to rent replacements?" he asked her.

She aimed a glance over her shoulder. "No. The first thing I did was phone not only the local costume shop, but every one in reasonable driving distance. No one had anything left that was suitable, so I had to, uh, improvise."

Improvise. He was still debating what that could mean when Jenna directed the group toward the upstairs sitting room.

Caroline frowned. "The dog's not there, is he?"

Jenna shook her head. "He's in the backyard. I think what happened this morning made an impression on him. He's been as good as gold all day."

"I bet Frisky's really sorry," Katie said.

Caroline seemed by no means convinced of that but kept her thoughts to herself until they entered the sitting room and she saw the two costumes draped over the chaise longue. Even several steps behind her, Ross heard her gasp.

"It's...beautiful," Caroline said with clear wonder as she stared at a floor-length child's dress made of several layers of creamy chiffon edged with gold ribbon around the ruffled neck and puffed sleeves. Although obviously far from new, it was also far more elaborate than the simple white satin dress with pale blue trim the rental store had provided.

Ross turned to Jenna. "Where in the world did you find it?"

"In the attic. Between you and me," she added, dropping her voice to a confidential level, "I was a long way from sure I could pull this off. In fact, I was at my wit's end until I remembered that we hadn't opened any of the old trunks we discovered there when we went up to wash the windows."

They'd also discovered some spiders in residence, Ross recalled, and he couldn't deny that he—and his male ego in particular—had gotten a kick out of playing hero and evicting what his wife had clearly considered to be less-than-desirable tenants.

He raised a wry brow. "Find any more spiders?"

She shivered. "Thankfully, no."

Caroline brushed a light hand over the dress. "Will it fit me?" she asked with a look back at Jenna.

"It should. I measured one of your dresses and managed to get the old sewing machine working so I could make a few adjustments. Why don't you take it to your room and try it on?"

Ross aimed a proud grin at his eldest daughter as she picked up her costume and carefully held it off the floor. He had no doubt that once she put on that dress and the clear plastic high heels that had come with her rented outfit, his little girl who was no longer so little anymore would be a knockout.

"You're going to be the best-looking Cinderella ever, princess," he told her.

As though she was coming to believe that, too, Caroline flashed him a brief grin in return before switching her gaze to Jenna. "Thank you," she said. Her voice had resumed its usual calm politeness, but her expression was suddenly serious enough to leave no question about the fact that she meant it.

"You're welcome," Jenna replied, her expression sobering, as well. "If you want to, it wouldn't hurt to also offer up some thanks to the long-ago Hayward girl who once wore that dress. I wouldn't have been able to do it without her."

Caroline nodded her agreement and headed off to her room. As she left, Ross settled his gaze on his other child, who was studying the same clown suit they'd rented the week before. Now, however, it displayed some obvious additions in the form of a haphazard mix of multicolored patches.

Jenna brushed her hands on her jeans. "I didn't find any clown suits in the attic," she told Katie, "but I did come across some pieces of old fabric that looked as shiny-bright as new. It had me thinking that there might be something even better than being just a plain clown."

Katie's brow knit in puzzlement as she looked at Jenna. "What's that?"

"A hobo clown."

"A...hobo?" Katie tried out the unfamiliar word.

Ross explained. "Hobos are people who travel from place to place and sometimes wear clothes with patches on them." Bums, some would call them, including his late mother for whom cleanliness had been next to godliness. "They don't seem to take a lot of baths," he allowed, and left at it that.

"But, for one night, that can be the best part about being a hobo," Jenna said to Katie. "You can get as grubby as you want and it's all right. We can even put some fake dirt on your face to go along with the red clown nose that came with your costume."

Obviously intrigued, Katie cocked her head and considered that plan. Once again she studied the altered clown suit, as though trying to imagine herself as a jolly character in need of a good washing.

"How did your first day back at the office go?" Jenna asked Ross while they awaited Katie's verdict.

He crossed his arms over the front of his suit jacket. "Fine," he replied. Which was true enough. He could have added that he'd received a phone call after lunch that had provided quite a surprise. Instead, he said nothing, reminding himself that he'd already decided to keep that news for later.

Still, something in his deliberately casual pose must have alerted Jenna. Her gaze rapidly turned as intent and thoughtful as Katie's. But Jenna's brown eyes were firmly fixed on him.

"Why am I thinking that in this particular case, the word 'fine' holds a wealth of meaning?" she asked.

He could say she was mistaken, but he had no intention of lying. "I do have something to discuss with you," he said. "It can wait until tonight, though, when we have more time."

Jenna hesitated, then gave in. "Okay," she said softly.

"Okay!" Katie repeated in a near shout, more to herself than anyone else. Nevertheless, it regained the adults' attention in a hurry. "Maybe I could win a prize if I'm the only hobo clown with a fake dirty face!" She glanced up at Jenna. "How are we gonna make it look dirty without dirt?"

Jenna stepped forward to close the gap between them and crouched beside Katie. "I'll take a piece of cork and put in on the stove to make the tip black. Then I'll dab it here and here and here." With those last words, she raised a hand and brushed a finger over Katie's forehead, cheeks and chin. "You'll be looking positively grimy in no time."

It won her a giggle. "I think I'm gonna like being dirty," Katie said.

Jenna offered a brief chuckle in response. "Somehow I'm getting the feeling you're right." Again she reached up a hand, this time to brush it over a mass of golden curls. "I want you and Caroline to have a wonderful Halloween."

Katie dipped her chin in a confident nod. "I'm gonna. And I think Caroline will, too, Jen— Uh…"

Ross sucked in a quick breath as Katie's voice trailed off. He noted that Jenna had gone as still as a statue. He'd been aware for some time, just as she clearly was, that neither of his daughters felt comfortable calling his wife by her first name, even though they'd both been invited to do so more than once. He had to wonder if that was finally going to change.

One second stretched to five before Katie spoke again. "I know when you and Daddy got married it didn't really make you my mommy," she told Jenna with a young child's simple frankness. "I had a mommy, but I can't remember her much."

"You couldn't be expected to," Jenna said, her tone equally frank yet gentle. "So don't feel bad about it."

Katie shook her head. "I don't feel bad, not about that." She paused. "But most of my friends and Caroline's friends, too, have mommies. And sometimes I feel bad 'cause I don't."

"Oh, honey," Jenna murmured. She lifted her eyes to meet her husband's gaze over the top of Katie's head.

"So," Katie continued in the next breath, "even if you're not my real mommy, would it be okay if I called you…Jenna Mom?"

The request was more than Ross had expected, and Jenna plainly felt the same way. Her eyes widened and a startled silence ruled for a short moment before she managed to speak. "I would never try to take your mother's place," she said, once again looking at Katie. "She's special, and she always will be. But I would be very happy if you called me Jenna Mom. In fact, I can't think of anything I'd like better."

Neither could he, Ross had to admit as he made no effort to hide a satisfied smile.

JENNA MOM. Those words, now hours old, repeated in Jenna's mind as she closed the front door after answering yet another merry ring of the bell and handing out more Halloween treats. Happy didn't begin to describe how she felt. The only thing that could have made her happier at the moment was if Caroline had chosen to join Katie in offering a cheerful farewell to their stepmother when the girls had left the house with Ross, proudly wearing their costumes.

Bye, Jenna Mom.

Maybe—just maybe, she told herself—Caroline would follow her sister's example…someday.

Right now, however, Jenna knew she ought to be grateful down to her toes for the sheer joy Katie had given her. And she was.

"What started out far from promising has turned into a great day," she told the dog who had accompanied her to the front door again and again and been nothing less than a courteous canine host to a stream of young witches, wizards, fairy queens, cowboys and spacemen arriving on the doorstep. He hadn't even tried to lift his leg on the tall, gangly boy dressed as a tree.

"I do believe you're growing up, Frisky," Jenna said

as she resettled herself on the plump cushions of the high-backed parlor sofa. Her companion stretched out on the rug at her feet and issued a wide, doggy yawn. "I'm tired, too," she confessed with feeling, "but it's getting late and I don't think we'll have many more trick-or-treaters."

She was sure that Ross and the girls would be home soon. Tomorrow was a schoolday, so the children couldn't stay up too late. Katie would probably relate a few of her adventures and start to nod off. The full story would be told over breakfast, Jenna was all but certain, and she was content to wait.

What she found it far harder to patiently wait for was the discussion Ross had promised they'd have tonight.

Something had happened. Something important, she more than suspected. But what?

Jenna was still mulling it over when Frisky lifted his head at a sound only he heard. Then the front door opened and Katie ran in, followed at a more sedate pace by her father and sister.

"Everybody liked my hobo clown suit and my dirty face!" she told Jenna. "I won a prize at the party and Caroline did, too!"

Jenna smiled. "That's wonderful."

"It was the best Halloween ever," Katie proclaimed. She gave her pet a hearty pat and placed an old pillowcase filled with goodies on the sturdy mahogany end table standing next to the sofa.

"They made out like bandits," Ross offered with dry humor. He shrugged out of his tan leather jacket and draped it over a wing-backed chair in a rich shade of forest green. "After the party, we hit what seemed like every house in town."

Rolling her eyes, Caroline took off the pale blue cardigan she'd worn over her Cinderella dress. "Not *every* house, Dad. We would have to be out all night to do that."

"I feel as though I've been out all night," Ross said in a mock grumble.

Katie pulled off her red clown nose. "You said the same thing last year, Daddy. I remember."

He crossed his arms over the front of the short-sleeved knit shirt he'd changed into before heading out with the girls. "Do you remember that I got to eat part of the loot you hauled in for my efforts?"

"Uh-huh." Katie sat next to Jenna on the sofa. "You can have some of my candy, too, if you want."

"I just may take you up on that," Jenna told her. "I've been keeping some apple cider warm on the stove." With the chill in the night air, she'd thought a hot drink would be welcome. Not that she'd been worried about Katie getting too cold with the thick sweatshirt worn under her clown suit. "You can have a glass while you tell me about the party."

The group headed off to the kitchen at that point, but, as their stepmother had thought, it wasn't long before both girls began to droop. Neither objected when their father said it was bedtime. After they gave him a goodnight kiss, Jenna went upstairs with the girls and a yawning dog to help Katie get out of her costume and to remove the fake dirt with some cold cream.

"Good night," she told Caroline at the door to the older girl's bedroom. "Sleep well."

"I will," Caroline said, still looking like a lovely child who'd stepped out of a fairy tale despite the slight slump of her narrow shoulders. She hesitated, as though trying to decide whether to say more, then continued. "It was a good Halloween."

Not the *best ever,* as Katie had proclaimed. But then, Caroline had memories of other years when the mother she'd clearly adored and whose framed photograph continued to occupy a prominent place in her room had been around to share the holiday with her.

No, you can't expect *best ever,* Jenna told herself.

"I'm glad you enjoyed it," she said to Caroline. "I'll see you in the morning."

Jenna left with Katie and her pet, and by the time the clown costume was off, the little girl's eyes were at half mast.

"I'm sleepy," Katie mumbled. "Frisky is, too."

"I know, honey. We'll have your face clean in a jiffy."

Once that was accomplished and Katie headed off to bed with her faithful dog trailing after her, Jenna returned downstairs. She found Ross in the parlor, his mug of warm cider replaced with a short crystal glass half filled with ice and an amber-brown liquid.

"I decided I deserved a Scotch," he told her from his seat on the sofa. "Maybe I'm getting old, but I'm worn out."

He didn't look old. Not hardly, Jenna thought. And even as the years passed, she was sure Ross Hayward would remain a dashing sight guaranteed to please a woman's eyes. Hers certainly weren't complaining at the moment.

"I think you'll survive," she assured her dashing husband as she sank into the wing-backed chair across from him. She folded her arms under breasts covered by the long purple top she wore with matching cotton pants. It was the same outfit she'd had on the night of the fire, making it one of the very few of her possessions that had escaped the blaze. Another, thankfully, had been the wedding gown handed down to her, which had gone to the cleaner's in preparation for being stored away.

Jenna wondered whether Caroline or Katie would want to wear it someday—not because she had, but because it had been their great-grandmother's gown originally. She hoped at least one of them would. Jenna sighed, remembering the undeniable sense of pride that had come from walking down the aisle in a Hayward family heirloom. Yes, she had to hope another bride would choose to wear it.

Ross leaned back in his seat and stretched out long legs clad in khaki pants. "I don't doubt that you've had a lot harder day than I did," he said. "Although," he added after a short study, "you seem to have perked up." His eyes took on a wryly amused gleam. "When I got home after picking the girls up at school, you looked like you'd been put through a wringer."

She had to laugh. "I felt as if I had, too. This has been a day to remember."

"In more ways than one," he added.

She knew his comment could hold a double meaning—an acknowledgment of what certainly seemed to be the beginning of a better relationship between his wife and his daughters, and a reference to another matter entirely.

Jenna's curiosity rose to new heights. "You told me earlier that you wanted to discuss something when we had more time. What is it?"

He lifted his drink for a brief swallow and set it down on the end table at his side. "I got a call from our mayor shortly after lunch today."

The mayor? Of all the possibilities she'd mulled over, none had involved the man who'd been Harmony's top official for many years. "What did he have to say?"

"Although he sounded chipper enough, he told me that he'd had a routine physical late last week and his doctor had found some early indications of a potentially serious heart problem down the road—one that could eventually mean major surgery if some lifestyle changes aren't made." Ross met his wife's gaze. "The upshot is that he's decided to take it easier and not run for re-election."

"I see," Jenna said after a moment. And she did. At least she now felt she had a good inkling of what he wanted to discuss.

"Apparently," he told her, "I was among the first people His Honor phoned with the news because he'd heard via the grapevine that I might be interested in succeeding him."

"Which you were at one time, I know," Jenna acknowledged. "I remember your mentioning it a while ago."

On their first date, in fact. Yes, she recalled it quite well. Back then he'd said in reply to her query that his grandfather would have wanted him to run. But that wasn't the question she'd asked him.

Now she had to ask it again, because the answer was important. Too important to just let it go.

"Ross," she said, choosing to be frank over beating around the bush, "do you really and truly want to be mayor?"

Chapter Ten

Did he really want to be mayor?

Ross considered that question one more time the following morning. He had just heard it repeated in his office and now offered the same reply he'd given Jenna the evening before.

"I think I'd make a good candidate," he told his shrewd and sharp-eyed assistant, "and public service is something my family has seldom shied away from."

Thelma Carter lounged back in a tweed visitor's chair and studied him across the width of his desk. "I suppose that's your story and you're sticking to it," she said in her typically blunt fashion, as though she knew he was skirting the issue—just as Jenna had.

Last night, after going 'round and 'round on the subject without tackling it head-on, he'd put an end to their discussion by reaching out to pull his wife off her chair and into his lap, after which he'd proceeded to make love to her, right on the parlor sofa. They'd finally headed up to bed more asleep than awake, and by this morning she'd seemed resigned to the fact that he had no intention of rehashing the matter.

As to why he was skirting the issue, well, maybe he wasn't all that eager to analyze it, he admitted to himself.

But then, he didn't have to. The bottom line was that only several weeks ago he'd been set on throwing his hat into the ring if he got the chance, and he saw no reason to have second thoughts now.

"What I'm sticking to," he told Thelma, "is the feeling that I can be an asset to this town if I wind up in the mayor's seat—and I don't think I'm alone in that regard."

"Not hardly," she agreed. "Plenty of Harmony's voters would feel the same way, I'm sure."

"Do you?"

Thelma dipped her graying head in a brisk and business-like nod. Nothing about Thelma, including her short, no-nonsense hairstyle and the simply tailored suits she favored, would ever be described as frivolous. "If it's something you're truly interested in doing, I think you'd make a top-notch mayor."

He flashed her a grin. "Then how about being my campaign manager?"

She stared at him for several seconds, plainly surprised. "Well, it would be a new experience," she admitted at last, her expression turning thoughtful.

"One I believe you'd be good at," he didn't hesitate to tell her. And it was no more than the truth, as far as he was concerned. The woman who'd spent the better part of her working life in a tidy office just outside the one he now occupied wasn't only efficient but had a talent for organization. "There's no one I'd trust more to handle the job," he added, and meant it.

That last statement won him a small smile. "Then I suppose I can take it on."

"Good." Ross shifted in his chair. "With the election coming up in March, we'll have to get started soon."

"Yes, indeed." Thelma arched a brow. "I imagined

you've thought about how this might affect Hayward Investments.''

''I have,'' he allowed. ''And I don't see it as having a major impact. Once the campaign is in full swing, I'll have less time to spend here, true. But you and I both know that the rest of the staff can take up the slack.'' If he'd had any doubts about that, Ross knew that the time he'd taken off for a crash course in home improvement would have put them to rest. Hayward Investments, with a solid base of competent and well-paid employees, didn't need a heavy hand on the reins any more than it had in Thornton Hayward's time. ''Even after he assumed office, my grandfather managed to run the company and be a conscientious public servant at the same time. And if I'm elected mayor, I have every intention of following his example.''

Thelma braced her elbows on the arms of her chair and steepled her nimble fingers. ''I see you're saying *if* you're elected—not *when*.''

''You bet. I don't think I'll be a shoo-in by any means.'' Ross paused for a beat. ''And, despite your feeling that plenty of voters would look favorably on my running, I'm guessing you don't, either.''

Thelma's response was, as always, straightforward and to the point. ''No, I more than suspect it won't be all that easy. With the race now wide open, you're sure to have some competition, and at least one of the candidates could prove to be a particularly effective opponent.''

For a moment their gazes locked, then both spoke at the same time. ''Warren Bennett.''

''Somehow I have little doubt that we're right,'' Ross added with a low chuckle. It hadn't escaped his notice—or Thelma's, as it turned out—that the longstanding, and by and large friendly, business rivalry between Bennett Enterprises and Hayward Investments could well lead to some formidable competition between the heads of both companies in another area entirely. "I've been of the opinion for a while now that Warren had his eye on the top seat at city hall. Since a Hayward once occupied that spot and no Bennett has so far achieved the same distinction, it seemed like a natural move on his part to try to rectify that situation."

"Mmm-hmm." Thelma nodded wisely. "And he'll go all out to do it, too."

Ross flashed her another grin. "Still game?"

"If you are," she replied in short order.

"I am," he said, matching her speed. "Which means we need to map out a strategy." Ross sat forward and rested his forearms on his desk. "I'm thinking we should announce my plan to run as soon as possible and jump-start things with a party hosted by the new candidate and his wife."

"Makes sense," Thelma allowed after a brief consideration. "That way we'll get voters' attention in a hurry, and with the holiday season not far off, it can only be smart to put your agenda out there before people get too caught up in the Christmas rush."

"Exactly," he agreed. "Then we can take a break and enjoy the holidays ourselves, and gear up again after the first of the year."

"Works for me." Thelma crossed one slender leg over the other. Despite the fact that she'd left her youth behind her, she still had a neat-and-trim figure. "I may never have married and had children, but I still have plenty of family and friends to buy gifts for."

Gifts. For some reason the word had Ross recalling the wedding presents he and Jenna had received. Especially one present. It had been lost in the fire, of course, but he just might have to see if he could find a duplicate.

"I don't have to tell you that friends and family are important to me, too," he said to Thelma. "No matter how busy things may get in the coming months, I have no intention of neglecting my daughters, or my wife."

Thelma cocked her head slightly to one side. "Speaking of your wife, I only met her at the wedding, but I liked her. How does she feel about your running for mayor?"

"I think she's still adjusting to the whole thing," he admitted with complete truth. "But once the campaign gets going, she'll be behind me one hundred percent."

Somehow he had no doubt about that. Jenna would stand by him. He hadn't forgotten that the woman he'd married for many logical reasons had "sticking power."

She would be the hostess he needed. He realized it was only one of the ways that he was coming to need her more and more as time went on.

JENNA WAS BY AND LARGE a stranger to one of her hometown's oldest institutions. Which wasn't surprising, despite her status as a Harmony native. The Founders Club had always limited visitors to its members and their guests, neither of which distinction had ever applied to any of the Lorenzo clan. Once, she would have never expected to find herself on the other side of the stately oak double doors she'd only gotten glimpses of across a wide expanse of beautifully landscaped lawn lush with tall trees that had seen endless seasons come and go.

Yet here she was.

Tonight the distinguished-looking doorman wearing a crisply pressed uniform and smart cap had welcomed her as the wife of a longtime member, as he surely would every one of the Haywards' special guests numbering well over a hundred this evening—even more people than had been at their wedding.

"How long has it been since you've been here?" Jenna asked the man at her side, who was looking especially attractive in a dark suit, white shirt and subtly striped tie.

"Years," he said. "Between you and me, I always thought the place was a bit...stuffy." The admission came with a wry slant of his firm lips. "Still, it's one of the few places in town that can hold the number of people we needed to invite tonight."

"True." And if the club was on the stodgy side, Jenna had to acknowledge that it nonetheless was a sight to behold with its large foyer leading to an even larger dining room, both sporting high, elaborately carved ceilings and wide, smoothly plastered walls holding a variety of landscape paintings framed in ornate gold.

There was no denying, either, that it had been built to last. Jenna had little doubt that it could withstand an earthquake, or anything else Mother Nature could come up with to test its resolve to remain a Harmony fixture far into the future.

She was still glancing around her when Ross leaned over and whispered in her ear, "Did I mention that you look terrific in that dress?"

Despite the fact that she would have preferred to be back at home making dinner and looking forward to a relaxing evening where fashion played a distant second to comfort, she couldn't help but smile. "Yes, I remember your saying something along those lines."

A shopping expedition with her friend Peggy had led to her buying something with a price tag that, to Jenna's practical mind, was a lot higher than it should be—even if, as Peggy had pointed out, she could now afford it. But Ross had been well pleased with the square-necked, shimmering-russet silk dress with its long, fitted sleeves and a short, flared skirt. His appreciation had gone a long way to justifying the expense in Jenna's eyes.

Although she might not be entirely at ease in her current surroundings or in her new role as hostess to hundreds, she was suitably dressed for the part, and she was bound to feel more comfortable with the whole thing as time went on—wasn't she?

Of course, she was, Jenna told herself. Now if she could just silence the niggling voice in the back of her head saying that another woman—the woman Ross had married first—would have handled everything so easily, so competently, so graciously.

"But she's not here and you are," Jenna murmured under her breath. "So just get on with it."

And she did. In the minutes that followed, she helped her husband welcome a stream of guests, including Hester Goodbody and Tom Kennedy, who arrived together.

"So nice to see you two young people again," the veteran schoolteacher told the Haywards.

"Glad you could make it," Ross said, bending a considerable way to place a brief kiss on her cheek.

"Oh, I would hardly have missed it," Miss Hester assured him as he straightened. "Luckily, Tom felt the same way and was so kind as to escort me."

The police chief grinned at the woman who was a good twenty years his senior. "You would have had my hide if I said I wasn't interested in coming."

Miss Hester smiled sweetly. "Fortunately that wasn't the case."

"Uh-huh." Tom shook Ross's hand and slanted his

head in greeting to Jenna. "Look's like there's going to be a crowd."

And as if to prove that point, more guests soon arrived in another wave that included Peggy and Jack O'Brien. "I told you you'd knock 'em dead in that dress," Peggy said to Jenna in an undertone as the men exchanged greetings. "I'll bet your hunky husband's fingers are itching to take it off you."

Since Peggy already knew that things had taken a definite—and far more intimate—turn in what had started as a marriage of convenience, thanks to having wormed some pertinent details out of her friend the day they'd shopped, Jenna felt free to be straightforward. "He liked the dress—and maybe you're right about his plans for later tonight."

"Darn right I am," Peggy declared, a knowing glint sparking in her eyes. With that said, she aimed an assessing glance around her. "This is quite a place."

"Not too stuffy?" Jenna asked with a lifted brow, using Ross's earlier description.

"Maybe," Peggy allowed. "But I'm impressed away. And now that I've finally made it here, I plan on giving it more than a once-over," she added before she and Jack moved off to join some of the other guests.

Ross watched them walk away. "That reminds me," he said, switching his gaze to Jenna, "I have a present for you."

"For me?"

"Mmm-hmm. I bought it a couple of days ago, but I've been saving it for a…special occasion." His voice turned just husky enough with those last words to have her blinking.

"Why am I thinking it's something, uh, personal?" she asked after a moment.

"Because it is," he informed her.

"But you're not going to tell me what it is," she summed up as he assumed an oh, so innocent expression, as though he had no inkling that he'd set her mind to wondering about all manner of things—personal things. "You're just going to stand there and let me drive myself crazy speculating, aren't you?"

His lips twitched. "I prefer showing to telling. You'll get your present later tonight, I promise."

"I suppose I'll have to be content with that," Jenna murmured a scant second before a man she recognized as a member of one of Harmony's long-established families walked over to bid a courteous good evening to the Haywards. She had no trouble recalling that the latest arrival had also taken on the role of her husband's chief opponent in the mayoral race by declaring his intention to run only days after Ross had made his own announcement.

"Glad you could make it," Ross didn't hesitate to tell Warren Bennett, repeating the phrase he'd now used several times to welcome his guests.

"Glad you invited me," the other man replied with a friendly smile that seemed genuine. "It never hurts to keep an eye on what the competition's up to when it comes to winning votes."

Ross chuckled with frank amusement, appreciating Warren's candid admission. Although two more Harmony residents had also recently tossed their hats into the ring in a bid to occupy the top slot at city hall, Ross knew—as Warren surely did—that the person they most likely had to beat was the other.

"Just remember to keep shaking hands and kissing babies," he remarked with dry humor before formally introducing his chief rival to Jenna.

"Sorry my wife couldn't make it," Warren said. "She had to go out of town for a few days."

"I'm sorry, too," Jenna replied politely.

"I do, however, have someone I'd like you both to meet," Warren told the Haywards as another man stepped up beside him. Like Warren, he appeared to be in his middle forties with a fit and trim figure. But there any resemblance ended.

Where Warren had a thick shock of dark brown hair Harmony's veteran barber did his best to tame, this man's hair had already turned to a gleaming silver and was far from thick yet expertly styled, probably by an exclusive salon. Where Warren wore one of his usual conservative three-piece suits fitted by the same local tailor Ross used, the height-of-fashion cut of this man's suit said "well-known designer" in no uncertain terms.

And where Warren's wide smile had been matched by a genial glint in his intelligent gaze, this man's sudden smile, although even wider, didn't begin to reach eyes narrowed in a shrewd and savvy stare that seemed to take in everything around him.

"This is Emery Slade," Warren explained. He paused for a instant, then added, "My new campaign manager."

"Pleased to meet you," Emery said smoothly in a cultured voice that held no hint of an accent. "Warren has told me a great deal about the Hayward family."

I'll just bet he has, Ross thought, meeting the other man stare for stare while they shook hands. "I take it that this is your first visit to Harmony."

Emery nodded with easy grace. "Yes. Delightful place." His tone was as sincere as a Boy Scout's pledge.

Nevertheless, Ross didn't believe it for a minute. This man, obviously a professional in the political arena who took on clients willing to pay him—probably steeply—

for his services, hardly seemed the type to appreciate the benefits of spending time in a city that was well off the jet-set track. Whatever the case, though, and despite the fact that he seldom made snap judgments about people, Ross knew that he'd already come to the conclusion that he didn't like Emery Slade.

And neither did his wife. It didn't take him long to figure that out when he performed the introduction and she pulled her hand away after only the briefest of handshakes. "I hope you'll have a pleasant stay here," she said in a strictly neutral voice.

Emery studied her for a moment. "I understand that you yourself returned to this part of Arizona not too long ago after being away for some time."

"Yes. And I'm very glad I did. Living in a smaller city might not be to everyone's taste, but I find it...delightful." Just enough emphasis was placed on that last word to indicate that Jenna had as many doubts about the sincerity of Emery's earlier remark as her husband did.

"I suppose we should mingle," Warren commented. "Will you excuse us?"

"Of course," Jenna wasted no time in replying.

The men were barely gone when Thelma Carter approached, walking in her typically quick fashion and looking as no-nonsense in her plain, dark blue dress as she did in one of her simple work suits. She held a glass filled with bubbling champagne in each competent hand. "Thought you two could use a little liquid refreshment before the party gets into full swing."

Ross took one of the glasses she offered while Jenna took the other. "You're an angel, Thelma."

His assistant met that remark with a delicate snort. "Just remember that when it comes time for my raise."

"If he doesn't, I'll remind him," Jenna said. The women exchanged a brief grin before she continued. "I think you did a wonderful job organizing this."

"Thanks," Thelma told Jenna. "But you did your share, too."

Actually they'd pooled their efforts to make it happen, and it was clear to Ross that they'd formed a mutual admiration society in the process. He'd been more than content to watch it happen. Still, he contrived to look left out. "What, no praise for the hardworking candidate?"

"You've gotten a lot of good publicity already," Thelma informed him. "Too much praise and you'll get a swelled head."

"Don't worry," Ross said, his tone turning wry, "Warren Bennett will probably try to make sure that doesn't happen."

Thelma's gaze sought and found Ross's chief opponent. "Who's that with him?" she asked.

Ross's mouth quirked up at the corners. "His new campaign manager. Emery Slade is his name, and unless I miss my guess, he's a pro who's developed a reputation for being worth what he charges. Whether he is or not, is another story."

"Humph." Thelma conducted a swift yet what seemed to be thorough assessment of the man in question. Then she snorted again, this time far less delicately. "The guy smiles like a shark."

"I think that about sums him up," Jenna agreed.

"And I'm thinking that we'd better watch our step," Thelma went on. She looked at Ross. "From all indications you're currently the front-runner, but that could also make you a bigger target."

Ross lifted one shoulder in a slight shrug. "Right now, I'm not overly concerned about it."

Thelma's expression sobered. "Maybe you should be. If Mr. Pro decides to go after you, he'll probably hit hard. And sooner rather than later, too."

Ross couldn't deny that she had a point. Still, what could Slade hit him with? Even if his father's hardly admirable behavior and the black mark it had left on the family history was brought up again, that was now old news in Harmony. Whatever Martin Hayward had done, Ross thought, it didn't seem to be affecting the way voters thought about his son. No, Slade would be barking up the wrong tree if he decided to go that route.

"Whatever the guy chooses to do," Ross said, "he won't be doing it tonight, so let's concentrate on making sure our guests have a good time."

As to his own good time, he was saving that for later, when he and Jenna were alone. A very male grin of pure anticipation spread across Ross's face at the knowledge that he still had a present to give her.

HE WAS STILL GRINNING, at least to himself, when he handed over the small package one of Harmony's trendy boutiques had wrapped for him in striped lilac-and-cream paper tied with matching ribbon. He had just pulled it out of the bedroom closet where he'd hidden it behind a row of shirts and was now champing at the bit to have his wife open it.

Thankfully, they had the house to themselves with Caroline spending the night at the home of one of her girlfriends, and Katie and her dog staying overnight with another friend. And since tomorrow was Saturday, nobody had to be picked up early. He would have the rest of the night and most of the following morning alone with Jenna.

He planned to take advantage of it.

Jenna sat on an edge of the bed, which no longer squeaked thanks to her husband's efforts with an oil can, and undid the fancy ribbon. "You didn't have to buy me anything, you know."

One corner of his mouth slid up as he braced a shoulder against the closet doorjamb and looked down at her. "Oh, yes. I did. And," he confessed, "it's as much for me as it is for you."

"Hmm." Jenna mulled that over for a second, her hands stilling. "Did you…" She paused for a beat, as though deciding whether to go on before she spoke again. "Did you give many presents when you were married before?"

It was the first reference she'd made to his earlier marriage since becoming his wife. Maybe that's why the question took him by surprise. Yet, for all of that, he responded instinctively, without having to think about it. "I gave gifts on occasion, yes, but that's all in the past. Right now, I want to see you open your present."

For a brief moment their gazes locked and Ross had little doubt that Jenna had gotten the message, even though he hadn't said as much. He had no desire to discuss his first marriage. In fact, he had never discussed it, not with anyone, and he saw no need to make an exception now.

"Then I'll get on with it," Jenna said softly. Dropping her gaze, she set her hands to removing the paper. Then she opened the flat, cream-colored box and removed a layer of tissue to reveal its contents. Her mouth formed a startled "Oh" before her eyes again met his. "I'd forgotten all about this."

"I did, too, for a while. But then something reminded me, and after that I was determined to do my best to replace the one that went up in smoke."

And maybe he'd go up in smoke once he saw her in it, Ross allowed as she lifted the black silk teddy from the box. It was a duplicate of the one the O'Briens had supplied as a wedding present, or so the saleslady had assured Ross, telling him that she had helped Jenna's friend Peggy pick it out.

"There isn't much of it," Jenna said, conducting a short study.

He chuckled, low in his throat. "Yeah. That's the whole idea."

She ran her tongue around her teeth. "I suppose you want me to try it on."

"Truer words were never spoken," he assured her. "Why don't you change in the bathroom? I'll wait." *But not patiently, so for Pete's sake don't be too long about it,* he added to himself.

With a nod of agreement, she carefully set the box aside, then rose with his present in her hand and walked toward the bathroom, the wide skirt of her russet dress gently swaying with each slow step. It seemed that she was in no hurry. Or not nearly in as much of a hurry as he was.

The door had barely closed behind her when Ross started stripping off his clothes. By the time the door opened again, and not anywhere soon enough to suit him, he was standing beside the bed wearing no more than his cotton briefs.

What he saw then had his breath catching in his chest, and he could only hope his jaw hadn't dropped to the floor.

"Well, it was worth the wait," he told her at last,

now letting his eyes roam at will over a full figure with abundant curves somehow enhanced by their skimpy covering. "You look…" He searched for a word and finally came up with "Spectacular."

Jenna gave her head a quick shake and followed it up with a wry smile, as though she didn't quite believe him. He thought about taking the time to convince her that he well and truly meant it, but the more demanding parts of him were quickly gaining the upper hand, and they were flat-out set on less talking and more touching.

So he touched, crossing the room in a few swift strides to take her into his arms. And he tasted, first slanting his mouth over hers for a deep, hard kiss, then stroking his lips down her body and over skin and silk. A now familiar floral fragrance filled his senses, and the warmth he'd come to expect whenever she was close—close enough to touch and taste—seemed to surround him as she brushed her fingers through his hair.

"Oh," she said on a gasp when he took the tip of her breast into his mouth right through the thin fabric barely concealing it. "I'll give you three days to stop that."

He didn't stop. Spurred on, he tasted her in other places, lower places, won more gasps, and kept on going.

He only stopped when his patience was at an end. Straightening, he again looked down at the woman in his arms. "I'll be lucky to last three minutes once I get you under me," he told her with total truth. "You'd better take the lead."

Jenna took in a quiet breath in response to that suggestion. She'd never, she recognized, really taken the lead when it came to the most intimate aspects of their relationship. She'd been an eager participant, yes. But a leader? No.

What had held her back? she wondered. Not inexperience, certainly. Although she'd done no more than casually date for some time before taking on the role of wife, she'd been no innocent. She had experienced intimacy with a few select men, and, in one memorable case, something far more serious.

So why had she hesitated to take the lead?

Maybe—just maybe, she thought as a possibility occurred to her—she hadn't been able, deep down, to come to terms with who the man she'd married was. Or, probably more to the point, who he had been. *Ross Hayward, former Golden Boy.*

Maybe she had been intimidated by that knowledge. And maybe it was time for that to change.

Yes, she decided, looking straight into the navy eyes that had captured her attention the very first time she'd seen them, it was definitely time to show her husband she could blaze a trail when she chose to.

"I want you stretched out on that bed without a stitch on in five seconds flat," she told him in a soft yet firm command.

His brows hiked up. "I take it you're…taking the lead?"

"Mmm-hmm."

And with that, she cupped her palms around his broad shoulders, gave him a small shove to get him started, and began to walk him backward. Once they reached her goal, she wasted no time in getting him out of his underwear and onto the bed. Then she stood looking at him and slowly removed the black silk teddy, letting it slide down her body inch by inch.

"You're killing me," he told her, gritting out the words.

She had to smile. "Then I'll have to make you all better."

And she did her best to do exactly that once she lowered herself on top of him wearing no more than a thick flow of hair down her back. She had to touch and taste him as he had her, and earned herself some low and very male moans in the process. Still, it wasn't long before she joined her body with his.

He'd said he wouldn't last three minutes with her under him. It didn't take her much more than that to feel the beginnings of something stirring deep inside her as she established a steady rhythm and gazed down at him in the soft glow of the small bedroom lamp.

Ah, it did feel good. No, far better than that, she thought, it felt…spectacular. Maybe she didn't look that way, but she could feel that way when she made love to Ross Hayward. When she heard his harsh breaths coming faster and faster. When she saw his jaw tightening and his expression turning steely with need. When she knew she was pushing him—pushing them both—to the point of no return, and once they'd reached it they would find something wonderfully special and totally satisfying.

Satisfaction. Yes, that was it, Jenna decided as she picked up the pace, her body steadily gearing for release. Making love to her husband was giving her a wealth of satisfaction, and more.

The truth was that she loved making love to him. In fact, she loved—

It hit her then, wiping her mind clean as it sent her body shuddering. Then he was joining her and both were shaking with the impact of it. Boneless now, she slid down to rest her head on his chest and soon heard his heavy breaths turn softer, until they slowed in a way that said he was either on the verge of sleep or had tumbled over.

Reason returned as she listened, and suddenly she recalled where her thoughts had been headed moments earlier. She loved making love to her husband. But even beyond that, she...

She loved him.

Jenna accepted the truth of that with a heartfelt sigh. Despite telling herself only weeks earlier that it was too soon to even begin to know how much he could come to care for her, she had not given in to a starry-eyed infatuation, but the real thing.

She had fallen in love with Ross Hayward.

And he, she couldn't help thinking, could very well still be in love with someone else.

There was no denying that he seemed more than reluctant to discuss his first marriage, which might well be because the loss remained too painful for him to talk about. After all, how would she feel if she lost him now?

No, she wouldn't even consider that, Jenna told herself. They'd both said "I do" intending to spend the rest of their lives together, and the coming years would be good ones. They would see Caroline and Katie blossom into lovely young women. And they would, hopefully, have more children. Right this minute, she realized, a child might be growing inside her. The thought brought a soft smile to her lips even as Ross stirred under her.

"I want you to wear my present when you make breakfast in the morning," he murmured near her ear.

"We'll see," she murmured back.

He yawned. "I like it when you take the lead."

"Me, too." At least, Jenna thought, she'd gotten past any tendency to view this man as the Golden Boy she'd known. Which, unfortunately, didn't mean that she'd forgotten the shining example of womanhood who'd once been the other half of the Golden Couple. Or that she herself was neither beautiful nor perfect.

Jenna sighed again. How could she ever tell Ross she loved him if he couldn't return the words?

Chapter Eleven

His wife had looked very fetching in that teddy when she'd fixed him breakfast, Ross recalled on a blustery Saturday afternoon. Two busy weeks had come and gone since that memorable morning, yet the sight remained etched in his memory. He might've had to coax her out of wearing her terry-cloth robe over that scrap of black silk as she'd stood at the stove, but it had been well worth the effort.

Ross leaned back in one of a pair of well-worn leather chairs in the library, sitting where his grandfather had probably sat countless times. He was feeling damn good at the moment, he had to admit. The campaign was going well, and when his wife and daughters returned from doing some errands around town, he could look forward to spending a welcome evening as a family man rather than a candidate.

"You look like the cat who fell into a bowl of cream and licked his way out," his campaign manager remarked from her seat in the chair across from him.

"Maybe I do," he allowed. "Having some free time tonight after the last couple of weeks makes my day, I'll admit. And it's probably making yours, too, even though you seem hearty enough for a woman who's put in some long hours lately.''

Thelma's mouth quirked into a wry smile. ''What I've done is work my butt off on the campaign trail,'' she said with blunt directness. ''In fact, you and I have both worked our butts off, and Jenna's been no slouch, either. Still, I've enjoyed it, by and large.'' She studied him with a lifted brow. ''Have you?''

Ross tossed the draft of a new brochure scheduled for a later mailing to voters onto the lamp table beside him and crossed his arms over the front of his V-necked sweater. Could he really say that he had enjoyed it? he asked himself.

He enjoyed spending time with his family. He enjoyed heading up Hayward Investments. These days, he even enjoyed tinkering around the old Victorian and tackling the continual minor repairs that seemed to go along with living in a far-from-modern house.

But the campaign and all the hand-shaking and speech-making that went with it?

''I like meeting people,'' he said, and left it at that, recognizing that much to be true. Given Harmony's genuinely friendly atmosphere, he had always liked meeting new people and catching up with old acquaintances, as well.

And if he liked it even more when he wasn't trying to convince anyone to vote for him, well, he hadn't let that stop him from doing his best to win votes. Which had paid off, he knew, because he continued to be the front-runner, even though Warren Bennett had gone into high gear with several rounds of handshaking and speech-making himself.

''Well, I'll be off and leave you to your free time,'' Thelma said, rising. She picked up the draft of the brochure. "I'll make the final changes and get this to the printer on Monday."

Ross stood. "Maybe I'll get a beer, put up my feet, and do some reading before Jenna and the girls get home."

His assistant aimed a sweeping glance at the tall bookshelves lining two sides of the room. "You've got plenty of reading material, that's for sure. How long did it take to dust all those books?"

His mouth twisted into a wry grimace as they walked down the hall toward the front door. "Too long."

They were steps away when the doorbell rang. Seconds later Ross found Tom Kennedy standing on the doorstep, looking far from happy. Even with the wide brim of his Western-style hat shading his forehead, there was no mistaking the police chief's deep frown.

"Afraid I've got some news," he told Ross, "and it's not the best." He held up a letter-size sheet of white paper. "You need to see this."

"I was just leaving," Thelma said. She hitched her shoulder bag higher on a slender arm covered by her beige knit jacket.

Tom's gaze shifted to her. "Might be smart if you stayed for a minute. This has to do with the campaign."

Ross blew out a breath. "Well, come on in and we'll take a look. Whatever it is, I suppose Thelma and I can deal with it." He closed the door behind Tom and turned to his visitors. "Let's have a seat," he suggested, and led the way to the front parlor.

Tom waved the paper as he settled himself in the wing-backed chair next to the fireplace. "As far as I've been able to tell since I saw it an hour ago, this is starting to be passed out all over town."

Ross sat on the sofa while Thelma perched on the

cushion beside him. "I take it it's something that casts me in a bad light," he said.

"Not you specifically," Tom replied, still sporting his deep frown. "This has to do with…your wife."

Ross was surprised and knew it showed. "With *Jenna?*"

"Afraid so." Tom's broad jaw tightened. "As chief of police, I have to remain officially neutral in this race, but between the three of us I think this is just plain dirty campaign tactics in action."

"We'd better see it," Thelma told Ross, her tone turning grim.

Tom leaned over and extended the sheet to Ross. "It's a copy of what looks like the front page of a Las Vegas newspaper dated several years back." The chief left his explanation at that, clearly feeling there was no need to elaborate.

And there wasn't. One glance at the black-and-white photo spread out over the top half of the paper was all it took for Ross to see that the woman he'd married had made major news in the past. The bold words stretched above the photograph told the story in one succinct statement.

Casino Cutie Caught Cuddling Coed's Man, the headline blared. The man in question was plainly the one featured in the center of the photo, with a wholesome-looking blonde on one side of him and a striking-looking brunette on the other. Both women were young, yet as different as night and day, with the blonde wearing a simple sweater set over tailored slacks while the brunette wore what might have been called a uniform in the waitress trade, one that displayed much of her full figure and well-curved legs to maximum advantage.

All three people in the photo had a somewhat disheveled look about them, as though they'd been in a scuffle. The blonde's short ponytail was off center and one side of the brunette's upswept hairdo had tumbled past her shoulders. But the fair-haired and slightly older man wedged between them, handsome in a clean-cut sort of way, seemed to have gotten the worst of it, his white dinner jacket and dark bow tie badly rumpled.

The blonde was staring daggers at the brunette, who in turn regarded the man with a narrow-eyed expression that seemed to hold equal parts temper and embarrassment. For his part, he gazed straight ahead at the camera with a large indoor fountain and a crowd of curious faces in the background, looking for all the world like a guy who'd been caught with his pants down—if not literally, then figuratively.

"Uh-oh," Thelma muttered, plainly noting that Jenna wasn't the "coed" who'd apparently been wronged.

No, the woman who had returned to Harmony after a well-documented career as a professional housekeeper had at one time made a living in an entirely different way.

She'd been a "casino cutie," no doubt about it.

JENNA STUDIED the thickening clouds, hoping she and her companions got home before it rained, because when the rain hit, it would probably pour. Still, despite what appeared to be a major storm gathering overhead, she wasn't allowing the weather to spoil her mood. She felt good—too good to let it matter. And she deserved to feel that way, she reflected with assurance.

After all, not only had she spent the past few weeks dividing her time between standing at Ross's side when he spoke to Harmony's residents at various locations throughout the city and playing hostess to some of those same people in the Hayward home—she'd done it all without so much as a false step as she'd diligently pursued her role of both firm supporter and caring helpmate to the candidate.

Even better, though, she'd somehow wound up with a supporter and helpmate of her own, and that support had come from someone she'd have once considered the last person in Harmony who would volunteer to help her. It was Ross's eldest daughter.

Caroline, much to Jenna's delight, had shown no reluctance to quietly step in and do what she could—not only to aid her father's effort to become mayor, but to lend a hand with whatever her stepmother had on her agenda. In the process, the lovely girl and the woman she'd held at a polite yet determined distance had slowly and surely become friends.

"Friends," Jenna murmured under her breath as she strolled down a busy street with Caroline at her side and Katie and her dog leading the way. Friendship was indeed a good thing, even if, in her heart of hearts, Jenna longed for a closeness beyond the bounds of friendship. The same type of closeness she seemed to be finding with Ross's youngest child, who now regularly offered hugs and was happy to receive them in return. Who called her "Jenna Mom" more and more as the days went by.

Yes, that kind of closeness with both of Ross's children was what she really wanted. She wanted them to be *their* daughters in a small and very special way, not just his.

Nevertheless, right now she was counting her blessings for the fact that she had a new friend.

"I think the asparagus will be nice for the lunch you're having next week," Caroline told Jenna. That observation, which might have seemed too adult for the average ten-year-old yet fit this one to a T, referred to the luncheon Jenna had scheduled with a group of women handpicked by Thelma Carter as potential volunteers to be called on later in the campaign.

"I think the asparagus was a good choice, too." Jenna shifted the paper bag she held. "You were right about the market having better produce than the grocery store where I usually shop." She dropped a grin down at the girl who had passed along what she'd recalled hearing one of her friend's mothers say about the downtown market. "Thanks for the tip."

"You're welcome," Caroline replied, her typically courteous words followed by a small and appealing grin of her own that had never been directed at her stepmother until recently.

"I don't like asparagus," Katie said with a backward glance.

Caroline released a patient sigh. "Grown-ups like asparagus," she explained to her younger sister.

Katie shook her head over that piece of news, as if she couldn't imagine why anyone would choose to eat something skinny and green. "As long as I don't hafta eat it."

Jenna had to laugh. Then, in the next breath, that laughter died a quick death as she recognized the well-dressed man in his lightweight cashmere coat approaching them, looking as though he'd just stepped out of a fashion ad.

He came to a smooth halt when he reached the group. "Good afternoon, Mrs. Hayward."

Emery Slade's smile, Jenna noted, still didn't reach his eyes. She didn't even bother trying to come up with one of her own. "Mr. Slade."

He raised his cool gray gaze to glance at the sky above them, then switched it back to Jenna, ignoring the children and the dog who had all stopped in the middle of the sidewalk. "I believe we're in for a storm," he told her, his tone casual yet somehow sly, as though hinting that he meant more than the weather. "Things could get rocky around here."

A sudden chill wiggled down Jenna's spine, one that owed nothing to the brisk wind swirling the hem of her raincoat around her knees. She had little doubt about how much "Mr. Pro," as Thelma referred to him, wanted his candidate to win. What she didn't know was just how far Warren Bennett's campaign manager would go to make sure that happened.

"Well, we've weathered storms in Harmony before," she replied, keeping her own tone light. "We'll make it through this one just fine."

"One can always hope so," he said, his voice still underscored with more than a hint of innuendo.

This time Frisky growled a response from his place at Katie's side. He didn't try to strain at the leash she held, but the slight baring of his teeth was by no means sociable.

It won Emery's attention in a hurry and had him fixing the dog with a wary look before he offered a small nod of farewell and continued on his way. Where he'd been strolling down the wide and sparkling-clean sidewalk with measured steps, he now moved along at a fast clip.

Jenna regarded Katie's pet with approval. What surprised her was that Caroline did so, as well.

"I don't think he's a nice man," Katie said. "Frisky never growled at anybody before."

Caroline turned and looked after the departing campaign manager. "I don't think he's nice, either," she said softly.

"Could be that Frisky is pretty smart, hmm?" Jenna asked Caroline with a lifted brow.

"Maybe," the older girl allowed. For the first time she reached down and gave a furry black head a brief pat.

For a scant second Frisky looked astonished at being petted by someone who had never given him any encouragement before. Then he issued a soft bark and wagged his tail a mile a minute, as if to say, *Of course, I'm smart.*

Jenna nearly laughed again. Somehow, though, she couldn't quite manage it. Emery Slade was up to something—something that would do her husband's chances of being the next mayor no good. She was sure of that much.

She just didn't know what.

THEY MADE IT HOME before the rain. Once again Katie and her pet led the way as they walked up the front porch steps. In addition to the vegetables she'd purchased at the market, Jenna held a plastic bag that contained something she hadn't been able to resist slipping in to buy when they'd passed a familiar downtown boutique and she'd remembered what had originally been the other half of Peggy's wedding gift.

Her husband, although he had no idea of the fate in store for him, would become the owner of a pair of silky black boxer shorts as soon as she found the right moment to spring it on him. He wasn't the only one who could give presents, Jenna thought with a small and undeniably pleased smile.

Maybe later tonight would be a good time, she told

herself. She brought up the rear as the group trouped into the house, nudged the door shut behind her and started down the hall toward the rear of the house. She could leave the wrapped box on the bed for him to find. Or she could just whip it out and put it under his nose. Either way would get the job done.

Jenna was still debating exactly how she would produce her gift and surprise the man she'd married when Ross stepped out of the front parlor. After one look at his face, something told her that he'd already been surprised—and in a way that had wiped his expression clean.

"I have something to show you," he said, his eyes meeting hers over the heads of the children. "Tom Kennedy brought it over a little earlier." Dropping his gaze, he added, "Why don't you girls have some cookies and milk while Jenna and I go into the library for a few minutes?"

"Okay," Katie happily agreed.

Caroline turned to Jenna. Where her younger sister had clearly noted nothing amiss, the older girl seemed to sense that all wasn't fine and dandy. "I can put the vegetables in the refrigerator," she offered in a quiet voice.

"Thanks." Jenna handed the paper grocery bag to Caroline, schooling her own expression to display none of the unease swiftly building inside her. Whatever the police chief had brought over, it wasn't good news. She knew that even better than the ten-year-old did. "Don't let Katie give Frisky any cookies," she murmured just loud enough for Caroline to hear. "They're not good for him."

Caroline nodded. "I won't." And with that, she headed to the kitchen with her sister and the dog in tow.

Jenna went into the library and set the plastic bag that contained the box with Ross's present on the card table standing in a corner, then took off her raincoat and draped it over the back of one of the small chairs grouped around the table.

Ross closed the door behind them and seated himself in a high-backed leather chair across the room. As Jenna turned toward him, she noticed for the first time that he held a folded sheet of white paper.

"Is that what you wanted to show me?" she asked, straightening the hem of her green knit pullover.

"Yes. Tom said that copies of this were beginning to be passed out in town." His even tone displayed little emotion. Nevertheless, the set-in-stone look still on her husband's face as he extended the sheet to her had Jenna more certain than ever that he'd not only been surprised a short while ago, but maybe even stunned.

She walked over, took the sheet and opened it. And then it was her turn to be stunned.

"The Incident" in her past had come back to haunt her.

What she'd thought long behind her was staring back at her in the form of a stark photograph topped by a blaring headline. She'd never forgotten either, even if it now seemed as though it had all happened in another lifetime. She would have liked nothing more than to tear the sheet she held into a hundred pieces, but it was only one of many, she'd just been told. They were being passed out all over Harmony.

"I think Emery Slade is behind it," Ross said.

I know he is, Jenna thought, recalling the campaign manager's oh, so sly reference to a storm. "Yes," she replied, her voice soft and sober in the quiet broken only by the steady tick of an old pendulum clock on the wall.

"He must have done a background check on me, trying to dig up something he could use to his advantage, and he found…this."

"That's my take on it, too," Ross agreed, maintaining his even tone.

Jenna let out a long breath. "I owe you an explanation."

He frowned. "You don't have to go into it if you don't—"

"Yes, I do," she said, breaking in. "I owe it to you to explain how I wound up on the front page of that paper." She refolded the sheet and let the memories come. "It started when I decided to quit college—not the wisest thing I've ever done, I can see in hindsight, but juggling school with a part-time job became more and more of a drain on me. After all the time I'd spent taking care of my three younger sisters when I was growing up, I wanted to have some fun while I was still young myself."

Ross shifted in his seat. "Even as an only child, I suppose I can understand that," he said.

"And I did have fun when I went out on my own and rented a small apartment in a quieter section of Las Vegas." Jenna went on. "Although I worked hard, too. First as a regular waitress, then serving cocktails in one of the large hotel casinos." She could still recall the first time she'd stared around at the flashing lights, sparkling colors and eager buzz of conversation coming from people trying their luck at a variety of games of chance. For all that she'd considered herself an adult, she'd still been somewhat naive when she'd met someone who would change her life—first for the better, it had certainly seemed. Then for the worse when she'd been forced to learn a hard lesson.

"It was while I was working at the casino that I met Brad Summerfield. He was an assistant manager at the hotel and originally came from a small city in Nebraska. That was something we had in common, both being born and raised in smaller towns." Jenna resisted the urge to sigh. "I came to care for him and believed he cared for me, as well. He said he did."

She shook her head. "But what I didn't know was that he'd gotten engaged the year before to a young woman whose very successful father owned a good portion of Omaha."

Ross's lips thinned into a grim line. "And I take it she found you two together."

"Yes," Jenna said, forging on. She was still determined to tell the whole thing. "We were in the hotel lobby just outside the casino area, making plans to meet once we were both done working. Brad had placed his arms around me—something the management frowned on but he nonetheless seemed to enjoy trying to get away with—when someone who probably everyone in the crowded lobby would say was the image of the all-American girl came storming up to us. Brad looked astonished. He'd plainly had no idea that his fiancée had decided on the spur of the moment to fly in from a Midwestern college for a short visit."

"And you?" Ross asked quietly, his low voice now edged with what might well have been sympathy.

"I was…flabbergasted, especially when she began shouting at me, saying she had no intention of letting me step in and steal the man she was engaged to while she was off getting her hard-earned college degree. Then she made a grab for me and we somehow wound up in a tussle, with Brad in the middle. He'd just separated the two of us when someone with a camera, obviously sensing a photo opportunity, took our picture. By then, what the fresh-faced coed had been saying was starting to sink in. She was Brad's fiancée, and to her mind, I was in the wrong."

The sigh Jenna had held back earlier broke through. "That's the way the paper played it, and since it happened on a slow news day and the young woman's father was well-known in financial circles even outside Nebraska, it became the headline story."

And so she'd been labeled the "other woman" even as her heart broke, Jenna had no trouble remembering. Still, her pride hadn't allowed her to let Brad Summerfield get away unscathed. "I hope that, in the end, the coed was smart enough to break off her relationship with Brad. At least she'd stopped glaring at me long enough to scowl at him by the time I'd had enough and pushed him into the lobby fountain shortly after that first picture was taken." Jenna's lips twisted into a brief and rueful smile. "The second photo wound up on page two. It featured Brad as I saw him last, hauling himself out of the water."

She stopped at that point, seeing no need to go into the short yet horrible media circus that had followed, when she'd been hounded by the more sensational elements of the press to tell her side of the story—not because they were interested in the truth, but merely to provide fodder for another article. At least she hadn't given them that satisfaction, preferring to say nothing. Instead she'd quit her job, probably only a step ahead of being fired, and had wasted little time in leaving Las Vegas with the goal of finding another means of earning a living far removed from the lights and glamour—and from the man who'd turned happiness to heartbreak in the space of one evening.

"I'm sorry the jerk hurt you," Ross said, bringing her back to the present.

She gave her head a quick shake. "I'm the one who's sorry for not telling you before," she countered, feeling as though her heart were breaking for a second time when she considered how what had happened in the past could affect the future of the man she'd married—the man she now knew had touched her emotions on a far deeper level than Brad Summerfield ever had. Although he'd left her with some major wounds to lick, she'd gotten over Brad and gone on with her life.

If she lost Ross, would she ever get over it? No, everything inside her said. She wouldn't. If she had to, she would go on with her life without him, but a part of her would always be missing.

"I should have told you before we were married," she continued, still standing a step away and gazing down at him. "And I would have if I'd had any idea that it could be important after all this time." Jenna swallowed against a sudden tightness in her throat. "I can't change what happened back then, but I never imagined it would be used against you."

He released a gusty breath. "Jenna—" he started to say.

She cut him off with an upraised palm. "I can't talk any more right now." She managed to get the words out with another swallow. All at once tears threatened, pricking at the corners of her eyes. She didn't want them to fall while she was standing in front of the man who'd been brought up to value the exacting standards passed down to him by his ancestors.

Haywards didn't make headlines unless they'd achieved something notable. And now people in Harmony would not only be reading about Jenna Lorenzo

Hayward's far different brush with fame, they'd be seeing her dressed in an outfit that displayed a good portion of her body—the same body she'd been a lot less than comfortable displaying too much of in public, and sometimes even in private, ever since that time. She could only imagine the combined effect on the town's residents—and voters.

"I know Cynthia would never have put you in the position I have." Jenna had to say that much as she handed the folded sheet back to him—because it was true. The other half of the Golden Couple would have made the ideal candidate's wife—polished, poised and charmingly persuasive. "She would never have raised a ripple of notoriety, would she?"

"No," he said after a thoughtful moment, his even tone once more displaying little emotion, "she wouldn't."

Jenna turned away and started for the door. Her hand was on the knob when she glanced back over her shoulder. Ross was still sitting there, staring straight at her. She knew what he might very well be thinking. She didn't want to believe it. Yet it was entirely possible—even probable.

"You must be sorry," she said, opening the door and ready to head for the privacy of her bedroom as fast as her feet could take her. "You must be so sorry that you married me."

Chapter Twelve

Ross watched the door close behind Jenna with a quiet click. Her last words still echoed in his mind. *You must be so sorry that you married me.*

She clearly more than suspected he could feel that way. Did he?

Hell, no.

The swift, simple and succinct reply came straight from inside him. There wasn't even a maybe involved, he recognized. He was an educated man, but he didn't have to put his brain to mulling the matter over. Down deep at the core of him, he knew—had known from the day he'd made her his bride—that he had done the right thing in marrying the striking-looking woman who had first applied to be his housekeeper.

So go find her, Hayward, and tell her so. Whether she wants to talk or not, she can listen.

Ross dipped his head in a brief nod, silently agreeing with the inner voice that urged him on. He rose to his feet just as the phone on the lamp table rang. Since he didn't want Jenna, or the girls, to have to deal with what might be a call regarding the article probably still being distributed around town, he wasted no time in picking it up. "Hayward here."

"Ross, it's Warren."

His chief opponent's voice was as serious as Ross had ever heard it. "Hello, Warren," he said. He had no trouble duplicating the sober tone as his hand tightened around the receiver.

"I take it you've seen…"

"Yeah, I've seen it," Ross supplied at the other man's hesitation.

"God, I don't know how to say this, except I had no idea what Slade planned to do before he went off half-cocked and put the thing out." Warren heaved a lengthy sigh. "I gave him his walking papers. In fact, I just threw him out of my house."

Ross's mouth twisted. "I'm glad you fired the bastard."

"Which doesn't mean," Warren admitted, "that I can undo what harm he's done. Not that I won't try," he added in the next breath. "I'll put out a formal apology tomorrow and do my best to see that it gets on the front page of the *Harmony Herald*."

Ross chuckled, a sound that held little humor. "I suppose the front page would be appropriate."

"Right now," Warren went on with clear chagrin, "I want to personally apologize to you…and most especially to your wife."

"I'll tell her," Ross said after a moment. "I don't think she's much in the mood to talk to anyone right now."

"When she is, I'm ready to meet her wherever she chooses, and she can kick my butt, if she's so inclined."

That won another chuckle from Ross, this one far more genuine. "I think she'd rather kick Slade's butt," he murmured. Then his voice hardened. "As a matter of fact, so would I."

"I don't blame her—or you," Warren said. "Besides Slade, the only person I'm blaming at the moment is myself for involving him in my campaign." He paused for a beat. "Jeez, I want to be mayor, Ross. You know just how much, I'm sure. But I don't want it badly enough to resort to the kind of thing Slade pulled."

Ross believed him. He'd known, and respected, the current head of the Bennett clan too long to doubt his sincerity. "Well, I guess I don't have to beat you up," he said wryly, "you're doing a pretty good job of that yourself."

"I deserve it."

"Maybe," Ross agreed, allowing himself a faint smile.

"The rest of this campaign is going to be totally aboveboard," Warren didn't hesitate to declare. "I swear it."

"All right. And may the best man win." There was no point, Ross thought, in belaboring the issue. Emery Slade was probably headed out of Harmony right now at the wheel of his expensive sports car. It was time to let it go.

"And please," Warren said in a parting statement, his sober tone returning, "be sure to give your wife my, uh, regrets."

After goodbyes were exchanged, Ross hung up and again started for the door, still intent on finding Jenna. He would pass along Warren's regrets. He had to hope it would make her feel better.

With that thought, he opened the door and started for the stairs, then halted in midstride, suddenly realizing as he once more recalled his wife's parting words and her reference to his earlier marriage that he bore his own share of regrets.

Or one major regret, anyway.

If Jenna believed she should have told him about what had happened in her past, then he in turn should have been frank with her about something else entirely, something he'd been determined to keep strictly private.

It had been a mistake, he was now dead certain. As his wife, she deserved to know. And there was no time like the present, he decided, to put things right. While he was telling Jenna a few things, he might as well tell it all.

"Dad," Caroline said, winning his attention as she poked her head out of the front parlor. "I think something's wrong."

"Wrong?" Ross didn't miss the worry knitting his eldest child's brow.

Caroline stepped into the hall with Katie close behind. The six-year-old's expression, usually so cheerful, was no less anxious than her older sister's. "We saw Jenna Mom crying when she went upstairs, Daddy. She never cried before."

Ross let out a breath at that news, certain that the woman in question didn't cry easily. "I'm going up to see her now. Everything will be all right."

"Okay," Katie murmured in a tiny voice.

Although they said nothing more, neither of the girls looked convinced by his attempt to reassure them. But everything would be all right, he thought as he left them and took the stairs at a fast climb. It had to be. He certainly planned on doing his damnedest to make sure it was.

And that, he knew, would include being frank about one particular portion of his own past.

JENNA WAS WIPING A LAST tear away as the bedroom door opened. She was certain who it was before she even turned around in her seat at one side of the bed. "Ross, I can't—"

He cut her off, smoothly yet firmly, as he closed the door behind him. "If you can't talk, just listen."

She would far rather have been left alone so she could finish putting her composure back together. Unfortunately the man who stood a few feet away with his gaze trained on her wasn't going to accept that. The tight line of his jaw told her as much. Whatever he wanted to say, he was set on saying it.

"All right," she said on a small sigh, "I'll listen."

"Good." He pushed up the sleeves of his tan sweater and folded his arms across his chest. "First of all, I'm not sorry that I married you—so don't even think it for one minute."

Jenna's heart reacted first, doing a small leap, but before she could even begin to respond, he took a resolute step forward and spoke again, never taking his eyes from hers.

"In fact," he said, measuring out the words, "the only woman I came to regret marrying was Cynthia."

Cynthia. Jenna hadn't thought she could be more stunned than she'd been at the resurrection of that long-buried newspaper article. She'd been wrong.

Ross regretted marrying his beautiful first wife!

Her mouth opened, snapped shut and opened again. With her mind still reeling, it took another moment for her to string enough of a sentence together to ask a halting question. "What exactly do you mean by that?"

He replied without so much as a breath of hesitation. "I mean that to the outside world she seemed like the best wife a man could have, but in the privacy of our home it was a different story."

"Oh." That was all Jenna could manage to come up with, still half in shock.

For years, ever since seeing them together for the first time, she'd been so sure—probably as sure as most everyone in Harmony—that the Golden Couple had been meant for each other. "She was a lovely girl who became an even lovelier woman," she said, not even realizing she had voiced that thought out loud until Ross replied.

"Yes, but an attractive exterior is little indication of how a person is inside. That knowledge didn't come easily to me, I'll admit, because when we first started to date, I was bowled over by her. And so were my hormones," he added with blunt directness. "At the same time, my teenage ego was basking in the fact that I was the guy she'd picked to squire her around."

His gaze went to the window, where he looked out at the rain now steadily beating on the clear glass panes. Rather than studying the storm in progress, though, he seemed to be caught up in memories of an earlier time.

"We saw each other a lot during those high school years," he went on, "but after we both headed off to different colleges, I got involved in other things and sometimes even forgot about her for long stretches. Then we'd both come home for vacations and holidays, and I'd be bowled over yet again, just as if we'd never been apart. We got engaged during one of those times and decided to get married shortly after we graduated—a plan that was heartily approved by both of our families."

Ross inhaled a quick breath and amended that last statement. "Or by most of our family members, at any rate. My father seemed to have some misgivings, but he never voiced them, and I was so dead set on what I wanted when I first put an engagement ring on Cynthia's finger, I'm not sure I would have listened if he had said something."

Jenna supposed she could understand that, even though she had to wonder what Martin Hayward might have seen that apparently everyone else close to Ross had not. Still, she said nothing. Although she hadn't wanted to listen when Ross had first walked in, it was, she realized, a time for it. She was all but certain that he had never spoken as he was speaking now to anyone else.

"Then, when I was in my senior year in college," he said, still looking out at the rain, "I began to have… maybe nothing as concrete as doubts, but some niggling reservations about getting married so soon after graduating."

He smiled a faint, wry smile. "Maybe my hormones had calmed down and my ego had matured enough to let me take some other things into consideration. Anyway, I came home for the winter break and broached the subject with Cynthia, but she was already up to her ears in planning a summer wedding—right along with her mother and mine. She reminded me how many arrangements had already been made, how much our families were looking forward to the wedding." He heaved a sudden sigh. "And I set those niggling reservations aside."

But… Jenna knew it was coming as she folded her hands in her lap and waited.

"But I shouldn't have," he said in the next breath. "Maybe it takes living with someone on a day-to-day basis to really get to know them. Whatever the case, after less than a year of marriage, I discovered something about Cynthia."

Ross pulled his eyes away from the window and once again locked his gaze with Jenna's. "She was...cold."

"Cold," Jenna repeated softly after a moment, testing the word.

"Yes. Beneath the undeniable beauty and the outward charm, there was something missing. A basic warmth, I suppose you could say. By the time I'd come to that conclusion, though, she was pregnant with Caroline, and there was no going back."

He lifted his broad shoulders in a slight shrug. "I became determined to be the best father I could, and tried to be a caring husband, as well. Sometimes Cynthia didn't make that last goal easy to achieve, I'll admit. But she took good care of Caroline, and then Katie. I have to give her that. As it turned out, she was a lot better suited to be a mother than she was a wife."

Which was why he'd been familiar with what it was like to sleep on the daybed in that stylish master bedroom suite, Jenna concluded, recalling what he'd told her on the first night she'd spent under his roof. She wondered how many nights he'd lain there. Alone.

And here she had once believed... "I thought you'd had it all," she said. "I was so sure that you had lost the love of your life when you lost her."

His expression turned grim. "The children did lose a good mother, and the accident that took her didn't have to happen. Even though it had been snowing pretty badly in the mountains on and off for days, Cynthia was set on driving down to Phoenix to take advantage of the after-Christmas sales at some of the major department stores. She and my mother went every year on the first Saturday after the holiday."

He took a deep breath before continuing. "It had become a tradition that neither wanted to skip, but I told

Cynthia flat-out on Friday evening to skip it that year. It would be damn foolish with the roads as risky as they were. She reluctantly agreed, but when I woke up the next morning her car was gone. She'd left a note saying the weather looked a little better and she was going to try to make the drive. Less than an hour later I learned that her car had slid off the road, and that my mother was with her.''

"It must have been terrible," Jenna said, "to lose them both at the same time."

"It was rough," he agreed, "but it wasn't surprising that they were together. They usually were. Sometimes I think Cynthia was closer to my mother than she was to her own."

They were a lot alike. All at once the memory of those words surfaced and had Jenna's brow knitting in a thoughtful frown. Martin Hayward, the only person who'd seemed to have doubts about his son's first marriage, had issued them on his brief visit to Harmony, during which Ross had vowed to maintain the breach between them. She'd decided soon after not to try to change his mind.

Was she going to change her own mind now? Yes, Jenna thought, she was.

She cleared her throat. "Have you ever considered that, as much as your mother cared about you, she might have, like Cynthia, been less suited to be a wife?"

Ross stilled completely for a moment as his mind grappled with the unexpected question. In the end, he shot back an instinctive reply. "She was a good wife. And she certainly didn't deserve a husband who just packed up one day and walked out on her."

Jenna sat straighter. "Will you hang on to your temper if I suggest something?"

He dropped his arms and shoved his hands into the pockets of his khakis, wondering where along the line he had lost control of the conversation. "Weren't you supposed to be listening?"

"I did listen," she reminded him. "Did you want to tell me more about your earlier marriage?"

He shook his head. "I think I did a fairly thorough job." And felt the better for having done it, he admitted.

"Then..." Jenna paused for an instant. "I just remembered something your father said when he was here that seems to indicate he felt your mother and Cynthia had a lot in common."

"Humph. I suppose he did feel that way," Ross acknowledged, recalling that his father had implied as much, although he himself had been too angry to give it more than fleeting attention at the time.

"Your parents were together for many years, weren't they?" At his short nod, Jenna went on, her voice soft yet steady. "If your father was right and the women you both married had one particular thing in common, that's a long time to be cold, Ross."

A low groan broke from his throat. "What you're saying is that I should give him another chance."

Her gaze never wavered from his. "I think you should at least give it some serious consideration."

He mulled that over, admitting, at least to himself, that what Jenna had suggested about his parents' marriage just might possibly be true. And if it was? What then?

"Okay," he said at last, "I'll consider it."

She was off the bed in a flash and threw her arms around him. "I don't think you'll be sorry."

"What I know," he said, tugging her closer, "is that I'm not sorry I married you."

She beamed a smile up at him. "So you said before."

Then her smile faded. "But what about the article that's being passed around town? I can't help being concerned about the effect it may have on the election. I know how much you've been determined to follow in your grandfather's footsteps."

Not how much you want to be mayor, Ross reflected to himself. No, that hadn't been what she'd said. And he knew the difference, although he'd been skirting the issue, even in his own mind. It was one thing for a person to further their private goals and another to feel obliged to follow family tradition.

"You once asked me if I really wanted to be mayor," he said.

"Yes." Jenna's eyes lit with a knowing look, as though she remembered how he had given her a roundabout reply. "I thought the answer was important. And I still do."

"So," he finally conceded, both to her and himself, "do I."

She bit her lip. "Do you still have a chance to be elected, even with the article?"

"Yes, I think I do," he said, and meant it. "It may even backfire and win me some votes, because Warren Bennett phoned a short while ago. He fired Emery Slade once he found out what his campaign manager had done without his knowledge, and he's issuing a public apology tomorrow." His mouth quirked up at the corners. "Oh, and by the way, Warren especially apologies to you and says you're welcome to kick his butt anytime you feel like it."

That won him another smile, although it, too, quickly faded. "I'd rather dump a load of the fertilizer I bought for the garden on Emery Slade's head," Jenna said with feeling.

"Well, I never thought of that option, but it sounds like a fine idea," Ross agreed. "But to get back to the matter at hand, yes, I believe I could still get elected." If he truly wanted to be elected. Which, he realized, was the crux of the matter.

His grandfather had wanted it, Ross knew.

Warren Bennett had made no bones about wanting it.

As for himself?

He…didn't.

Ross accepted that truth of that with an inner sigh. "I could give it one hell of a try and might very well wind up winning," he told Jenna, "but I don't truly want the job."

She looked deep into his eyes. "You're not just saying that because of what happened today?"

"No," he assured her, "although it's taken me a while to come to that conclusion. What I'd really like to do is to keep running Hayward Investments, tinker around this old Victorian in my spare time, give Caroline and Katie some brothers, or maybe some more sisters. And," he added, holding Jenna's gaze as firmly as he held her in his arms, "spend the rest of my life with you."

"Oh, Ross."

"Now don't start crying again," he said in a hasty bid to head off further tears.

She sniffed. "I won't. It just that…most of what you said you wanted is exactly what I want, too."

He kissed her then, long and hard, and once again that now expected warmth flooded through him. Yet as familiar as it had come to be, it was also somehow different this time, he sensed. Sharper and sweeter and stronger.

This time, it touched places in him it never had before—because this time he wasn't only on the receiving end. It also came from gut-deep inside him, he suddenly recognized. And it sprang from more than physical desire. Much more. All at once he was as certain of that as he was of his own name.

It was more than want. Or even need. It was—

"God, I love you," he told his wife. "I've just figured that out, as well."

A few tears did fall then, but he didn't panic because they seemed to be happy ones. He started to brush them away with the tips of his fingers, but Jenna's next words had him stopping in midstroke.

"I love you, too," she told him on another sniff. "I couldn't say it before."

She loved him. He thought about giving a triumphant shout, then scrapped that plan in favor of kissing her again.

He'd have liked to do far more, and would have with no hesitation whatever if it weren't for the fact that Caroline and Katie were probably still worrying. "We have to go downstairs and tell the girls that everything's okay," he said. "But after they're in bed for the night…" He left the sentence hanging with a pointed lift of his brow.

"After they're in bed, I get to give you a present," Jenna told him.

"A present, hmm. Will I like it?" he asked.

"I think so." Her eyes sparkled. "I know I will!"

"Hmm," he said one more time before they left the bedroom, hand in hand.

THEY FOUND THE GIRLS seated on the front parlor sofa with the dog stretched out nearby on the rug. The anxious looks on two angelically fair faces came as little surprise to Jenna. Ross had told her on their way down-stairs that Caroline and Katie had seen her in tears earlier, although she hadn't even noticed them in the hall as she'd hurried up to her bedroom.

What a difference only minutes could make, Jenna thought. All it took was the love of a woman's life to tell her he loved her in return and no amount of rain blowing in from the mountains could put a damper on her spirits.

She had a wide smile on her face as she stepped into the room with Ross at her side. "I know that you were worried," she told the girls, "but everything is fine."

The small frown marring Katie's brow eased. "You're not gonna cry any more?"

"Well, I may cry now and then," Jenna allowed, "but that doesn't always mean a person is sad. Sometimes they can be tears of joy, too."

"But she's done with any tears for the moment," Ross said, sounding relieved by that fact. "And I have something to tell you."

He studied his daughters. "You know I've been running for office. And you especially," he added with a private nod to Caroline, "have been a big help. But as much as I appreciate it, I've decided that being mayor isn't something I want to do."

Katie cocked her head. "If you don't want to do it, then you shouldn't, Daddy," she explained to her father, oh, so reasonably.

Ah, out of the mouths of babes, Jenna thought, knowing she couldn't have said it better. A brief, sidelong study of the wry look on her husband's face told her he might well be reflecting along the same lines.

"I think Katie's right," Caroline said in her typically well-mannered voice.

It earned her a startled look from Katie, as though the little girl was far from used to winning such ready praise from her smart-as-a-whip sister.

"Well, I think you are," Caroline told her.

"Okay." Katie accepted that with a quick nod and switched her gaze to Jenna. "If Daddy's not gonna try to be mayor, will you still have the lunch for the ladies?"

"I'll probably cancel it," Jenna replied after a moment. She and Ross would have to call Thelma Carter next with the news that there would be no further campaigning. Despite all of Thelma's hard work, something told Jenna that Ross's shrewd assistant wouldn't be too disappointed with his decision.

Katie screwed up her face in thought. "If you don't have the lunch, does that mean I hafta eat the asparagus?"

"No, you do not," Jenna replied with a small laugh. She walked over to the sofa and crouched. "But I would like a hug," she told Katie.

The six-year-old didn't hesitate. She slid off the cushion and stepped straight into Jenna's outstretched arms. "I like to hug," Katie whispered.

"I know, honey," Jenna whispered back, holding on tight. "Me, too."

Frisky jumped to his feet and got into the action then, trying to wiggle his furry body between woman and child. He nearly knocked them both over before Jenna regained her balance. "Okay, okay," she told the dog, "you get a hug, as well," and barely evaded a sloppy doggy kiss as that was accomplished.

Katie hopped back onto the sofa. Frisky looked as though he wanted to join her but didn't dare risk it, and

Jenna was about to stand when Caroline slowly rose to her feet. "Can I have a hug, too?" she asked softly.

Jenna hesitated a bare instant before again stretching her arms out wide. "Oh, you certainly can," she said, and in the next moment she held close to her breast a smaller version of the woman her husband had first married.

Caroline would in many ways always be Cynthia Morgan's child. Nevertheless, she hoped that this beautiful girl would be able to be a loving wife someday, as well as a caring mother. She longed to do everything in her power to help that happen—if Caroline would let her.

Reluctantly, Jenna released the ten-year-old when she eventually pulled away. "Any time you want a hug, I'm available," she said, keeping her voice light.

Caroline studied her for a moment with a small smile. "Then everything really is all right?"

"Yes, it's—" She almost said, "Perfect." Then she realized that wasn't the word she sought. Once, she'd thought that Ross had had the perfect marriage to the perfect wife, but perfection, she was beginning to realize, wasn't in the cards for most mortals. Certainly not for wife number two.

And that was fine with her.

"It's wonderful," she went on, picking the word she felt best summed up the situation. "Right now, everything is just plain wonderful."

Caroline dipped her head in what seemed to be a nod of understanding and acceptance. "I'm glad…Jenna Mom."

She hadn't expected to hear those last words from Caroline's lips. Not now. Not yet.

It had Jenna's eyes swiftly misting. But she wasn't

shedding any more tears that day, she told herself. Not even ones of joy. Still, she needed a second to regain her composure and was relieved when Ross broke in.

"I wanted to tell you girls something else," he said. "Jenna and I have started another project."

Caroline looked at her father. "Like fixing up the house, Dad?"

He grinned. "No, more like giving you and Katie a new brother or sister."

"A baby!" Katie suddenly exclaimed, clearly delighted at the prospect.

"You figured that one out, sunshine."

"I figured it out," Katie repeated, looking as pleased as punch with her achievement.

"How do you feel about babies, princess?" Ross asked his other child.

Caroline gave it her usual calm deliberation. "I think a baby would be good," she allowed at last.

"When do we get it?" Katie wanted to know.

"As soon as Jenna and I can make it happen," Ross replied with a deep chuckle as he crouched next to his wife. "Now, can I get some hugs, too?"

Caroline and Katie didn't hesitate to comply, and Frisky again attempted, and failed, to slip in a sloppy kiss. "Nice try, pal," Ross told the dog, "but I've got a woman who can do a much better job."

With that, he pulled Jenna to her feet and slowly lowered his mouth to hers as his strong arms came around her to hold her close.

"Do they hafta kiss to make babies?" Katie asked her older sister.

"I'm not sure" was Caroline's thoughtful reply.

"It may not be strictly necessary," Ross murmured

against his wife's lips, ''but we can get to the other part later.''

Oh, yes, Jenna thought. They would indeed get to the other part. Right now, though, the sound of his—no, *their*—daughters' muffled giggles rising in the background as the soft yet lingering kiss went on and on was the sweetest music she'd ever heard.

Jenna Lorenzo and Ross Hayward were going to have a far from perfect but very happy life together.

She just knew it.

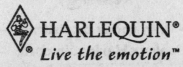

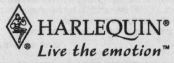

If you enjoyed what you just read,
then we've got an offer you can't resist!

Take 2 bestselling love stories FREE!

Plus get a FREE surprise gift!

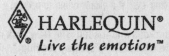

MIRA®

Once you cross that line, there's no turning back....

Judith Arnold

Heart
on the Line

Hip, savvy Loretta DeAngelo and sexy thirtysomething Josh Kaplan are just friends.

Josh and Loretta are just friends because Josh has a girlfriend, Melanie—1,200 miles away in Florida. They're just friends when he agrees to become Loretta's "arranged" blind date for a ratings-boosting show. They're just friends when he pretends to be her boyfriend to get her marriage-obsessed family off her back. They're just friends when they fall into bed...and in love.

Now what? Sometimes, if you want something badly enough, you have to put your heart on the line, even if it means doing something a little crazy....

"Charming, humorous and loaded with New York references, this lighthearted tale is satisfying subway reading."
—*Publishers Weekly* on *Love in Bloom's*

Available the first week of August 2003 wherever paperbacks are sold!

Visit us at www.mirabooks.com   MJA702